For Sarah and Georgia

Crumps Barn Studio
No.2 The Waterloo, Cirencester GL7 2PZ
www.crumpsbarnstudio.co.uk

Copyright © Anne Buffoni 2024

The right of Anne Buffoni to be identified as the author of this work has been asserted in accordance with the Copyright, Designs and Patents Act 1988.

All rights reserved. No part of this publication may be reproduced, stored in a retrieval system, or transmitted in any form or by any means, electronic, mechanical, photocopying, recording or otherwise, without the prior permission of the copyright owner.

Cover design by Lorna Gray

All our books are printed on responsibly sourced paper from managed woodlands. Printed in the UK by TJ Books, Padstow.

ISBN 978-1-915067-35-7

ANNE BUFFONI
KIRIN OF THE DOBUNNI

Crumps Barn Studio

KIRIN'S FAMILY TREE

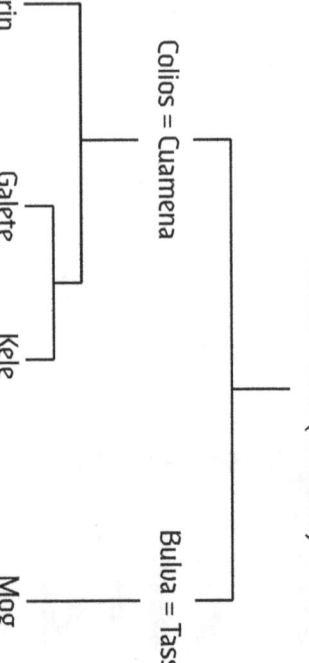

BEINDUBN

Touisac = Tana (first wife)

Colios = Cuamena
- Kirin
- Galete
- Kele

Bulua = Tass
- Mog

COMELRIS

= Assuna (second wife)
- Tirtos

PART ONE

AD 8

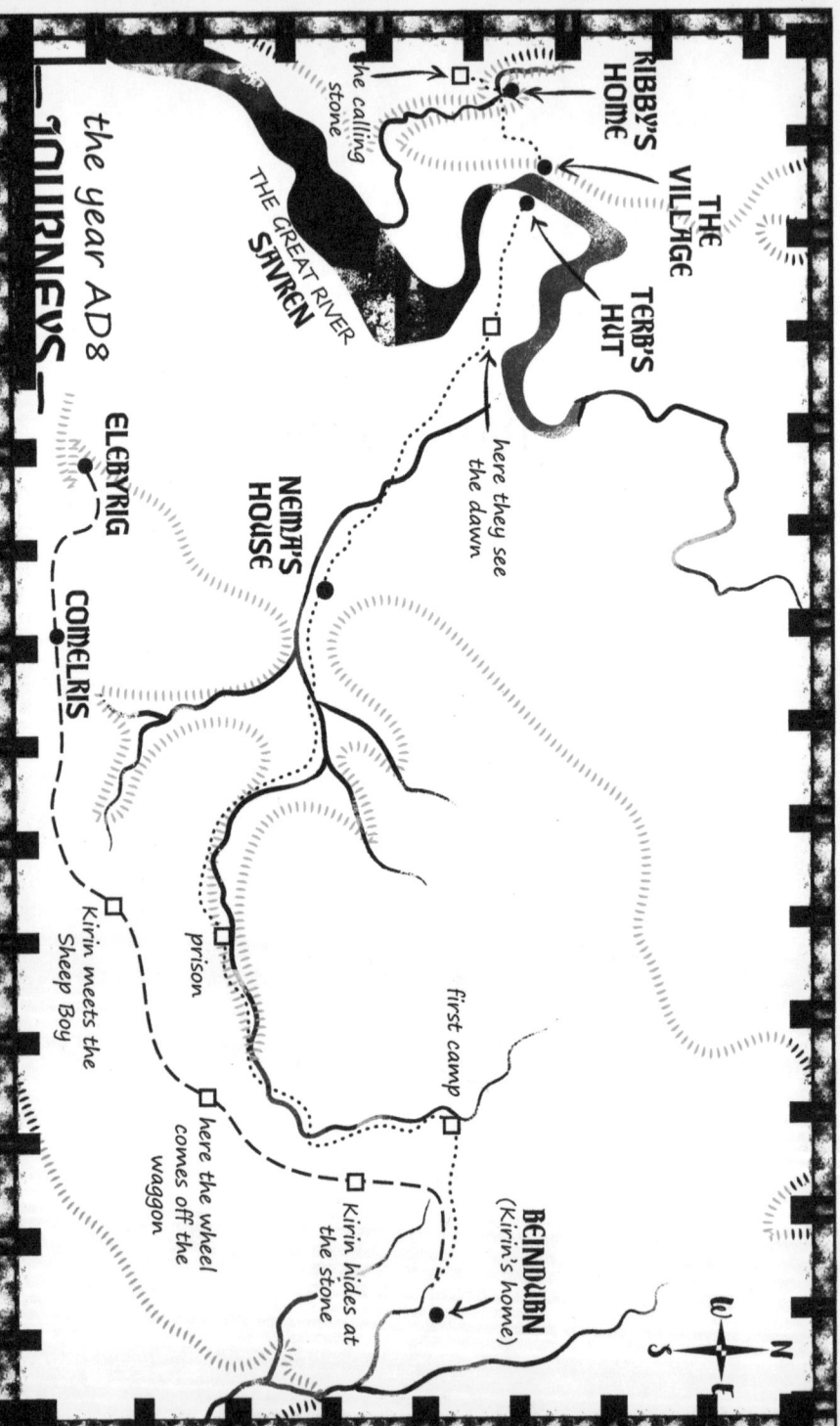

1

Kirin lost his battle with the wind. It was making him crosser than it should, whipping his hair about his face and making his eyes water. This was not a good morning for studying the horizon. Low clouds were playing with his view, scudding up the valley beneath him between the flat topped outliers. The great river Savren could only be glimpsed for a grey moment. She wanted to keep her own counsel today.

He shrugged and turned his back. Perhaps he had better get on with looking for early hazelnuts, as his aunt had asked, before anyone found him just standing there.

As if to tease his surrender, the wind suddenly dropped. In the lull, the boy heard new and exciting sounds. Shouts of greeting rose up from the wooded slopes below, answered by the dogs in the village behind him. The tight worry, deep inside him, melted just a little. Could it be his father, at last?

Kirin sprinted for the main gate, running around the wide grassy platform that cut into the side of the hilltop just below the bank and fence of the settlement. As he turned into the sheltered side, a creature exploded out of the trees, charging at him, tongue and tail lashing. It leapt over stacked wood ready for palisade repairs. It neatly dodged the drying skins stretched over low bushes. Kirin stopped and braced himself for impact.

"Kuno!" he yelled, grinning widely.

Heavy paws landed on Kirin's shoulders. The large dog licked his face while his rear wagged dangerously from side to side, threatening to bring them both crashing down.

"You've missed me then," the boy managed, "and I've

missed you!"

A great deal of ear-rubbing and tummy-scratching was needed before his long-legged friend was satisfied and Kirin was released. He ran on to the wooden gate, tripping and laughing, as Kuno showed his delight by leaping up in his path and barking to the sky. As he entered the enclosure, Kirin could see that the Elebyrig people, his cousins, had put aside their work. From all directions they were rushing in relief and excitement, like him, to welcome the first of the returning men and horses that plodded wearily into view through the north entrance.

Kirin was sure of it. His father was there and all would now be well.

2

Kirin had been staying in the village while his father and uncles were making the most of good weather with their horse-trading. From Elebyrig they could spread wide. Plenty of trade was found northwards up the valley and across the powerful river flow of Savren. They were all the people and communities of the Dobunni, linked over generations by blood and tradition, their authority unchallenged up on these hills. Home for Kirin was usually at Beindubn, the family's settlement a good day's ride away. Once the frosts had disappeared and Uban's passage across the sky grew high and strong, it had been time to bring the ponies westward. And this time he had been included. Well, for the first part anyway. It was a start.

The men's final trip this season had taken them longer and further than usual into the western hills. They needed to trade there for the metal stone, so important for their winter forging back at Beindubn. They knew where to go for the deals and where there would be a welcome for their sturdiest breeding mares, but that meant reaching out to the very edge of Dobunnic influence. There was some risk in that. The men had been due back for some days and the delay had begun to cause concern.

At ten years of age, Kirin was considered too young to be included in the low voiced deliberations around the fire. He had to keep his worries for his father to himself. In the subdued atmosphere that had hung over recent evening meals that had been hard. Now, finally, his wait was over.

At the sight of his son, a smile spread across the tanned and rumpled face of Colios. He handed his horse to one of the children and gave Kirin a hefty squeeze.

"Pona's blessings on this happy return!" he boomed. "How goes it, my lad?"

Taking a step back, he surveyed his son from top to toe and laughed. "You've grown like black binding-weed again! Any food left for us? I hope you've been earning your keep."

Kirin could only grin back. By his feet, Kuno was gazing lovingly from one to the other, quivering with excitement. This was a fine day for the hound; his two favourite people were in the same place once more and he had definitely heard the word *food*.

But Kuno's supper was a long while coming. Despite many willing hands, it took some time to sort out the pack ponies and their baggage. Then the group with the heavier cattle-drawn waggons arrived a little later at the level pasture beyond the enclosure. They were exhausted by the final effort of trundling their way up the long track from the valley floor, and one look at their loads of iron-rich stone tied down under stretched hide showed why. The children rushed backwards and forwards with water for men and animals, while their parents separated the traded goods for the Elebyrig settlement from those for Beindubn.

Eventually there was time to get a meal prepared. It was after sunset before the families could sit down together round the fire, under a clearing sky, to eat and exchange news.

Kirin studied the faces around him. His father Colios, the oldest of the brothers and respected leader, seemed never to have been away. His bulk cast a shadow wider than most as he tucked into another large chunk of roasted meat and wiped the juice from his long moustache. Aunt Tass was smiling happily, with Little Mog cuddling up in her lap, while her husband Bulva waved his arms about in excitement as he told his tales with his usual enthusiasm; stories of black rock that burned red, of the bent and grimy people who burrowed into holes to find the metal stone, and rivulets and streams that followed the god Uban so closely they ran with the colour of his last golden rays, before disappearing with him into the underworld.

Kirin's other uncle, Tirtos, who was much younger than his half-brothers but already an experienced trader, added to the tales with details that made the older girls giggle and hang on his every word. The young boys listened to it all with envy. Like Kirin, it would be their turn one day to go further than Savren and see these places and people for themselves. Until then they had to practise their horse handling, and be content with their play fighting and imagination after a day's work.

With a belch of pleasure, Colios threw the remains of his meal over his shoulder for Kuno and the other dogs to squabble over. He took a swig of brew, wiped his hands on the grass next to him, and cut into the chatter.

"It's time for more practical matters." As usual, an expectant hush followed.

He looked across at his son. "Kirin, by chance we met an outrider from your grandfather, as we began the climb up here. The news is good. I hear all is well back at Beindubn. Your mother and your baby sisters are thriving. I've sent word that we will leave in the morning and spend tomorrow night with Father and Assuna on our way home. Tirtos, I'm sure you will be glad to see your mother."

"Indeed," smiled Tirtos, "and she will be glad to welcome her stepsons, too. Bulva, will you come with us as far as Comelris?"

Bulva looked at Tass and Little Mog, his wife dozing in the last glow of the fire and his child fast asleep in her arms. He shook his head.

"No, Brother, I'm sure the old man will forgive me if I stay here. I see the grain is gathered, Cuda be praised, but there's much to get started on to prepare for winter. And I can pay my respects more easily than you; the ride is nothing. You're going to be slow. The worst is over, but your beasts are tired."

"Very true," nodded Colios, "With that in mind, I suggest sleep and an early start tomorrow."

"I'll check on the carts and the watchman on the north ridge," said Tirtos. He looked up at the star scatters that now pierced the dark velvet between the clouds. "And there's enough light for a timely gift-giving to the gods at the shrine, I think." He reached out and pulled a little meat from the bones left on the warm stones. "Let's not give them any cause for anger now," he yawned.

Tiredness had been weighing heavily on them all for some time. The party broke up quietly, dogs and people clearing up the leftovers without a fuss.

Colios rose to his feet and stretched, watching Tirtos go. He grunted in approval. "Your uncle is a fine young man, Kirin, a good example to follow." He reached out to ruffle his son's mop of hair. "But I have no worries about you, my boy. I can tell you have stood well for me while I was away. I am proud of you."

Kirin glowed inside at this unexpected show of praise. "Thank you, Father," he managed sleepily.

His father smiled at him and lifted the thick, woven cloth to enter the large roundhouse. The two of them, and Kuno, found their own places along with the rest of the family on the bed frames and heaps of dried grass and rugs against the low walls. When Tirtos returned, sometime later, only the dog was alert enough to open one eye at the young man's careful movement across the earthen floor to a pile of bedding. Soon all was still.

LITTLE MOG CLAMBERED over Kirin and blew in his ear, chuckling at the chance of surprising a favourite cousin.

This morning Mog had extra support from Kuno, who also landed on Kirin, panting and licking. From the depths of sleep,

Kirin realized the time for rest was over. He sat up as best as he could, wiping his face with his sleeve. "Alright, alright!" he groaned, "I'm awake!"

As he got to his feet, tickling the squealing toddler away and heaving the dog to one side, he remembered the importance of the morning. He would soon be leaving Elebyrig and heading for home. Sunlight shafted through the doorway, picking out the mounds of folded rugs and a wicker tray of freshly picked greens on the wooden bench for cooking later. The day had been here a while. He needed to catch up before his father noticed. After a hasty splash with water from the leather bag that hung under the thatch, and a visit to the latrine pit behind the midden, he went in search of the others with Kuno at his heels. In the bright light, he gazed around him. It would be his last look for a while.

Elebyrig, this grassy table-top of land, perched high on the hill edge above the impressive Savren river valley. It was so familiar now. Sturdy roundhouses resisted the weather with thick cones of soot blackened thatch. Darker teeth-gaps of doorways cut into their low walls of stone and turf. Around and about the roundhouses were woven hurdles linked into fencing for managing the animals. Thatched workshops and fodder stores clustered, some raised on posts above damp and pests. As he strode past the new straw ricks, Kirin felt a glow of pride for his tribe, for all their skills and knowledge passed down through time.

It was an old fort. At one time its fences and deep ditches had been made to protect the Dobunni from enemies and disguise war-mongering preparations of their own. Times were now peaceful. Oaths made before tribute lords were now broken at peril and calm had spread throughout the region. The tribal families had been able to settle and farm beyond their hillforts. Now Elebyrig was a useful place for corralling and resting the ponies. From there it was a straightforward drop down to the profitable settlements on either side of the great river.

Outside the north entrance, Kirin followed a ridge, where the land fell away on both sides. Beyond was a patchwork of fields, cleared for now after the recent harvest. There at the start of the upland levels began the drovers' trackways, that set off to the north east and then turned south and east under a wide horizon. Soon they were to follow one of those ancient routes homeward, above the wooded valleys that cut their way down through the limestone.

The line of animals and transport was being put together near the mound of the Old Ones, an ancient monument of earth and stone which lay close to the edge before the land fell away sharply. Colios and his team had already started to yoke the cattle and tie them to the shafts of the waggons. The results of their successful trading were tied securely to the rough wooden planking in great bundles. Mostly it was raw material for the metal tools and objects that were always in demand - iron wheel rims, farming tools and weapons, copper and tin for the fine bronze pins and brooches. The Beindubn family had developed minting skills that had brought respect and notice from the tribute lords. The coins that the leadership had authorized Colios to make and use, as tokens of trust, gave him a reputation for fair dealing. He held a respected position among the Dobunnic elders that he did not want to lose.

Kirin knew there would also be bags of rough ochre, ready for pounding and diluting for dye, and salt kept dry in clay containers in closed carts. But there were other packs, in panniers tied to the ponies, that he knew would be more exciting to open with his mother once they got home. His father always managed to find something new and interesting on his travels. Once it was a fish trapped by the gods in stone with flattened skeleton and sharp jaw, gaping blindly as the wrapping of leaves around it came away.

Often it was a small but weighty polished stone for Kirin's collection, drilled with a hole ready to thread onto his leather belt. This time he was sure his father would have tucked in something for his new twin sisters Galete and Kele. At the thought of returning to them as a seasoned traveller like the older men his excitement grew, and he half skipped and hopped up to the busy scene.

Tirtos spotted him over the head of the pony he was harnessing.

"So the sleepyhead is up and about, then. Are you ready to join the real men at work? There's plenty to do here, so get yourself organized. Have you packed your things?"

He broke off suddenly and scowled at Kuno, who was sniffing around his cart and trying to jump up at the rear, unsettling the small horse as the wooden shafts shook. "Dog! Stay away! We've enough animals to manage here without stupid ones!"

Kirin caught hold of the scruff of Kuno's neck and rubbed his chest to distract him. The dog had picked up on Kirin's excitement and seemed destined for trouble this morning.

"I've nothing to carry. I've grown out of the clothes I brought with me. Aunt Tass made me these from Uncle Bulva's tunic and trousers."

"Well, you'd better keep that dog of yours out of my way. Stay at the head of the line near your father. You can help chivvy the cattle pulling the biggest waggon; you can always ride then if you're not up to the walking. I'm going to bring up the rear with this salt cart." Tirtos turned back to concentrate on fitting the bridle.

Kirin wandered along. He found his aunt handing out food for the journey.

Tass put down her platter at the sight of him. She enveloped the boy in a warm hug. "I will miss you, Kirin." She released him and wiped her eyes. "And what will Little Mog do without you? Please come and stay again next season!"

"I will, aunt, if my father lets me."

Tass smiled a watery smile and gave him another hug. Kirin felt a lump in his throat. He had grown very close to his aunt over the past months. As she stood for a moment with his hand in hers, he realized how much he was going to miss everything and everyone. And the western horizon of the green-etched hills beyond the river, so close on a clear day but always out of reach, when would he get to go there? Suddenly, he knew what to do. He looked over at the birch woodland nearby.

"Could I have some bread, aunt? I want to visit the tree."

Tass looked at the boy standing there with his chin up. She understood, and bent to break off a chunk for him. He took it, and told Kuno to stay where he was.

Kirin walked towards the trees and headed for a small gap between them, parting the low branches as he made his way in towards the clearing. He didn't really want to enter on his own; it was too close to the gods to be comfortable. Inside, the light was diffused by the interlacing of leaves that almost met overhead. The air felt trapped, with a particular damp coldness and smell of fungus and decay that caught in his throat. His arrival startled two large black crows from their stalking as they looked for food. He caught his breath, then held it with heart hammering as they clattered in surprise and flapped their way up and out through the canopy.

Despite his fears, Kirin made himself approach the gnarled and twisted tree at the centre of the clearing. It was protected by a ditch and partially screened by panels of woven hazel. Kirin reached it across a narrow causeway. There it grew, just about alive; pointing a jagged finger of ancient shattered trunk to the tiny patch of sky above, and sending thick ropes of root turning and drilling into the moss below. This was a special tree. This tree had been honoured by the gods, scarred by their lightning, marked forever. This tree connected the overworld to Uban's passage westward across the sky through the day, and to his return back along underworld rivers in the night. It hovered between life and death, and had done so for generations. This tree accepted a gift for the gods and gave a promise in return that no request would go unnoticed, if not granted.

Trying to ignore his shaking hands, Kirin carefully placed the bread in a cleft in the exposed roots, amongst the rotted remains of past petitions. There was no sign of his uncle's fresh offering from the night before, but he was not worried. He knew, whether the birds had found it quickly or not, that the message would have been acknowledged. Uban and Hatane who lit the sky by day then night, Pona and Cuda who watched and provided for horse and home, even mighty Volkos, quick with anger and merciless in his revenge – all the spirits of above and below would have appreciated the offering and blessed the giver.

For a moment Kirin wished he could just turn and leave, forget this impulse, and leave the serious work of talking to the gods to his elders. But that was childish. He wanted to speak for himself now. This is what adults had to do. He took a steadying breath and closed his eyes. How would Tirtos have done it?

So he began by asking the gods to protect his family and his tribe this day, surely the right beginning. But his innermost feelings, that only he seemed to have, were they important enough? The burning for action that had started to shoot and spread, like spring growth inside him, was hard to explain to anyone. Was there a chance the gods could sympathize with his impatience? Would they forget him, once tucked away back at home at Beindubn, or would they help him to new adventures as soon as possible?

Somehow he shaped the words in his head and let them go free. After a final promise to earn the right for such favour, Kirin opened his eyes. He shivered as a cold breeze suddenly whipped through the clearing and rattled dying leaves. He turned and escaped thankfully back down the path through the undergrowth.

3

In the bustle of the departure, and the joking farewells between the Elebyrig and Beindubn kinsmen, the boy's mood soon lifted again. It was a joy to be on the move, strolling alongside the cattle and ponies as they drew the swaying carts and rumbling waggons step by step along grassy swathes and the soft curves of the hilly uplands.

This first stage of the homeward journey was going to be a short one. They could not pass through the estate of Grandfather Tovisac at Comelris without visiting him. Tovisac was old, as old as the hills themselves, or so it always seemed to Kirin. He had lived through many more than fifty winters and bore the scars of his youth as a warrior at Elebyrig, fighting for the tribute lords in the old days. Tovisac's loyalty and his belief in the Dobunnic leadership had helped bring the settled peace to their lands. He had been able to put down his sword and develop other ways to make a living and bring up a family. His way was horse breeding. He knew everything there was to know about the short, sturdy local breeds. From his new home on the Beindubn hillside he had become skilled at developing strains with strength and speed. It was at Beindubn that he had met his first wife. Together they brought up their two boys Colios and Bulva, until her death. After that, he had soon heart-bonded again with another woman. As soon as his sons were old enough, he handed over the control of both settlements to them and moved to Comelris.

All this Kirin knew from fireside tales of the family's past. He had never really understood why his grandfather would have wanted to leave the sunny hillsides of Beindubn for the windy upland fields of Comelris, but he guessed it must have been the influence of his second and much younger wife, Assuna, the mother of Tirtos, whose family came from there.

Kirin looked across at Colios, who was striding away, straggling hair flowing back and humming tunelessly to himself. He decided not to bother his father with questions. He knew Colios had accepted Tovisac's new family, for Assuna came from the same Dobunnic tribe and there was no conflict in the match. He had taken his younger half-brother Tirtos to live at Beindubn to learn the family trades and skills, and had always treated Assuna and her kinsmen with respect on their occasional visits. But Kirin sensed Colios was never as relaxed with his father at Comelris as a son should be. He thought it a pity; he loved his father and would never want anything to come between them like that.

Anyway, today was not a day for problems. Today was a day for enjoying the clean air of late morning and the mewling cries of the buzzards from high above. Ahead of them, Uban had not reached as high in the sky as Kirin remembered from their earlier trip. The trees in the wooded valleys that fell away to either side were starting to patch with brown and bronze. The signs were there that the long summer days were over and winter was on its way.

The boy whistled for Kuno, who once again had decided to go off and annoy others, judging by the complaining from the rear. The dog soon bounded into sight and together they settled into a regular pace with the animals, glad to be together in easy company, making their way through the landscape.

By early afternoon, the sounds of a farmstead reached them as the roofs came into view. The light haze of wood smoke hanging above Comelris had been visible for a while. Horses and cattle snorted greetings, and a few children left the stones they were rolling into a muddy puddle and wandered towards the visitors as the cavalcade lumbered to a halt.

Assuna appeared in the doorway of the roundhouse, followed by her sisters. She bustled over to meet them, wiping her hands and fixing her plait more securely to her head.

"There you are, then," she said, "Pona's blessings." She frowned at them all. "Tovisac has been pestering me for an age, sure that you were delayed by trouble. He can't come out to meet you, his bones are aching and the herbs aren't helping today. I'm glad for the company. I can't get on with my work for all his fussing."

"Now, Mother, have good cheer and give your wandering son a smile," laughed Tirtos, coming up and putting his arms around her. "Where's the welcome for us thirsty travellers? Relax and leave the old man to us now. Open a pot of your best cyser. We'll celebrate a successful summer with him, and wash down some of your spiced meats too, I hope."

He squeezed his mother until she pretended to push him away, softening in pride at her son. She turned and smiled more easily at the rest of them.

"Well, sort yourselves out then and find a welcome inside when you're ready. My sisters here will show you the necessary. The children will help with water for your animals." Assuna waved vaguely at the women and children and took hold of the arm of her son. "Tirtos, come now and greet your father." She started to march him towards the roundhouse.

Then she paused and half turned. "Oh, and Colios too, of course," she sniffed. She carried on her way, grumbling to her son, "I see Bulva hasn't bothered himself."

Colios missed nothing of this. He turned and winked at Kirin. "Better do as I am told, my boy," he grinned. "I'll leave you to check the watering and get the animals onto grass. We'll feed them all later."

With that, the great leader followed meekly in their wake,

bent his head under the low edge of the thatch and disappeared into the shadowed gap. Kirin watched for a moment, and then started his familiar chores alongside the other men. He wondered vaguely why it was that life seemed more complicated the older he got. He had thought it would get clearer.

WORK STARTED AGAIN before dawn. Colios was keen to move on from Comelris as soon as possible. He knew that to reach Beindubn by nightfall with those heavy waggons was going to be a challenge. And the begrudged hospitality that Assuna and her family offered was no incentive to stay longer. Tirtos was just as happy to get going. He had fed and harnessed his own pony quickly, with time left to help others.

The previous evening had gone well enough. Tovisac was distracted from his aches and pains by his visitors. The old man had taken interest in the men's trading tales; he was also clearly delighted to see how his grandson Kirin had grown. He tired quickly, however, and had soon gone to his wooden box bed, built into the recesses under the slope of the roof. The men took their chance to settle early for the night around the fire at the centre.

Just before sleep came to Kirin, he thought he heard his grandfather call his name. Unsure, and hardly awake, the boy stepped over the mountain of sheepskin and rug that was his father, and groped his way in the shadows over to the old man.

"Grandfather?" he whispered.

Tovisac's eyes were sharp and bright and fixed on him. He reached up for the boy's hand and grasped it firmly in his twisted fingers, pulling Kirin down to him. The boy sensed the old warrior will in him, the determination that was now approaching its final battle with failing flesh and bone.

"Boy!" His voice rasped against Kirin's ear. "Uban calls me. I am not long for this world, you can see that." He stopped and breathed in deeply, almost a sigh. Then he gripped Kirin's hand even more tightly and continued.

"My old heart swells with pride. My sons prosper. The gods favour us. But you are the future, boy. Heed your father well, and your uncles, and take my bloodline into the next age." Tovisac paused again for breath. The light in his eyes grew sharper at memories from the past. "I've seen changes, boy, and more are bound to come. You will need to use your wits – and your heart – to find the right path. Now, I have something for you …"

With both hands he opened Kirin's fingers and placed an object there. He closed the boy's hand over the metal, and patted it abruptly.

"Take this," Tovisac grunted. "I want you to have it. It's not for one of Assuna's scrawny pack. They'll be picking over me like rats, once they get the chance." He scowled over Kirin's shoulder, as if looking for trouble. "I see how she just puts up with me. Pona only knows how I've kept my tongue …"

His hands dropped heavily, releasing Kirin as he stretched back thankfully into his bedding. "I got that from a trader once. In fair exchange. Came upriver from the ocean, from another world." A sudden and surprising chuckle rattled dryly in his throat. "Do not fear. There's no man's blood on it, it was made for other reasons …"

His voice trailed off, exhausted with the effort. Sleep lay on the old man's eyelids. The conversation was over. He waved his hand for Kirin to go, as he turned his face to the dark once more.

Kirin crept back to the others and curled up again in his place. No one else seemed disturbed and he was very relieved. He wanted time to take in what had just happened. In the dim light of the dying embers he opened his hand to look more closely. There, relaxed in his palm, lay a little creature with long neck and rounded muzzle, gazing pointedly back up at him. Not alive, but … In his sleepy state it was hard to be sure. He rubbed his eyes and held the smooth metal to the firelight.

It was a small knife, light to carry and perfect for tucking away out of sight. The creature formed the handle. In the half-light he saw two dark sockets slanted back beneath ball-ended horns that stuck cheerfully upright. The eyes were shadows, but not lifeless ones. The sockets seemed to draw the remaining light in, pulling at your thoughts, then laughing back at what it had found.

From where and for how long had it travelled to be here in his hand? He should have been wary of it, scared of this strange character grinning out at him, looking from one world into another. But he wasn't. He knew without reason that this knife was an explorer. Through his grandfather it seemed to have chosen him next as companion. The gods themselves seemed to know.

Kirin hid the gift under him and turned over to sleep, but the whole event unsettled him. For a long while he shifted and fidgeted, bothered by his thoughts and for once resenting the hard dirt floor so close under his shoulder. He felt proud to have been singled out for this honour, but he knew now that he might not see the old man alive again after this visit. And the knife creature? Was it an honour or a burden? Did it carry a message from the gods, that his plea at the shrine had been heard? Could he hear Pona close by, watching his reaction and whispering to Hatane? He slept poorly for the few remaining hours before Colios called for action.

4

There was tension in the air. Colios was tired and impatient to be home, and he set a fast pace. Kirin walked on aching limbs. The knife was wrapped in a scrap of hide from one of the baskets in the roundhouse and tucked away inside his tunic above his belt. He still did not feel like telling anyone about the conversation in the night, and the men were too busy and weary themselves to notice he was quieter than usual. Devoted Kuno noticed, though, and kept a watchful eye on him as the straggling group made their way on along the high droving way.

Gradually the distance was covered. Over their shoulders, a band of brighter sky marked where the wind rushed upwards and lifted the cloud cover at the scarp edge, a memory of the steep drop behind them down to the great river plain. Heading southeast, they kept a different horizon to their right now; a low line of hills at the farthest limit of a wide forest. The woods stretched away from them as far as Kirin could see. This route had been preserved by the regular moving of herds and flocks for generations. It was the most efficient path for covering longer distances, curving along the high ground, above the trees and folds of valleys that led off below like the veins of a leaf. Kirin remembered some of the shared jokes and events of the outward journey. How different the mood had been then. It was a quieter party that now revisited the route on their return.

The boy and his dog were kept busy encouraging the animals and looking out for the landmarks that kept them on the right track for home. This was safe country. The authority and influence of the Dobunnic tribute lords went unchallenged in this region. Here people could go about their daily lives, and their partnership with the land and the seasons, without looking for trouble at every turn.

Occasionally they came upon one of the great solitary stones that had been fixed on their ends by the Old Ones, above the springs that fed the watercourses, placed with a strength and purpose that was hard to think of as human. As well as the stones, Kirin marked in turn more of their occasional grassy mounds, sitting like great upturned bowls. There were many legends attached to these, and ancient stories of sounds and spirits from deep within. Some of the long ones had doorways sealed with huge slabs, but Kirin knew of no one who had ever dared prise them open and enter.

All these landmarks were at the same time familiar and strange. Once mighty, the Old Ones had had their time and passed on. Uban and the gods had the power then, and the power now, to take life on a whim. Who could say what had been caught or driven under those mounds and stones in the past? Kirin had been taught that life above ground was short and the passage below was forever. He was determined to get the most from his life above.

Late in the morning they reached a watering hole, formed from a lively spring and marked by a low wall of ragstone built into the slope. Its position, just above the thick woods, saved the drovers from struggling down through the undergrowth to the streams below. The procession came to a halt, to the relief of Kirin. He had been wondering for some time whether or not to face the inevitable teasing and sit up for a while on the nearest waggon.

Their arrival broke up a small flock of wiry brown sheep that had been drinking from some hollowed log troughs. The little animals scattered in alarm and reformed at a safe distance, grumbling and occasionally stamping their front feet. Their young minder, who had jumped to his feet as they came into view over the brow of the hill, seemed to have the same attitude.

"Ere, mind me sheeps! We ain't finished. We come a long way an' we needs this!"

The boy was about the same age as Kirin. He stood there defiantly in dirty tunic and bound leggings, with grubby face and eyes just a little too far apart. He stared at them through a lanky fringe. He was not frightened. The clothes and hair of the travellers marked them as Dobunnic like him, although the ochre designs on the men's forearms told him they deserved respect. He knew he would have to give way, but not without protest.

Colios laughed loudly, for the first time that day.

"Don't fret, my lad! There's water for all. And perhaps a share of our honey cakes will make a difference. Kirin, come and distract this young nettle and we'll start with the buckets."

Kirin felt grateful to the boy for lifting his father's spirits. He ran over and smiled at him, Kuno at his heels. The boy was not to be won over easily. He looked Kirin up and down and gave Kuno a suspicious stare.

"Ope that dog'll keep away from them shearlings." He sniffed and wiped at his nose with the back of his hand.

Kirin wasn't sure, but didn't want to admit it. "Oh, he'll behave. Won't you, Kuno?"

The dog looked up at them and then across to the uneasy animals, while they half-heartedly nibbled at the grass and kept an eye on the intruders. He suspected that good behaviour would get him more reward than bad. He decided to flop down in a heap of legs and tail and close his eyes.

"There," grinned Kirin, "I told you."

The boy was no talker. He seemed to have no interest in finding out more from Kirin. Instead he sniffed again noisily, and wandered along to watch the men as they pulled out iron-bound wooden buckets from the carts and collected water in turn for the thirsty animals. As this seemed distraction enough for the sheep boy, Kirin was free to do the same for Kuno, his father's pony, and then himself.

It wasn't long before Tirtos was pushing to get going again, but Colios stopped him.

"Hold, Brother," he said. "The gods have been with us so far, and these animals need a while longer to rest. The sky is clear enough. We will have light to get us to Beindubn tonight. We will sit to eat."

Tirtos looked as though he was ready to argue, but thought better of it and strode off back to his cart.

Suddenly there was a yell. The sheep boy appeared clutching his ear and bellowing loudly, tears making grimy tracks down his cheeks. "Ee 'it me! Ee 'it me! I was only looking, I was!"

The boy rushed up to Colios, instinctively seeking refuge with the leader. Tirtos followed him, red in the face. "That boy is trouble! He was poking around!"

Colios cut him off, bemused at the fuss and obviously disappointed. "Enough, Brother. Food is needed now, and this lad must remember us for our friendship, not ill temper." He sighed impatiently. "Go over and sit with Kirin, boy, and wipe your face."

The men gathered together for a few minutes of rest, but the atmosphere had got very uncomfortable. They chewed on strips of dried meat, followed by chunks of Tass's sweetened barley cake from a woven wrapper, passed around the group from hand to hand. Tirtos, his brow furrowed in frustration, kept out of the way of Colios and sat deep in thought as he ate.

As the food was passed around, Kirin noticed the sheep boy hesitate. He reached for a handful of meat and gave it to him. The boy finally smiled a careful smile and tore at it. He was clearly very hungry. He guarded the food close to his chest, as if he was afraid that someone might decide to take it off him.

"What's your given name?" asked Kirin.

The boy looked sideways at him then swallowed a mouthful. "Name? Don't 'ave one, I don't think."

"So what do your elders call you when they want you?"

He shrugged. "They don't want me oftentimes. They says I eats too much. If there's sheeps to be minded I'm alright. I loves the babs. I loves they wigglin' tails an' hard gums tryin' to milk yer fingers. Yep, I'm alright when I'm up here on the hilltops with them sheeps."

This rush of information surprised both of them and was enough for the sheep boy. No more talking for him. He carried on eating as much as possible, as quickly as possible, to Kirin and Kuno's silent admiration. He came to a stop reluctantly when Colios ordered the remaining food to be wrapped and tucked away in the panniers.

"That's it," the boy said, in satisfied acceptance. He wiped his mouth on his sleeve and got up. He looked directly at Kirin. "I likes you." He nodded across at Tirtos, who was heading back to his place in the line. "I don't like 'im. An' I dunno about *'im* ... " The latter was directed at Kuno, who tilted his head with his most appealing expression just for a moment. Kirin felt rather pleased to be approved of, though he wasn't sure why the opinion of this rough boy should matter. The boy went over and stood back with his straggly flock, watching as the travellers tidied up and got on their way once more.

As they set off alongside the waggons, Kirin raised his hand in farewell and the sheep boy lifted his hesitantly in reply. Kirin thought about his own comfortable life and the boy's lonely days. He felt sorry for his uncle's angry outburst. He knew his father must have felt sorry too; it had caught both of them by surprise. But the boy was probably used to rough handling. He had recovered quickly, and they had given him a good feed. Kirin decided to put it to the back of his mind as the work animals lumbered up to speed and the creaking carts began to eat up the grassy track once more.

During the afternoon the track turned more to the north. When the light was able to gleam between the new layers of thin cloud, the pale shadows stretched thinly across the uneven track. The turf was ribbed here by exposed tree roots from a tree line on either side and a colder breeze gained strength against their backs.

There was an air of concentration now as the weary group found their own ways of keeping up pace and focus. They were more than halfway, but this next stage was going to be a proper test for man and beast.

Tired and edgy, his attention distracted by a yell from one of the men handling the alarmingly jolting carts behind him, Colios forgot that the ground beyond the copse dipped away sharply. Without warning and before he could do anything about it, the double pair of oxen pulling the lead waggon decided to take the downward slope at a shuffling run. The wooden shaft and yokes strained to their limits with the combined mass of animal and load, and the waggon started to skid relentlessly sideways and down.

"Father!" Kirin yelled desperately.

He, and the nearest of the men, rushed forward to help Colios get control. But it was too late. There was a splintering crack that rang in their ears and echoed back to them from the trees.

Their difficult journey had suddenly turned impossible.

Moving closer, Kirin saw that an axle had broken on the waggon and one of the great front wheels was now lying wedged at an awkward angle, gouged turf lapping at its rim. Its partner wheel, on the other side, was giving alarming signs of giving up as well, and the strapped sacks of iron ore were straining against their ropes on the tilted planking, ready to slide at any moment.

Tirtos strode angrily to the front and inspected the damage while Colios and the men unharnessed the oxen. To their relief the animals appeared to be unharmed.

Colios was cursing himself for his lack of attention as he joined his brother. The look on the young man's face gave no relief to him. It was all Tirtos could do to control himself. He glared at his brother, fists clenched, breathing hard.

"That's done it! We won't make Beindubn now by nightfall! You wouldn't listen, hanging about, fussing over worthless scum. And now this!"

The rest of the party stood with Kirin and watched in awed silence, aware of the importance of this moment. The younger brother challenging the senior? This had never happened before. Kuno slunk down on his belly, his head between his paws. Kirin held his breath.

Colios was leader, there was no doubt. His icy response whipped back at Tirtos. "Close your mouth and open your ears! We need to work together, not argue like crows over a corpse! This is not welcome, for sure, but no one is injured. We are within reach of home and can send for help. Some of us will have to camp here till the morrow, we can ferry the load then or fix the break. So, calm yourself!"

"Well, I'm not staying!" Tirtos retorted. "I'm taking my cart and heading home, the rest can do as they will!

"I shan't stop you. In fact, it would make sense to take Kirin with you," ordered Colios. "I was thinking of sending him as messenger. He's a light load for my tired mount. Go together, if you must go yourself. Double weight to the call for help."

At his father's words Kirin turned to the pony, but Tirtos was still fuming, and in no mood to take orders.

"No, I won't. I'm not going to be held back any more by a

child. We are wasting time. I'm leaving, and on my own!"

The young man turned on his heels and marched back to his cart. Leaping up on to the front bench, he snatched up the leather reins and urged his pony into motion. He sped off past the silent group, cart wheels rattling and clods of turf flying.

Colios looked down at Kirin. The boy was wide-eyed at the cheek of his uncle, and unsure of what would happen next. His father sighed and looked at the company of men waiting, like the boy, for him to take full charge of the situation. After a moment, he spoke decisively. "Kirin, you're still to go. I need to know the call for help has been given, and Tirtos could add to our problems with that reckless speed. The rest of us will stay here and do what we can for the animals for now. Take my horse and follow your uncle, there's daylight enough yet and you'll catch up." A hint of amusement appeared in his voice once more. "Well, maybe not catch right up. He's ready enough to spark at anything, so try not to strike his flint. I'll help you unload the panniers and get you on your way. Your mother will be grateful to see you sooner rather than later."

A few minutes later the boy was astride and heading off in the same direction as his uncle. His mount had a fresh spring in his step, having been released from his heavy pack, and Kuno trotted beside them with ears pricked, determined to protect his friend from all possible dangers.

Kirin could not believe the important task that had just been given to him. He was sure he could prove himself up to the job. How impressed his friends at home were going to be! However, he was relieved that Beindubn could not be too far away. The clouds were thickening now, which meant dusk would not wait and there would be little chance of Hatane casting her light tonight.

And that raised a problem. He did not like to admit it to himself often, and never to others, but the truth was he did not much care for the dark. The times he had left the safety of firelight at night were always in the company of the other children, caught up in games and shared nonsense that distracted him from his own imagination. Today he would hurry to catch up with his uncle, even if it meant facing his anger. He patted at his ribs to feel for the little knife, hidden above his belt. Its presence was comforting; a talisman for success.

"Kuno? I hope you are ready to stretch your legs!" he called down to the dog, then clinging on again tightly he nudged the pony forward faster with his heels.

The route home was starting to flatten out a little and Kirin realized that softer valleys were beginning to form on his right, pouring gently down and away. The horizon spread wide again, more obvious now, as much of this upper land was grazed regularly. He picked up smoky hints in the air of home fires being stoked for evening meals in the roundhouses below. The pathways made by sheep and local farming families crisscrossed the drovers' way in front of him.

He made good time, and was surprised not to catch sight of his uncle very soon, especially in this open country. His father was worried about Tirtos and his hot-headed speed with a weary horse and loaded cart, and now so was he. Had Tirtos not learned from one accident today already?

It was not long before he came up to another group of familiar landmarks, which helped his confidence. The Old Ones must have valued this area. They had left a series of three large, long mounds moulded to the slopes at the watershed, not too far from each other. These, and the trackways leading off from them in all directions, he knew well. Home was just beyond the approaching line of hill. Kirin had a favourite of the three mounds, one that had a large stone standing out at the top at one end. He had enjoyed jumping off it and rolling with Kuno on his journey out to

Elebyrig. He remembered his father had shouted at them to show more respect to his ancestors, and to stop frightening the ponies.

I was just a boy then, of course, he thought, embarrassed at the memory. *Not a horseman with an important mission.*

That mission in mind, he stopped and dismounted. A little stiffly, he and Kuno clambered onto the top of the mound to look ahead. And at last, there was his uncle. Well, there he should be, he thought. Some distance ahead, Kirin could see his cart. It was stationary to one side of the trackway, in the long shadows cast by the tall bushes at the edge. As Kirin watched, surprised that his uncle should now be wasting any time at all, Tirtos came into view around to the back of the cart. The boy reacted instinctively, dropping down to watch, half hidden behind the standing stone with his hand on Kuno in a warning for quiet.

Tirtos seemed to be manhandling something, an awkward bundle. At that distance Kirin could not see for sure but it did seem to be giving him some trouble. His uncle finished pushing whatever it was up and into the back and fastened the rear wicker panel. Glancing quickly over his shoulder, Tirtos then returned to the front and leapt up. After a moment the cart started off again and was soon out of sight once more around a bend.

After the cart had disappeared from view Kirin sat for a short time, trying to make sense of what he had just seen. Tirtos had not seen him when he looked back; it was clear that Tirtos did not want to be seen either. There was a shimmer left in the air of secrecy, of something suspicious. There was something else in that cart as well as containers of salt, he felt sure.

Kirin remounted and set off again, his head full of questions. He decided he had to get as close to his uncle as he could without attracting his attention. He needed some answers. He needed to know that the fanciful ideas now starting to fill his thoughts were ridiculous. It was not going to be easy. His uncle had increased his speed, and Kirin had to drive his poor pony and Kuno on at an exhausting pace to close the distance between them. Kirin wondered how Tirtos's pony could be coping with such lack of care.

As he rode, keeping a close eye on the view ahead, the boy began to revisit events and ideas that had lodged awkwardly in his memory. His uncle's bad mood and unexpected challenge to his father's plans ... He did not know what Tirtos was doing but he knew that things were not as they should be. Now Kirin's job to get help for his father seemed simple compared to this development. And how was he to tell his father about it without sounding like a troublemaker himself?

Thankfully, the route turned eastward and Kirin knew that soon would come the final drop before the rise to the Beindubn enclosure and home. With a silent prayer to Pona, the horse-spirit who watched over her subjects whether they had four legs or two, he pressed for the last of his mount's energy. In the fading light of the early evening, he and Kuno drew on their own reserves. Aching with weariness, more alert to trouble than ever before in their short lives, they carefully followed the young man with his cargo of secrets.

5

Kirin tied his pony to a low tree that overhung the stream in the near darkness of the valley floor. Then he felt his way up and through the tangled woodland towards what was left of the daylight, with Kuno silent at his side. There was no danger of losing touch with his uncle in the dusk, Tirtos was making enough noise to help the worst tracker in the land.

The cart had come to a stop. Kirin watched through the leaves as Tirtos jumped down and tried to force his exhausted pony to pull up the last, but steepest stretch to the open land above. The horse had had enough, and Pona took charge, giving the sturdy creature the will to resist the man's curses. Digging her hooves into the stony slope she refused to take another step. With a yell of exasperation, Tirtos lashed at the pony with the leather traces and stamped his foot like a spoiled child. He raised his fists to the sky and stormed off and up towards the enclosure gate, leaving the horse with head hanging, ready to drop where she stood in harness.

The animal's sudden refusal was a gift of time. It would take a while for the Beindubn folk to absorb the surprise of Tirtos's arrival, let alone the bad news of the stranded travellers left behind along the way.

"Now or never!" thought Kirin.

He didn't really have a plan. He just knew he had to see inside that cart, to try to find the reason for his uncle's strange behaviour. But Tirtos wanted to get it safe within the enclosure, that much was clear, and was bound to return for it as quickly as he could.

"Guard, Kuno!" Kirin whispered to the dog crouching at his

feet, ears pricked with tension.

Putting his exhaustion to one side, he parted the beech saplings in front of him, stepped onto the narrow track, and ran up quickly to the rear of the cart. Kuno, obedient as always when it was really needed, slunk further into a watchful position in the long undergrowth.

It felt like an age before Kirin's stiff fingers could loosen the twine knots holding the back panel in place, and the sound of his efforts seemed deafening in the quiet of the twilight woods. He swung the screen to one side and peered into the inner shadows. It was very difficult to see clearly. As the cart's sides wobbled against Kirin's efforts, splinters of dull light through gaps in the wickerwork played across the stacked cargo and confused his view. Taking a deep breath, he wiped his brow with his sleeve. He had to calm down and think.

It was then that he realized, with a shock, that he was not the only thing breathing hard. He could hear shallow rasps from the depths of the cart. Between the side panel and a wall of fired clay bricks stacked in straw, a bundle of rags was moving, trying to press itself as far back into the narrow gap as possible. With dry mouth and thundering heart, Kirin reached out a shaky hand and snatched at the nearest fold of cloth, poised for instant flight.

He found himself looking into a pair of dark staring eyes. With a gasp, he dropped the grimy cover and stepped back, thoughts whirling around his head in panic. For a moment he stood rooted to the spot. Then his brain cleared and his chest slowed. Those eyes were wide with panic. The creature was as frightened as he was.

He remembered his uncle. There would be no mercy in his rage if he discovered him there. The thought galvanized Kirin into action. He stretched into the shadows and took hold of the bundle, which in turn tried to wriggle weakly out of reach, whimpering. Its struggles were in vain, and Kirin was able to grab two handfuls of cloth and pull it to the edge of the cart. He got it to the ground, where it stayed in a heap, unmoving. As quickly as he could, he replaced and tied the rear panel to the cart, before dragging what now seemed a dead weight back to the undergrowth and out of sight.

Hidden by the screen of beech saplings once more, Kirin tried to take stock. He became aware of barking and calling that had started up from the enclosure above him during the last few intense minutes. His time was running out. He pulled at the folds of dirty homespun lying there in a heap in the ferns, and his nose wrinkled at the sour smell as he stripped away the last covering. What he saw in the shadows made his jaw drop.

It was a small girl, lying now with half closed eyes, white face pinched and pulled under a grubby cloth gag, hands bound at the wrists. Despairing, she turned her head away from him.

Kuno, who had been watching intently all this time, shuffled over and sniffed her greasy hair. Gently, he licked at her cheek and snuffled at her ear. The girl opened her eyes wide and struggled in alarm, trying to kick out at them both. Her feet had been hobbled together. Kuno sat back on his haunches and looked at her, unsure why his gesture of friendship had been rejected. Kirin was in shock as he tried to absorb the extent of her suffering.

But he had to think fast. They had to get further away from the cart before the Beindubn rescue party set off and his uncle was free to return. He knew the girl had no reason to trust him any more than his uncle, but any cry for help from her would be their undoing. Yet he could not leave that dreadful gag on her. He dropped down as close as he dared and looked into her panicked eyes with all the friendliness he could muster.

"Shh, shh! I won't hurt you!" he whispered, patting her knees even as she drew them up tightly towards her, gasping. "I'm a friend. A friend. The bad man's gone. But not for long. Let me help you, please!"

She froze, rigid, staring wildly at him. Kirin didn't know if she understood him, but he had to press on. He felt under his tunic for his new knife and pulled it out from its wrap. She made a little choking sound of fear and Kirin felt bad about causing her more distress, but quickly he cut through the gag. It took just a little longer to work his way through the thicker binding around her wrists and the length between her ankles. He sent thanks to the gods for keeping her alive. Even in that light he saw the white marks on her skin turn dark with returning blood. There must have been such pain to follow. Her defiant stare gave nothing away.

He sat back on his heels and balanced the smooth blade and handle in his fingers, his thoughts calming. He began to reason. They had surprise on their side. Tirtos did not know that he had been followed. Whatever her story was, the girl needed to be as far from the cart and his uncle as possible, and it would be easier to scramble her down the hillside rather than up. He tucked the knife away safely and gave the pieces of the girl's binding to Kuno to carry in his mouth. There would be enough evidence in daylight for Tirtos to piece together, without making it easy for him. He took hold of the girl and tugged.

"Get up!" he whispered urgently, "You're free ... But you must walk, do you understand? Get up and walk! Walk now!"

The girl's eyes went wide. There was still no sign that she understood him. Kirin gave her no time to think. He pulled her to her feet, propelling her forwards and, like a sleepwalker, her feet began to move one in front of the other.

Stumbling and sliding, they somehow started their descent back down towards the valley bottom, down into the protection of the night.

6

They reached the luminous thread of stream just in time. Suddenly the darkness was pierced by the flash of tallow torches through the trees from above. Stones scattered and hooves skidded as the rescue party set off in earnest down the track. Kirin gritted his teeth as the wave of noise rushed past somewhere above their heads and then headed up the opposite slope. His pony pulled a little at his tether and whinnied softly in recognition of familiar smells. The Beindubn men were wasting no time in getting to Colios.

The girl was in a bad way. Barely conscious, she drooped against him, drained by their scramble to safety. Kirin lowered her onto the mossy bank. Without a sound, Kuno dropped down next to her. She turned towards the dog's warmth and curled up against him. Worn out himself, Kirin slumped down next to them and tried to think.

It was all very confusing. He could not imagine what Tirtos would want with such a scrap of a girl. Where had she come from? What would his father make of it all? His head whirled. He needed help.

The pony fidgeted and nuzzled at his neck, comforting Kirin with a soft nose. The steady breathing of the animals and the constant trickle of the stream calmed him. All sensations seemed to amplify in the renewed quiet of the woods. Insects scratched in the bark behind him, the moss beneath them smelt heady and rich, the smooth stones strung on his belt lay more heavily on his hips, the soft hide around the little knife pressed against his ribs. He reached inside his tunic and felt the warm leather, and the head of the creature hidden inside.

He needed help, and now he knew where to get it. He summoned up some energy and struggled to his feet once more. Kuno lifted his head but made no attempt to get up. Kirin knew the girl and the pony would be safe for a while in his care.

"Good dog" he whispered, rubbing his head. "Guard. I'll be back soon."

Darkness had closed in completely. Kirin took a deep breath and started to make his way back, avoiding the main approach to the enclosure. The last thing he needed now was to bump into Tirtos on his return to the cart. He picked his way carefully with memory as his guide, winding his way up through the tangled coppicing and creeper. He sent up a plea to Pona that Tirtos would not think to check inside the cart until through the gateway.

As for him, there were many ways to get into the Beindubn enclosure if you were a resourceful boy who knew every little gap in the turf bank and fence around his home.

WATER HISSED AND spat on the stones at the edge of the fire as Cuamena dropped her wooden ladle in surprise. The appearance of her son in the doorway of the roundhouse, after the noisy rescue mission had departed, left her speechless. She was preparing a warming broth for the weary travellers when they were finally brought in. She had not expected to find Kirin sneaking in alone, dishevelled and pale.

For Kirin, the sight of his mother brought hot tears to his eyes. Words were impossible for him too. He rushed across and flung his arms around her, burying his face in her thick shawl. Cuamena held him tight for a long moment. Then she found her voice and took his pale face in her hands, brushing his hair aside to look at him properly.

"Kirin! What are you doing here? You're home already? I don't understand. I thought you were still with your father. Tirtos arrived a short time past with the news of the waggon. He has been charging about like a fly-stung beast since, but he said nothing of you. Oh my son, I'm so happy to see you!" She squeezed him again.

At the mention of Tirtos, Kirin remembered how little time he had. Rubbing at his tears, he struggled to recover his breath, and his control. "I've come for help too, please listen …" He grasped her arms and pulled her away from the bright firelight over to the shadows by the beds.

He lowered his voice. "Father did send me, but Tirtos doesn't know I'm here. There are many things to tell you. It's about Tirtos, he has been keeping secrets. Father doesn't know yet, I don't know it all—" He glanced over his shoulder at the doorway, the fear of his uncle's anger starting to cut into his thoughts.

"— There's a girl. A small one. I've just had to free her from his cart. I've left her in the woods with Kuno. Tirtos was hiding her. He must have had her in there for ages. I had to do something to help her. I had to! But if Tirtos finds out … He's been acting strangely. You would hardly recognize him, Mother, when he changes. When he finds out what I have done, I fear what he might do …" Kirin gulped and came to a breathless halt.

Cuamena sat down heavily on the lower bunk. It did not occur to her to doubt him. It was hard to see the carefree boy she had said goodbye to, so many weeks ago, standing there full of worry. All this bad news, coming thick and fast after happy plans for their welcome home, took a while to take in. But Cuamena's quick mind soon began to make sense of what he told her.

"Slaves," she whispered, almost to herself. "I wager he wants to trade girls. Someone has filled his head with dirt. That trip he made to Calleba; those tales of traders with their fancy wares and fine living that impressed him so much. Oh, the stupid boy,

Colios would never agree! And so arrogant to think he could get away with it. Well, he's proving to be Assuna's son alright!"

Cuamena stood up, thinking hard. She fixed her shawl more tightly across her with its bronze pin and then guided her son over to a low pile of bedding next to a wooden box.

"Kirin, you have done the right thing. Stay here and rest for a moment. And you need to eat now, while we think of the best course." She went back over to the fire, scooped out a bowlful of meat broth from a large blackened pot. Picking up a wooden spoon, she returned to her son in the shadows. She smiled as she handed it to him. "You are in charge, while I see what Tirtos is doing right now." After a brief look around the hessian hanging in the doorway, she slipped away.

The boy blew on a spoonful of hot broth to cool it. As he ate, the welcome warmth spread through him and he realized just how hungry he had been. The heavy air of the roundhouse, with its thick walls and soot stained roof poles reaching into the darkness above, was secure and comforting. The hissing of the logs on the fire and the occasional flurry of sparks that twinkled into nothing as they rose up into the shadows were like a sleeping potion to Kirin. His eyelids grew heavy and the spoon drooped in his hand.

A TINY WHIMPER broke into his consciousness. He sat up straight with a start. Kuno? The girl? Then he remembered.

The noise came from the wooden box. He put his bowl down and lifted the head of the box carefully to catch some light. Peeping in, he saw his baby sisters lying there. The twins were sleeping side by side with chubby arms outstretched, the larger one with the wrap of the smaller in a fist. Galete and Kele.

They had changed so much! His heart filled with love and he smiled as he remembered that day of spring sunshine, when his mother and the wise woman had returned from the birthing place with not one bundle, but two. There had been such celebration at Beindubn that evening!

Kirin watched as the smaller of the two, Kele, blew little milky bubbles of sleepy satisfaction. Her twin, Galete, wriggled slightly and frowned and murmured. He wondered what problems babies could possibly have to worry about, warm and safe as they were, and now with their older brother to watch over them. Then he thought of the girl in the woods. She must have a family too. Perhaps somewhere there was a mother or father looking desperately for her, or a brother frantic to find and protect his sister. For he would be, if it was one of his sisters, of that he was certain. Kirin tucked a blanket more closely around the twins and stood up. His decision was made. There was no more time to lose.

Quickly, he pulled down a length of homespun that was hanging from a hook on the roof post. Cuamena returned to find him laying it out on the floor.

"I'm going to get the girl home, Mother. I don't know where that is, but I'm going to try. I've got Father's pony and I know my way around more than I did. And Kuno is with me. Please don't tell anyone yet. Tirtos will find out, and you will not be safe from his anger. I've learned a lot this summer, truly, and I hope Father will understand when he finds out what's been going on."

He looked at her desperately and faltered. When Cuamena opened her mouth to speak, he added quietly, "Please don't stop me, I am old enough. If we wait for Father to come in, it will make things hard for him. He will have to hear what Tirtos has to say. I have to do this."

Cuamena looked from him to the wooden box and back again. She gave up what she was going to say and her shoulders dropped in acceptance. "Well, your uncle is putting up a fine show of temper over at the other house," she admitted. "There's not a body would get in his way tonight without suffering."

She paused in thought, then spoke briskly. "Get the girl to safety tonight. Find out what you can from her and wait in the woods for your father to sort all of this out. Kirin, I will help for now, but use the sense the gods gave you, please. I trust you to do that, and pray for Cuda's guidance."

She began to think aloud, gathering items from all directions and place them on Kirin's blanket. "Meat, bread, pottage grain ... fire maker and cooking pot, spoon ... knife ..."

Kirin quickly checked at his waist. "No, I have one."

"Then use it carefully. You'll need a water bag and some horse meal. They're outside." Cuamena looked up at Kirin. "The girl? Does she have anything with her?" Kirin shook his head. "Then I'll find a spare shift or two." She disappeared once more.

Kirin began to gather up the corners of the blanket to form a bag. Was it only this morning that he had set out from Comelris? Kirin felt he had lived half a lifetime in a few hours. So much for wanting adventure. Had the gods planned how this day was going to end? Now they were sending him back out into the dark.

His mother returned with two more bags and tied them across his back. She refilled Kirin's bowl with crumbled bread in warm broth to carry in his hand for the girl. As a last thought, Cuamena tucked some dried mutton bones into the top of one of his bags. "For Kuno," she smiled.

He was ready. Cuamena cupped his face with her warm hands and looked at him closely. "You don't have to do this, you know. Your father will deal with Tirtos soon. All will be put right."

For a moment Kirin hesitated, but then remembered the scenes of the afternoon; the clear challenge to his father's authority. His mother had not witnessed that. He could not explain to her the unease that remained with him. A thin crack had appeared in their secure world. Only time would tell if it was to be a fatal one. Kirin could not be sure that Beindubn would be safe for the girl even with his father around. He was sure that a long journey lay ahead of him, but this was not the time to worry his mother more. Kirin forced a brave smile for Cuamena. He picked up his bundle and disappeared out of the low doorway.

7

Kuno heard him approaching and came to guide him to their hiding place. The girl had not run away. Kirin was not sure if she had even woken until stirred by the dog's movement. Before she could flinch away, Kirin pushed the bowl of food into her cold hands. Unsure at first, she picked at morsels of the meaty bread pudding with her fingers and then tucked in hungrily.

Kirin fixed the leather meal bag over the pony's head and pulled out the bones for Kuno. It was a strange midnight meal amongst the undergrowth with companions he could not really see in the darkness. The boy sat chewing bread, listening to the little group eating around him. He was responsible for them now. It was up to him. The gods had decided.

Kuno padded off to lap water from the stream. Kirin realized the girl had finished her food. He took the bowl from her and followed the dog to rinse out the bowl. He drank himself and then refilled it, taking it back for the girl. He sat down heavily next to her, weary to his bones. She took the bowl from him and drank.

"Thank you," she whispered.

The unexpected sound jolted Kirin to the core. He could understand her, and she him! This was very good news.

Just then there was a low growl from Kuno. Kirin felt him at his elbow, nudging and worrying, and a minute later he knew why. Downstream, on the opposite bank, someone was approaching, muttering and crashing around in the bushes. It had to be Tirtos.

Kirin touched the girl's arm in warning, and raised a reassuring hand for the pony. They froze in their hiding place, listening intently as the sound of angry complaining found them through the trees. Wood cracked and snapped under clumsy feet. The noise got closer and louder.

"Just you wait! You wait till I get you! You'll know what trouble is then! Conjure up what you can you little wildcat – I'm ready for it!" Suddenly there was a splash, followed by a short silence. Then a burst of dreadful curses called down the wrath of Volkos on anything and everything.

Despite the tension, Kirin had to smile at the picture in his mind's eye. He could tell that Tirtos had been at the brew. To his relief, he heard the noises fading back up and away. Wet clothes and drunkenness had put an end to his searching for now. And by the sound of it, Tirtos thought the girl had escaped by herself. But he would work it all out when Colios returned in the morning. This long night was not over yet.

With a sigh, he took off and tied the pony's nosebag, and turned to gather together their things, fumbling in the dark. As he took the bowl from the girl he realized she was crying, the dread of that near miss with Tirtos shaking her thin shoulders. He took the blanket, shook it free of its contents and wrapped it around her. He did not know what to say that might help. There was nothing that could help, except action.

"Come on," he said gently. "We can't stay here. We have to move again, while the dark is on our side. Climb up."

Kirin helped the girl onto the pony and tucked the homespun around her for warmth. He repacked the bags as best he could and tied them on behind her. She lay forward, passive and unresponsive, with her arms around the animal's neck. Kirin took the reins and whispered him into motion.

Kuno led the way through the trees and up the steep hillside. Step by step they put distance between them and the Beindubn estate, between them and home. Somewhere, across the drovers' way above them, Kirin hoped for another little valley, sheltered and welcoming, dense enough for safety and sleep and perhaps the chance to think up some sort of plan.

8

Bright light flickered through the canopy high above and played on Kirin's upturned face. He turned stiffly and brushed sleep and hair from his eyes. The thick mattress of the woodland floor shifted and rustled under him. Kirin rubbed his face and opened his eyes properly. He pulled himself up and looked around him. The girl was sitting and watching him nervously.

He grinned at her, feeling a bit self-conscious. The daylight, and the sight of her, put reality into the dreamlike events of the previous night. She swallowed and spoke quietly.

"You have slept well?"

The girl had been busy. A small fire was burning some way in front of him on a wide ledge of packed soil, which she had cleared of its leafy layers and ringed with large stones pulled from a hole in the bank behind them. A large tree had fallen back from here at one time, and now the exposed and dry root system reached out protectively from the base like an open hand. On some of the wiry tendrils she had hung their bags.

The cooking pot was starting to simmer, and grey-green wood smoke floated gently away. Beneath the ledge of their camp, between the lines of tall and slender trunks, he could see glimpses of water meadow and then green banks rising up opposite them in the brighter light of open sky.

The pony wandered into view down below, cropping at fresh grass. Kirin guessed that Kuno would not be far away either, probably scavenging for his next meal. The world seemed to have left him behind, just a little. He must have slept well into the middle of the day.

Kirin looked back at the girl, who had got up to check the fire. She was older than he had first thought, perhaps closer to his age. She moved around the clearing with quiet purpose. Kirin took in her small size and undernourished state. She seemed fragile to him. But not broken, that was for sure; he was impressed with everything she had done while he slept. He watched as she dropped leaves and roots into the steaming water, followed by some crushed wheat meal from Cuamena's stores. The sores left by the binding of her wrists stood out sharply.

"Who are you?" he asked.

"Rianbe is my given name. Everyone calls me Ribby." She stirred slowly as she spoke. The long green leaves softened, folded and disappeared into the broth. She sat back and looked directly at him. "Who are you?"

"Kirin, from Beindubn. That's where I went last night, for help. It was my uncle Tirtos... who ... who ..." He fell silent again, embarrassed.

Tension strained her face. She turned again and poked at the embers with a stick. "I think the gods sent you," she said simply. "I was praying and praying, and they sent you. My father says that they will listen, if you have a good heart." Her voice grew stronger, and she frowned. "Your uncle has a bad heart." She shuddered.

"So," she continued. "Did you hear me, then, in the cart?"

"No, I was following. I was watching my uncle. He was behaving strangely. I had to find out what was going on." The need to defend his family came to him in a rush. "Listen, I don't know why my uncle did this to you. My father will be angry, I have no doubt about that! My family has honour. We trade ponies, good strong ponies. We don't take people. That's not right!"

The girl shrugged, unconvinced, pale face twisting with difficult memories. "Say that to your uncle. I heard him make the bargain, and I got the bruises." She smoothed at the sores on her wrists and blinked away fresh tears.

Kirin spoke more softly. "How did he get you? Where are you from?"

"I come from the long forest, between the sister rivers. It's a long way off, I think." She gazed around her. "My village is cut deep among the trees. My kinsmen dig for the stone with the metal in it. They came from over the high mountains and settled there before I was born. We have enemies. There are people, bad people, who think we should go back to the mountains and stay there. They say we have no right to the stone." She swallowed, the effort of speaking coming hard after her days of silence. "Oh, my mother warned me of trouble, but I did not think. They took me when I was alone in the woods, they covered my face with a sack. I thought it was the Green Man …"

"Green man?" Kirin had to interrupt.

"The Man in the Woods," she said, surprised. "You must know. He catches naughty children and takes them to his hideout. But there were two men, or three, and they were no spirits. They hid me in some village, then they passed me to *him.*" Her voice hardened from pain to anger. "They traded me like a horse, I heard them arguing. I heard the clink of metal and the deal was done."

Kirin was shocked at her story. Tirtos must have used a prized Dobunnic token; he wondered how he had got hold of one from Colios's bag. His uncle's secrecy and deception was unfolding with every word the girl spoke.

"I was a long time in the cart then, I shook off the sack but saw little. He said he would kill me if I made a sound," she continued. "Sometimes he got me out, and gave me water and scraps of food. Or to empty myself; he said he did not want to spoil the salt." Her chin trembled, she looked away into the trees.

Kirin knew now the reason for Tirtos stopping the cart yesterday. The girl went on, impatient to finish and push it away from her thoughts.

"I remember lots of bumping. Oh, so much bumping. And a crossing over the great river, I think, with the animals frightened and men calling. I felt sick. I let the river and her water spirits decide my fate." She fell silent.

Kirin had stood up and was pacing the clearing, his indignation rising, finding it impossible to sit still. He stopped and thought for a moment. Everything she was saying was making him more determined.

"Well, I have a good idea where your home must be now. Look, I'm not going to take you back to mine. I must get you back to Savren," he decided. "That has to be the great river you crossed. I've seen her, and the hills beyond. That's where we will go, we will cross again and find your family, and then everything will be as it should!"

The girl stood and joined him, bewildered. "Are you sure?" Her voice was choked. "Could we do that?"

"I know it!" he said confidently, to convince himself as much as her.

"Now? On our own?" She looked up through the trees. "How will we find the way?"

Kirin had not given a great deal of time to that problem yet, but it had to be faced. He fingered the collection of beads strung at his waist, thinking. His hand brushed against the wrapped knife under his tunic. Suddenly it came to him.

"This stream below will show us! We can't use the open paths on top – Tirtos may be searching – but we could return along this valley. We could start early tomorrow, when we have the morning light of Uban's path to show us the way. If we follow that, and the stream, we will find the mother river, Savren herself! And then we just have to get across somehow, and, and—" Kirin ran out of inspiration at that point.

"— And then we will see what happens next?" Hope lit up the girl's face.

"Um, yes," Kirin agreed lamely.

She smiled at the expression on his face. "Thank you ... Kirin ... It's a very good plan."

He blushed a little at her using his name for the first time.

"We need to get ready, then," she continued, happily. She looked down at her filthy clothes and picked at her torn skirt, sighing. "We have to get clean first."

Kirin was not sure why that was of any great importance, but he realised how uncomfortable she must be. He remembered Cuamena's bags. He went over to them and pulled out a small bundle.

"Ribby?" He tried out her name, holding the clothes out. "My mother sent these."

"For me? So you did tell someone at home." She was alarmed, and couldn't hide it.

"Yes, but she understands the danger. My uncle won't find out. She knows we are in hiding for a while. Although I think she may expect us back there soon ..."

"Kirin, I don't want to get you into trouble with your family," Ribby said cautiously. "It's enough to be free from that cart. Let me go on myself now."

Kirin shook his head. "No," he smiled, "and please don't say that again."

Ribby smiled back. She put down the clothes and went over to the scar around the tree roots. She took a handful of damp clay from the layers of soil and stone. Returning to the fire, she scooped some cool wood ash from the edge and began to knead it all together in her hands.

"Not as good as my mother's, but it will have to do," she said, worrying at her long greasy hair. "I must try something for this. I'll keep a bit for you, perhaps?" she added, teasing just a little. "Anyway, I'm going down to the stream." She picked up the clothes and set off down through the trees.

Kirin looked down at his scuffed hide boots and bindings and at his grubby tunic, all dirtied and dulled by their damp scramble through the woods. Maybe she had a point. They would be travelling through Dobunnic country; it would not do to appear like outlaws. He didn't want any awkward questions, or any word getting back to Beindubn too soon. Perhaps a little work down at the stream later would be a good idea.

He returned to the fire to inspect the broth, now smelling inviting and homely. He sat down for a while. Only yesterday, he had promised the gods that he would be a dutiful son. What was Colios saying about him right now? Was he being disrespectful by not waiting for his father to cast his judgement before leaving? The worm of doubt in his father's ability to control Tirtos was eating away at him. It made him feel disloyal.

But Ribby's happiness and hope had left an echo in the clearing. Last night he had felt alone; today things had changed for the better. He felt comfortable with Ribby. They would be in this together.

An instinct made him take out his knife. Once again it had prompted his attention. He unfolded its wrapping and considered the little bronze creature. "So you fancy a little daylight, do you?" As usual it looked back at him playfully, challenging his thoughts.

"Well, are you pleased with me this far, my friend?" Kirin quizzed. "I hope I am doing right, for Uban's blessings are needed now. You will need to work your magic with the gods. There's no turning back for us now, and that includes you!"

At that moment, Kirin's attention was caught by a disturbance high on the top of the bank opposite, silhouetted through the trees against the bright afternoon skyline. Two large birds had dropped like stones and were arguing frantically. They seemed to have some unfortunate creature gripped in their talons, and neither was ready to give way to the other. As he watched, Kuno appeared along the horizon, barking joyfully. The dog leapt in, all tail and legs, and frightened the birds into letting go. He snatched the furry prize as they abandoned it, and galloped off cheekily, ignoring their outraged screams and slap of powerful wings.

Kirin laughed out loud. He and Ribby were not the only ones who would get a meal inside them today. He felt like leaping about with Kuno. The prospect of redeeming his family's honour, with an adventure into the bargain, now filled him with excitement. Even the thought of a wash in the cold stream was not going to dampen his spirits.

9

By the time hazy sunshine had appeared over the top of the steep woods and touched the reed banks below they had been walking for some time.

Kirin's plan seemed to be working out well. Heading downstream felt right from the beginning. They could see the stream was growing. With cheerful confidence it bubbled down over shallow gravelly shelves and neatly skirted the outcrops of deeper limestone layers that fingered into the valley floor. Green tendrils of water plants swayed in darker pools caught behind natural stepping stones. Its course had meandered a little over time to give them a clear path along its banks. There was not enough workable land down there to encourage any farmer, so they had travelled since first light without meeting anyone. They took it in turns to lead the pony, quiet for the most part.

The damp smells of early autumn rose up as they swished through the long grasses and herbs, heavy seed heads catching at their clothes, morning dew darkening the leather on their feet. Insects worked to make the most of these final days before frost, and Kuno shook his ears in warning at bees that took too much interest in them. Every now and then he decided to make an exaggerated snap at one as he trotted along. Ribby laughed at the dog.

"I know!" Kirin laughed too. "Kuno loves a performance. There's not a fireside tale-teller that can keep an audience longer than that hound."

"Why does he have a name?"

"He is my brother, or feels like one anyway. My father found him. His mother had been killed by a wild pig. I've grown up with him. We look after each other."

"Do you have other brothers?"

"No, I have two baby sisters. Twins, would you believe. Cuda has blessed our family. What about you?"

"I am the only child. My mother's babies usually died but I did not. That's why I was called Rianbe. My father says it means I'm special. But I have many cousins at home." She took a sharp breath and looked away quickly. "They must all think I'm gone forever."

"Well, you are not," asserted Kirin firmly. "Kuno and I will make sure of that." The dog wagged his tail widely at the sound of his name and Ribby smiled again.

After a moment, she continued. "What about this horse, then?" She reached and patted the broad brow of the little pony that followed in Kirin's wake with their bags balanced and tied. "The horse should have a name."

This came as a surprise to Kirin. He had been trained from an early age to avoid getting fond of the ponies they bred and sold. They were Pona's bounty, a unit to be bartered or traded. It was hard work to provide for the people of the settlement from the fields and woods of the Beindubn estate, let alone keep the horses fed and watered and cured of ailments as well. It was hard work to keep the horse pastures corralled safely against thieves or against the occasional attempt of the liveliest to break free. Everyone at Beindubn, child or adult, respected the beautiful animals but had to consider them with trade only in mind. He tried to explain some of this to Ribby.

"We have horses too, where I live" she replied, afterwards. "We use them to pull the stone diggers' sledges and carts. They are better than oxen in small spaces. But only the most important families can get one, the ones who control the richest layers. My father hopes for one, but he never gets a chance."

She turned back to the pony and spoke gently in his ear. "If we had you, I'd call you Belin, the strong one."

"That's a new name to me. I like it. Belin it should be," nodded Kirin, patting the pony's flank.

Ribby smiled back. "Now we are all friends!"

She took the halter from Kirin and set off once more at a good pace, Belin and Kuno trotting behind. Kirin stopped for a moment to scoop and drink some of the cold clean water from the water's edge.

"Wait for me!" he called happily, as he raced to catch them up again.

THE UNCERTAIN COURSE of the stream began to create problems as the day passed by. At one point the narrow riverbank came to an end and the water suddenly disappeared underground into a dark stony fracture in the valley side. They had to clamber across higher ground for some time, around twisted tree trunks and through tangled scrub, hoping they would not lose their way. Belin needed sure and steady hooves to follow his companions. Many times the pony had to wait patiently while they freed the bags on his back that had snagged on low branches. Twigs caught on clothes and scratched at faces. Centuries of leaf mould and rotting wood slipped away under their damp feet as they clambered around. It was hard for all of them. Eventually they heard the welcome sound of gushing water further ahead, and Kuno guided them down to the source.

Uban's light stayed strong, though. As they came back out into more open woodland Kirin could sense from the direction of the afternoon sun that the valley was curving round and heading in the direction he had hoped for. It was more cleanly cut now, with faster flowing water at its base. A young river, rather than a stream.

He was very relieved. His nerve had started to wear thin as his tiredness increased; losing the track of the water for a while had confused and worried him. He looked up at the patch of sky above. There was now a much greater gap between the leafy canopies that swayed and rustled at the top of slender trunks on each valley side, catching the breeze. Kirin sent up a silent prayer to Uban that this would prove to be leading them to the destination that they needed.

He turned to Ribby. "Shall we rest here for a short while?" She nodded, sensing his worry, and glad for a rest herself. They allowed the pony to graze and drink freely, and pulled out what was left of their food from their stores for themselves and Kuno. But it could only be a brief respite, and it was not long before they had to get on the move once more.

They began to see signs of other people. As they drove themselves on, they would occasionally come across the flat stones of an old fireplace or the collapsed skeleton of branches and dried leaves that marked an abandoned shelter on a terrace. Sometimes they passed muddy patches of snuffled turf at the edges of the woods where pigs had been walked. The possibility of meeting someone made them both nervous, though neither had energy enough left to speak about it. The calm sanctuary of the hidden valley upstream had made their adventure so possible, so reasonable. Soon they were going to have to justify themselves to others. Soon they might be asked to tell a believable tale that would not send riders to Beindubn in the hope of a quick reward.

The sun had dropped behind the tree line before Ribby broke the silence between them. For some time she had been foraging for their evening meal as they walked, and had enough to make it worth lighting a fire for some soup. She suggested it carefully. After a moment's consideration, Kirin agreed. There was some shelter there at the edge of some tall river rushes, hopefully enough cover to spend the night unnoticed and room to have a fire on the bank. To his dismay, Kirin's fear of the dark had returned with the drop in his spirits. Anger and indignation had fuelled him through that first night of action, but now it was almost as though he had time free for worry. With every step he now felt more vulnerable, more aware of the enormity of what they were attempting. A comforting fire would be a good idea.

While Ribby gathered some of the dead dry wood hanging from the lower branches at the edge of the steep woods, he untied the bags on Belin and let him free to explore their new surroundings with Kuno. He rearranged some stones, took out the fire-maker of hazel and twine, then a few bits of dried grass and kindling, and finally his knife.

He thought of his mother's endless instruction, and his endless practice, until he was as quick as any of the other children at making fire. He set about spinning one point of kindling into a cut in another until the grass smouldered into wispy blueness and then into glowing red threads. "And yes, Mother, I will remember to dry more for the next," he thought, in answer to her voice in his head.

As Ribby set the fire he encouraged the small heap of smoking grass, balanced on a flat stone, and kept it alight until she was ready. Soon blue smoke was rising up into the early evening sky. Such an ordinary sight, and so reassuring to the tired group of travellers. It was a sign of home, and a sign of life.

10

Ribby became aware of the silent observer before Kirin, although Kuno had been watching the small child for some time with interest. He liked children and had not felt any particular need to raise the alarm. She touched Kirin's arm to alert him.

The child was standing half hidden by the trunk of a tree some distance away. Whether it was a girl or boy was hard to tell, the few scraps of weave that served as clothing had dressed many children before that one. What they could see of the child's bare legs and arms were dirty and thin.

Kirin got to his feet slowly. His movement broke the spell. With a loud giggle, the child turned and disappeared back into the shadows. He shrugged, and turned back to Ribby at the fire. "There must be a homestead close by."

They looked at each other. They both knew what this meant. They had to be ready now for the real world. With the morning sun they would be following a route past farms and foresters, taking their chance against prying eyes and inevitable curiosity.

"We had better decide now what to tell people," Kirin said. "Let's be brother and sister, taking our father's horse to meet him downstream somewhere …"

Before he could finish, their attention was caught again by the appearance of the same small child at the trees' edge, this time accompanied by a few more children of varying size and grubbiness. They stood and sniggered, trying to nudge each other to the front. Kuno wagged his tail and trotted across the clearing towards them. Kirin and Ribby stood up and smiled.

That was a mistake. Filthy hands seized them both from behind. They found themselves in the clutches of two men in rough clothes and even rougher mood. Their freedom was over, and much sooner than feared.

Without a word, and ignoring their struggles, the men bundled them along the riverbank. Kuno tried his best, but his snarling attempts to defend the pair were met with harsh sideways kicks. He retreated to some distance, worrying and fretting. The untidy pack of children trailed along behind with Belin and the bags.

They rounded a bend and arrived at a cluster of buildings. A few shabby huts stood between the river and the start of the rising woods, with a small paddock behind. A weary-looking cow raised her head over a wicker hurdle and looked mournfully at them as they approached. Two darkly spotted pigs, squealing and chasing, skittered past them and spattered their arrival with mud. To one side, a large mound of burnt turf and ash was being taken apart by two women. Black sticks were being graded and sorted into heaps. The acrid smell of smoke hit their noses and everything they saw was touched with black grime.

The scene held no surprises for Kirin and Ribby. With sinking hearts, they both realized they had fallen into the hands of charcoal burners. Both had grown up with charcoal burning at home and had helped collect wood from a very young age. A charcoal supply was vital for anyone with kilns and smithies. But so much was needed that many of the tribes could not produce enough themselves and had to barter for extra. Some of the poorer families had taken to wandering from place to place, setting up temporary burning sites until the good wood ran out, and moving on. It was a difficult life, and a bit of wheeling and dealing out of sight of any tribute lords was always welcome. And where there was no control, there was no protection.

The two men stopped and pushed Ribby and Kirin to the

ground. The women rushed over and stared in surprise.

"See?" grunted the larger of the two men, looking them over. "Here's a fine result for no effort. Two cubs and a good lookin' pony!"

The other man bent down and rubbed the cloth of Ribby's sleeve between his fingers. "Tis good weave, an' all. Perhaps there's a bit more of that in they bags." He turned and snatched a bundle from one of the children and thrust it at the women. They immediately started to rummage inside, whispering to each other.

"What's yer story then?" growled the first man, poking at Kirin's chest with his dirty boot. He noticed Kirin's leather string of polished stones around his middle. "All decked for a feasting, are you? Pretty bit of not much!"

Kirin stood up and lifted his chin, looking directly into the man's shifty eyes. He was determined to make a stand. "How dare you!" Ribby joined him and took hold of his hand. "My sister and I are going to meet my father and his men. They will come straight upstream if we are not there in time. And you will have to explain this treatment to them! Kuno, come here!"

The women and children stared at Kirin in surprise at his nerve, and both men looked at each other, shuffling a little with indecision. Kuno picked his way through the group and sat upright at Kirin's feet, his eyes watchful.

"Well, that's as maybe," muttered the large one. "Tis a fine father as lets his cubs wander about the land." He patted the nearest of his children roughly on the head. "Wouldn't find me lackin' like that, would you, my tiddlers?" The child's flinch at his touch told a different tale.

"He's not here now, though, is he," calculated the other, weighing up the advantage. "Reckon there's somethin' in this fer us, but we needs a bit of thinkin' time."

"Right enough, Brother, right enough. Let's us all have a bit of that thinkin' time till mornin'. No rush. These two, and that bag of dog bones, can roost in our store. Woman, tie that horse up with the cow …"

The large man's loud instructions continued, echoing back and forth around the clearing and sending the family in all directions. The other man ran to unfasten the door of the storage hut that was raised up on a crooked timber framework above the ground. Kirin and Ribby found themselves, once again, dragged against their will through the mud.

As they were being lifted and thrown into the hut, Kirin caught sight of a small flock of sheep emerging from the trees, followed by their shepherd. In the fuss and distraction of Kuno being made to jump up into the hut too, Kirin took another glance, and caught his breath, at the shocked face of Sheep Boy.

11

Ribby's heart had sunk at finding herself trapped once more. The memory of that salt cart was too raw for her to cope with this fresh imprisonment. She had wrapped her sore arms around Kuno and was weeping silently.

Kirin whispered, excitedly, "I know that boy! I met him the other day, up on the hills. I'm sure it is the same one. He upset Tirtos, poking around his cart. Of course! Now I know why!"

Ribby showed no interest.

Now Kirin did not know what to make of their situation, or how to comfort her. He turned to peer through the gaps between the uneven poles of the walls.

The dusk had brought shadow to the valley, and birds were singing their evening song. The family had disappeared into their hut, most likely to sort through their bags. There was no sign of Sheep Boy. Kirin wondered whether knowing the boy might help them. Probably not, as the women and children were all clearly scared of the men. As the quiet settled his thoughts, and his heartbeat, he realised once more that it was going to be up to him, if the gods should please, to find some escape from this.

He shuffled over to the door panel and felt in the twilight for any looped hinge of twine. Yes, the door was fixed in the usual way. With a rush of relief, he felt at his waist for his knife, wondering why he had not thought of it immediately. He patted at his ribs, assuming the package had slipped around behind. But he could not feel it anywhere at his middle. Had he not returned it safely to its hiding place earlier after spotting the child? The awful truth hit home: his talisman was gone. They were on their own.

It felt as if he had been doused in icy water. Like Ribby, any hope dropped away. Cold and exhausted, he crawled back silently and squeezed next to her and the dog as they slumped against a few dusty bags of grain. Kuno lifted his head and licked the boy's damp cheek, then sighed deeply and settled back against the girl. All they could do was wait, and they didn't know what to wait for, except an attempt at sleep.

THEN THERE WAS no mistaking scrabbling at the door. It sounded like a rat. Kuno growled and his muscles tensed, waking both Kirin and Ribby. They sat up in the darkness, confused and fearful. The door panel shook and then swung open. The half-light of the open space revealed the face and shoulders of Sheep Boy.

"Come now, you!" he whispered.

Without a word they scrambled down on to the mud. Kuno leaped past the three of them, relieved at being able to stretch his long limbs once more. Sheep Boy took hold of Kirin's arm and led him and Ribby, half crouching, along the line of paddock fencing that edged the clearing, putting as much distance between them and the huts as possible. He motioned for them to stay in the darker shadows behind a wood stack, and disappeared. Kirin squeezed Ribby's hand in reassurance, as Kuno pushed in between them.

"Good dog!" He ruffled Kuno's ears and whispered to them both. "I think it's going to be alright!"

The three of them crouched in silence, aware of faint sounds and movement not a great distance from them. Sheep Boy reappeared at Kirin's elbow. "This way," he muttered, a little out of breath, and turned into the undergrowth. They followed as quickly and quietly as they could. It was not many moments before they came up against the warmth of Belin, who nudged his nose into their faces.

There was no time to celebrate or talk. Sheep Boy set off at speed, picking his way ahead of the group from dark to lighter and back into dark, winding a path through the lower reaches of the woods. Kirin realized he was keeping the course of the river below them and to their right. It was clear that he knew the twists and turns of every track and ridge through these woods.

As the sky lightened above them he slowed the pace a little and turned more often to check how his companions were coping behind him. Both Ribby and Kirin were tired, but had managed to keep up. Neither had wanted to ride Belin in the dark and run the risk of injury from low branches.

At last the boy felt able to stop. He suddenly turned, grinned at them and dropped flat on the ground, stretching out his arms and legs in relief. He spoke at last, and with a joyful laugh.

"Ha! I ain't dared do that before!" He closed his eyes and breathed deeply, smiling widely.

Kirin realized that the charged flight through the night had not just been for their sake. Sheep Boy had been making his own escape too. He sat down next to him and laughed himself. "Well, the gods will reward you! And if they don't, my father will!"

"I don't understand!" exclaimed Ribby breathlessly, dropping down next to him and looking from him to Kirin and back again.

"Soon's I saw him and that dog I thoughts, that's the kind boy, so I knew somethin' bad was up." He sat up. "An' that made me think hard. I don't need them fer nothin'. So 'ere we is!" He laughed again with delight at his new freedom, and at the thought of the angry scenes probably playing out right now in that shabby homestead.

"But won't they come after us?" asked Ribby.

"Nah, they don't do nothin' that's too much hard work." He chuckled again. Then at another thought his expression dropped a little. "I got yer horse but not yer bags. Or food. So we might go a bit 'ungry for a whiles. Still, won't be the first time." He turned over and tucked his hands under his head. "Right now I needs a bit o' shut-eye." And with that, he was asleep.

The boy and girl looked at each other. So much had happened so quickly, it was hard to take it all in. How could they ever repay him? But that would have to come later. Right now there were practical things to think about; their group had increased by one. Kirin shrugged. "Five of us to feed. No fire maker, either. Ribby, this isn't going to be easy."

"It never was, was it?" she said quietly. "But we're still together. We're free. Belin is strong and Kuno is clever. And look, the river is still down there." She pointed to the sparkle of reflected dawn through the trees. "I understand how good of you this is, Kirin – what you are doing for me," she added, "I will never forget this."

"But … there's something I didn't tell you last night. I've lost my knife. There was something special about it. I had this feeling that it was given to me by the gods, that it was helping me. It's gone. I'm not sure I can manage without it." Kirin's voice trailed away.

Ribby held his arm. "Well, I know you can. Uban's strength returns every day, we can use that strength for ourselves." She jumped up. "We've been rescued, Kirin, haven't we, knife or no knife?" She reached to pull him up from the leaves. "Come on, we need to drink. You bring Belin. Water, then sleep, and then we start again."

She smiled and headed down through the bushes. After a moment, Kirin took Belin's halter and followed her.

12

"So what are you doin' then, what's you all about?"

Sheep Boy seemed completely refreshed after his deep sleep. The others had only managed to snatch enough to feel stiff and out of sorts. They struggled to sit up and answer him, leaves in their hair and twigs in uncomfortable places.

"I'm getting Ribby home again. My uncle bought her and hid her in his cart. We think he was going to sell her as a slave. I found her and got her away. We're heading for Savren. Ribby comes from across her water."

"Oh." Sheep Boy appeared thoughtful. Kirin could not be sure that he knew about the vast river valley that lay beyond his home patch, let alone the hills and woods beyond.

"Your uncle, was 'ee that man what 'it me? Just cos I was looking at the cart?" He shook his head at the memory of Tirtos and that painful blow, and then stared afresh at Ribby. "You was in there!" Then he grinned at her. "I can 'elp too. That's good. Serve 'im right!" Sheep Boy jumped to his feet. "Let's go!"

Kirin and Ribby were cheered by his enthusiasm, despite their tiredness. There was little point hanging around with empty stomachs grumbling, so soon they were walking once more. This time it was Kirin who set the steady speed. Sheep Boy would not accept the offer of a ride on Belin, insisting that Ribby should. He led the pony along, looking about him with interest as the unfamiliar landscape slowly opened out into an ever widening valley.

The riverside trackways were now well trodden. Paths joined from either side, out of smaller valleys and water meadows. They were able to find berries on tangled banks, and mushrooms buttoned in the damp grass. It was not much, but it helped. Occasionally they stopped to drink and Belin was given the chance to crop the short grass. Kuno found an abandoned waterfowl nest. From his reaction as he broke into the eggs they must have been there a good long while.

Occasionally they were hailed from distant doorways or paddocks. They always waved back cheerfully, but kept on the move to avoid talking to anyone. Once Sheep Boy suggested creeping back and seeing what he could steal for a meal, but when he saw Ribby's face he quickly dropped the subject. When they had warning of a farmstead ahead, they took a detour into the trees. Walking there was easier now as the woodland was coppiced carefully. Sometimes there was the bonus of new season beech nuts peeping from small prickly cases.

They were always glad to get back down to the river and its trusted route onwards. Now the path crossed the meadows at the neck of each meander rather than following the bank. At one point they avoided a small settlement ahead by crossing the river on a low bridge made from large flat slabs of limestone.

The day had grown cold and overcast. As the hills parted in front of them a strong breeze pushed into their faces. The wooded hillsides were stretching further away, curving off in all directions, their autumn colours rippling upwards to a sharp skyline. The chill in the air was matched by the chill in their stomachs.

For Kirin, the difference in the air brought an excitement that eased his emptiness for a while. This was the wind he remembered from Elebyrig. The wind that rarely dropped, that brought with it the salty hint of far away. The smell of Savren. He looked carefully, following the skyline on each side of them. A memory had been teased back into life by that smell. He was not disappointed.

"There!" He stopped and turned to the others. "Can you see? The Old Ones' mounds up there, guarding the valley? I've been there, so I know Savren is not far." He pointed to the bumps of turf, small from this distance but clearly outlined where the grey clouds met the edge of the hills. He was sure now that Elebyrig sat beyond. He pointed to the expanse of greying sky that had widened ahead of them. "Soon this river will join Savren. Look, the hills are disappearing and the land is flattening. We're nearly there." Sheep Boy and Ribby followed his gaze, lifting tired heads to take in the new stretch of sky.

Ribby dropped down from Belin's back. "But my hills? I can't see them. I thought we would be close. Oh Kirin, maybe I've not remembered it right."

"No, I think we are doing well. The cloud is coming in, which doesn't help. There's a short way to go, and Savren runs wide in places. She curves like a serpent, I've seen it from up there."

"I've seen that too!" realised Ribby. "I remember I was allowed to go with my father once. There was a feast day and no work. We walked for a long while and there was a place where we could see across. Oh Kirin, she was so beautiful. I just wanted to leap and fly into the air above!" Her exhaustion was forgotten just for a moment and her eyes shone. "And do you see what that means? If we get across her, I should be able to find the way home!"

But Sheep Boy had finally reached his limits. "Well, my belly is eatin' me insides like yer serpent! I ain't goin' to get much further without somethin' to shut it up." He sat down heavily in the tall sedges that had replaced the cropped meadow grass. Kuno agreed with him and flopped nearby, flattening a small patch of spiky reeds against its soft marshy base and sending feathery seeds whisking off in the strengthening wind.

Kirin thought hard, gazing out across the waving reed tips that stood waist high around them. Large white birds called, wheeling and circling in the wind. Now the river made more than one channel in its hurry to reach Savren. On the distant levels, where the valley sides parted away finally to the north and south, he could just see the thatched cones of a village. Stumpy trees dotted the horizon, offering little shelter. He made an instinctive move to feel for his knife, and the advice it might offer, and then remembered its loss with a jolt.

He studied his companions, drooping and hungry. What if he did as Sheep Boy had suggested and went to see what could be taken from that village? But he was no thief, and he didn't fancy setting anyone after them. They had enough to deal with right now. He looked back towards the village but it had disappeared from view. In a moment he found out why. Bad weather had closed in quickly. A harsh wall of icy rain swept down upon them without warning, piercing their clothes like bone needles, threatening to kill what little remained of their energy.

Kirin had no choices left now. He shouted through the downpour that he was going to find help by himself. Ribby was not happy but was too exhausted to argue. Kuno tried to look willing, but was told to stay and guard. Sheep Boy just hunkered down, eyes closed.

He headed in what he hoped was the direction of the village, head down against the driving rain. He knew he was taking a chance. If it went wrong, then he had only himself to blame. The gods had given him help through the little knife and he had not looked after their gift well enough. He had to take responsibility.

With numb fingers he kept the wet hair from his face as he went, trying to peer into the wave of rain that fought against him. Shivering, he stumbled his way upwards onto a low ridge to see if the roundhouses were in sight.

He found himself on the edge of a quarry cut into the side of the slope. He could make out heaps of stone beneath him, overgrown with creeper, and large flat stones piled against the rear. It seemed to be out of the worst of the wind. Here they could find some shelter at least, he thought. But before he could do anything about it, his wet boots lost any remaining grip and his feet went from under him. With a yell into the rain, Kirin slipped and slid down the quarry side and ended in a muddy heap at its base. Winded and grazed, it took a while for him to collect his thoughts. When he did so, shaking the water from his face, he found himself looking into bright eyes set in a bronzed and wrinkled face.

13

What had appeared to Kirin to be a pile of stones, stacked against the quarry side, turned out to be a small stone house half cut into the layered rock, with a narrow doorway and gaps in the wall for light. The bright eyes belonged to its elderly owner.

The old woman started to bustle him across to her little shelter, questioning and fussing, until Kirin managed to get out that there were others to worry about. Without hesitation she turned him around and headed straight back with him, out of the quarry, and Kirin was able to lead her to where he had left them. In no time at all it seemed, the old woman had taken charge of the bedraggled group and led them out of the storm to shelter.

Now the three children were sitting wrapped up by her fire, too tired to speak, their hands warmed by bowls of thick stew from a huge iron pot. The steam from their drying clothes joined the smoke, drifting up through a vent in the roof slabs above. Kirin could not be sure why he felt so safe. They had been taken in by a stranger; one with the oddest collection of keepsakes and tools hung around her tiny home. But outside, the rest of the rainstorm passed the quarry by. There was no point questioning anything right now. Kuno's grateful eyes followed the old woman as she moved around the small space. His stomach was full at last, his teeth gripping a mutton bone as if he was never going to let it go. They could hear Belin snuffling happily as he sheltered in the lee of the little house, his nose in a pile of dry grass.

The shelter and food did its healing work. The old woman let the children collapse in a heap, like puppies, as the night settled in. She occupied herself peacefully, chopping dried herbs here, stirring a little there, always busy. Polished bronze glinted as she moved delicate metal bowls back and forth from little shelves in the stonework, spooning this and that, always keeping an eye on her young visitors.

A log on the fire crackled and rolled to one side. The old woman reached to poke it to safety and Kirin and Sheep Boy moved out of her way. They lay there, blinking in the flare of flame. Ribby moved, but in her sleep, one hand resting on Kuno.

The old woman bent to the boys. Her lined face was etched like bark. She spoke softly and carefully. "Tis surely hard to sleep properly with worry on you, I'm thinking." She moved closer and patted Kirin gently on the shoulder. "Now, you are doing well, boy, be sure of that." She nodded towards Ribby. "I can see she's not your sister. Not enough arguing going on for that!" she chuckled. "Your quest must be a worthy one to have got this far, so take your rest while you can." Kirin was too surprised and sleepy to answer.

She turned to Sheep Boy. "And I think you have something to say before sleep will come to you. You are a good lad. Look into your heart sooner rather than later."

She sat down expectantly, her leathery hands resting in her lap. Sheep Boy blinked, his mouth open, tousled hair in his eyes. After a moment he shrugged and slowly reached forward to poke into the binding around his right ankle. He held his hand out to Kirin.

"I was goin' to give it to yer. Truly. It don' want to stay with me, it don't sit comfy. I found it in the mud by my house. I guessed it were yourn, but ... but I wanted it. At first I did, anyways." He dropped his eyes in shame. "Volkos is goin' to get me now, 'an I deserves it."

There in his hand was Kirin's knife, safe and sound. Kirin

could not believe his eyes, as he took hold of it once more. To Sheep Boy's surprise, he placed the knife down carefully and grasped the boy's hand with his own, not cross at all. "Thank you for finding it, thank you!" he whispered, beaming.

"There," declared the old woman happily, patting her knees and rising from the fireside. "I'm to my bed now. Can't say I'm always right, but I'm not often wrong. We'll all sleep better now."

She was right of course.

14

"How did you know he had the knife?" asked Kirin.

He was grazing Belin in-hand on the slope above the quarry, while the old woman studied the meadow for herbs. Belin was finding patches of rich grass for his morning meal while Kuno sniffed around, following trails of his own. The old woman bent and pecked with her fingers like a bird for grubs.

"The lad was distant from us. I could see he was not easy in his mind. But, mostly," she chuckled, "he would not let me dry his boots. No one likes wet feet when dry are offered. There was no secret to it. I was just using my eyes. Using the spirit knowledge must be kept for when the gods invite you."

Kirin stopped and looked at her. "Do you know how to talk to the gods?"

"Oh, indeed," she replied without any hesitation, picking a stalk and considering its leaflets. "And more besides. I help the villagers over there with my brews and treatments." She sighed and straightened her stiff back. "But what I say is not always welcome, and not everyone wants their business known. That's why I'm here, in my stone house, away from the others. It's the best for all." She laughed, and mimicked, *"'Let Nema have her space. Keep trouble out of our village!'* But they find me fast enough when they need something, Cuda knows."

She stopped and smiled reassuringly at Kirin. "Oh, I don't mind. It was the same for my mother, and her mother before that. Those chosen by the gods have to bear the load. The meat and stores, that I'm given to keep me happy, fair make up for the trouble."

Kirin smiled back. There was an air about the old woman which was calming and peaceful. Last night the surprise reappearance of his knife had been a joy. He was sure now that it was not chance that had brought them to the strange house and its wise occupant. The gods were happy with him. He felt refreshed, ready for more challenges.

"Now, boy, enough of me. I want to hear all about this journey of yours. If that horse has had enough we'll return to the others. Let's work out together how best I can help." Nema tightened the corners of her apron around her collection of leaves, and put one arm through Kirin's. They turned downhill together with Belin, and Kirin looked around to call Kuno to follow. As he did so he realized that, in the clear light of the rain-washed morning, a low cut green line was now visible in the distance. Ribby's hill world was within sight, and hopefully within reach.

THEY FOUND A busy scene back at Nema's house. Sheep Boy had dragged a long branch of dead wood back to the old quarry. He had discovered a small axe hanging inside the house and was cutting and breaking the firewood into pieces, adding the lengths of wood to her wood stack. Ribby had already wiped the large quern stone free of its puddle of rainwater to dry in time for grinding the day's barley meal. As they arrived, she emerged from the doorway carrying a beaker of nettle tea.

Nema untied her apron and tucked the herbs away safely. She took the tea from Ribby and plumped herself down on a large limestone boulder near her doorway. "Well, well!" she declared happily. "Cuda has blessed me this morn with such helpers!"

Sheep Boy stopped chopping and grinned shyly across at her. "It's a good place 'ere," he commented. "I ain't never seen a house like yourn before."

"I'm glad you like it," replied the old woman. "There's always space in Nema's home for someone with a big heart, who's not scared of hard work. That firewood will come in very useful. You're a good lad." Sheep Boy did not know where to look. His ears reddened at Nema's words as he turned back to his chopping.

"And you, my dear," she continued, turning to Ribby. "I've heard your story. You have a strength inside you that will always serve you well, whatever the gods decide for you."

"I pray they will let me see my family again," said Ribby. "I want to be home so much."

"Then we have good news," announced Kirin as he returned from tying Belin, with Kuno at his heels. "The hills on the other side of Savren are in sight. And Nema says she knows how to set us on the right path to cross her." Ribby's face lit up and Sheep Boy stopped and stared in surprise.

"All this is true," said Nema, carefully. She beckoned them over to sit by her.

"You must understand the way is going to be no easier than before. And Cuda knows that trial has already left scars." The old lady stroked Ribby's cheek in sympathy. She continued. "The river you have followed has been a trusty guide, but could now lead you astray with its threading and plaiting down to the big river. There are parts where mud and marsh can swallow an unwary traveller, and there's no rescue likely where the wind eats up any cry for help. I can take you part of the way, at least to safer tracks. Savren takes a mighty turn in the flats as she slides her way round a ridge to meet the edge of the world. There is higher ground, marked by the Old Ones, where you can get your measure and look ahead for the place to make your passage across."

She shifted in her seat, and smiled a little at the serious faces around her. "I have a name for you. Terb, the Ferryman. He was still working the passage to the red cliff when last I heard. You can find him and tell him old Nema sent you. He had better help you, if he knows what's good for him. I'm trusting that he's grown out of his youthful nonsense." Her wrinkled face softened at a memory, and then she waved the thought away.

Then her bright eyes narrowed. With a shrug to her shoulders she seemed to come to a decision. "Hmm. The gods sent you to me, so I think I can use their powers without offence." She tapped Sheep Boy on the shoulder. "Lad, you seem to be finding your way through my things without a problem." Sheep Boy looked embarrassed again and started to speak, but Nema cut him off. "Say nothing, I'm glad you're here to save my old legs. Go and look behind the homespun above my bedding. There's something hanging there. Bring it out here, but hold it carefully, mind."

Sheep Boy rushed off, but returned more cautiously. He was staring at the weighty object in his hands. He placed it gently in Nema's lap and Ribby and Kirin moved in more closely to see. It was an enormous bronze disc, round like the sun and perfectly flat. It was held within a frame of burnished metal that tapered and looped until tamed into a strong handle.

Nema caressed and turned it in her bent hands. The morning light flickered from the shiny surface and danced across the faces of her audience.

"See how you catch the light for us," she murmured, stroking the curves of the bronze rim, her voice dropping as if soothing a small child. "So beautiful …" Nema's voice tailed away for a moment, but then she remembered where she was and looked up from the polished surface to the three children. She sighed with pleasure, "This came to my mother and then to me."

"What is it for?" asked Ribby. "I can see reflections, but they are not clear."

"Ah, if it's detail that's wanted, this is not what you need," said the old woman. "The detail is for us to decide, here in our world. We have to use the skills our forebears gave us for that; with a bit of sense thrown in, of course. This beauty will send our thinking in the right direction and then add a god's blessing. It can set a person on a path with a lighter heart and the confidence to try." She turned to Kirin with a knowing look. "I'm thinking you've already had a taste of that?" Kirin nodded, and his hand went to his tunic where the hidden knife sat snug and safe once more.

She turned the heavy mirror over and showed them the other side. It was decorated with intricate engraving and colouring. Curving within curves, circling within circles, the delicate lines led finger and eye on a never ending journey. Inlaid drops of silky red made owl-eyes back at them, and tiny strikes like basketwork gave texture and depth to the polished bronze. It looked incredibly old, and unlike anything the children had seen before. In a low voice, Nema guided them through the design.

"See here how the surface eddies like wind on water, and here the wicker that's set to capture like trappers' baskets do. But this beauty is not set to trap a living bounty. Look again. The clues are there for those who want to see. Sky is brought to water, gold and silver turned to blood. This will capture things not usually of this overground, my dears, and bring them into it. This will capture the thoughts of Uban and Hatane themselves." She lapsed into silence. Even Kuno sat still, caught by her words.

Sheep Boy broke the quiet. "I wants to see that," he said. "Do it now for us?"

Nema rested her gnarled hands over the surface of the mirror. "Never think to use this, lad. It's dangerous for your eyes, do you understand?" She touched Sheep Boy's arm gently to soften her firm words and he nodded. "And I can't seek by daylight. Uban blinds the thoughtless and hasty. No, I will ask for the gods' guidance for you when Hatane shines, and when I am alone. That's how 'tis done, always and forever."

This was not completely accurate, but Nema did not feel

guilty. It was true that the only right time to use the bronzed reflections was with Hatane's moonlight, but it was not essential to be on her own. She had learnt to capture their power through watching her mother and had seen others witness the casting. However, experience had taught her that sometimes the gods offered visions and images in unsettling ways, ways that sometimes required thinking through or even just patience. These young people needed straightforward help and advice, not confusion. Did the gods favour their quest? She was not in any doubt, and would not waste time with the question. But would they be successful? She needed to investigate later by herself.

But here and now there were the daily chores to be done: water to be fetched from the spring, grain crushed on the quern, bedding shaken in the fresh morning and food to be foraged along the riverbanks below. Nema knew time spent on these would push cares to the back of young minds. She got to her feet. "Now, my dears, there's many little jobs that want doing round here. Cuda knows I could do with the help. I shall tuck this away safe and then heat up some oven stones for a bread baking."

She smiled as the little group jumped up willingly. Nema's weathered face crinkled as she turned it to the bright sky and called out cheerfully to the birds. "Yes, it's a blessed morning, indeed."

15

When the moonlight began to slant its way in through the narrow slits in the wall, alighting briefly on the gently breathing bundles of bedding and dog, Nema left her seat. She drew back the wall hanging and unhooked the heavy disk from its iron wedge between the stones. She stepped silently out through the door and into the clearing.

Out here, Hatane the moon shone down without interference, and Nema gazed up at her face. Hatane was the faithful partner of Uban. Only she could dare look at him directly and reflect his glory for the small people on the overground. Only she could be the agent of wisdom. Without Hatane's generosity Nema could not begin to commune or seek beyond the known. Tonight she was almost fully turned towards the old quarry.

Satisfied, Nema sat down on the same boulder she had chosen that morning, just by the door, and turned the mirror to lie flat on her lap, its polished side uppermost. Gently, she tilted the mirror very slightly backwards and forwards, keeping the reflection of Hatane within the frame, ensuring that the whole surface of the bronze disc was eventually touched by the image. Nema's long wiry grey hair, normally bound and tucked into a knot behind, swung freely forward. As she rocked gently in her seat, it swung in rhythm around the path of the light. Then she started to chant quietly into the night breezes.

"Cast light on this, cast light on me. Cast light on this, cast light on me …"

Again and again she repeated the simple words, whilst reflecting the glow this way and that. The moonbeam glanced out to the wooden overhang above her with its heavy weight of roofing stone; to a plucky little elder bush that clung for life in a crack in the quarry side; to the nettles dressing the midden heap to the side. Finally it flashed on the sudden stare of an owl, gazing without motion or emotion on the old woman caught up in her task.

Those icy points of light, returned so coolly, brought Nema's chanting to an end and she slowly rested the mirror once more in her lap. Staring at the moon's reflection in the bronze sheen, she was no longer trapped by her surroundings. Her hair dropped down like a curtain, protecting at each side like a veil. She could now reach across the space between her and Hatane, free to form her questions, and ready to receive any wisdom which the gods were willing to impart.

16

Kirin had to laugh at himself. He was usually far too fond of his bed, but there he was, up before the others and putting fresh water to boil in Nema's iron cauldron. What a difference the turn of just a few days had made. He put the wooden bucket away and headed again for the quarry entrance.

Kuno shared his enthusiasm. He was delighted to lead the way up behind the quarry in the fresh breeze, tail wagging and senses alert for an unwary breakfast. As they strode along, Kirin caught that smell again on the air, the salty freshness he could almost taste on his tongue. It was a smell he would always link to Savren and Elebyrig and his yearning for adventure.

But adventure was clearly a serious business. Now he knew why his family believed in protecting their young. Being able to deal with the unexpected, that was the test. You could believe you were as ready as you like, but the gods had a way of putting challenges in your path that would lead you beyond ready. Well, he had coped so far.

He turned and stood for a while. The hills and valleys they had emerged from, such a short time ago, were behind him. Ahead he could see the soft line of Ribby's homeland again, stretched in mist now at the foot of a wide sky. Kirin wondered once more about Savren. Between him and those hills she must be winding and widening her way as she consumed the flat valley floor. But where was she heading? Uncle Bulva had talked of Savren reaching the boiling water world of Uban, out at the limits of the overground; how her force helped him dive deep to return, renewed, on the other side of their world. But how far away was that? Had anyone ever seen it? How did they know?

He put a hand to his tunic and held the wrapped knife firmly against his ribs. "I'm sorry," he whispered into the wind, so the creature under his hand could listen or disregard at will. "Maybe I shouldn't question things, and I do believe now you are watching out for us. But Tirtos fooled my father, and might be leading my family into disgrace right now. I don't want to accept everything anymore. I want to see and decide things for myself."

Just then he caught sight of Ribby, running up through the grass and waving to him. He waved back and headed down to meet her, as Kuno came bounding along from behind, neatly dodging past him in the competition to reach her first. The hound did his usual trick of almost toppling Ribby with his greeting. By the time Kirin reached her she was breathless with the exertion and Kuno's slobbering welcome.

"Oh, Kuno! I do love you ... But that's too much! Get down!" Kirin wrapped his arms around the dog and eased him down, giving Ribby a chance to recover. She laughed and brushed bruised grass from her skirt.

"Nema wants you," she continued excitedly. "She was able to seek the gods last night and says it's timely to send us on our way today. Lad has come back from gathering wood, I've watered Belin, and there's cheese bread left for our morning meal."

The two of them had taken to using the name for Sheep Boy that Nema had started. 'Lad' had grown in confidence and cheerfulness with every kindness, and was starting to talk more, accepting happily when Nema mildly corrected his speech or provided a better word.

"Ah good!" Kirin was glad to hear it. Action was so much better than thinking sometimes. Ribby's excitement was catching. The three of them cantered back to the quarry where Nema and Sheep Boy – Lad – were waiting.

"No time to lose!" Nema rubbed her hands as they appeared in the clearing. "Come and eat. 'Tis a fine day for a walk and our way is clear ahead."

"So the gods were there? They told you so?" checked Ribby. Her eyes sparkled at the thought of getting one stage nearer home.

"To be sure, to be sure," bustled the old woman, bringing out platters and beakers. "There's a shining about your plan in the shadows of the night. That you young colts could attract such attention from the heavens? Well, it is a wonder."

If Kirin had known Nema for longer he would have recognized a forced cheerfulness in her manner as she handed out the remains of last night's supper, avoiding more questions. The thought of losing her new companions so quickly had raised surprising regret in her. It was surprising, because she had felt so content before with the quiet way she lived. But there was no ignoring that the visions and impressions she had received in the moonlight had left her with a general feeling of unease.

The spirit world wanted this journey to continue and wanted her to help them on their way, but the outcome was not clearly scried. Success was not denied in the bronze, but then neither was their safety assured. It was all very unsettling. Nema would have felt more confident if Cuda had taken interest, she who watched over children. Instead, Nema suspected she had heard Volkos laugh. She had been left with an uncomfortable feeling about the future, and disappointment that she could not know all of the present.

But she had not worked at her craft for so long without accepting that she was at the mercy of the gods as much as any other living creature. What must be done must be done, and today her duty was to set them towards the Savren passage with full bellies and cheerful hearts.

And who could not be infected with excitement around and

about that stone house as morning sunshine warmed their preparations? Nema did what she could to provide them with basic supplies, and once again Belin stood patiently as a bag and a bundle of homespun rugs were strapped across him. Kuno got under everyone's feet, until Kirin held up a long pull of binding weed and threatened to tie him up for a while.

There was an interesting moment when Nema insisted that Lad should go down to the river to clean up as best he could. The horror on his round face made Kirin laugh out loud, but after some persuasion from Ribby and Nema he gave in. He returned with wet hair and clearer evidence of Nema's good food and care in his shiny cheeks.

Each new departure on their quest had added to their numbers. It was a lively group that left the quarry cut under the noon sky: Nema, Lad, Kirin and Belin, Ribby and Kuno. The old woman set the pace with unexpected nimbleness. The value of her local knowledge was soon obvious. They skirted the village that Kirin had glimpsed in the storm, and from then on the pathways, if they existed at all, were very different from the ones they had followed down from the hills. Now they were nothing more than firmer ridges between the sodden moss of marsh and bog, marked by occasional pollarded willows and dry tipped grasses rustling in the strong wind. There was little protection out there in the open.

Nema picked her way through this wet maze unerringly. Sometimes Kirin thought they were heading to a dead end, and then a patched causeway of wicker hurdles would appear, laid on a wooden frame and set on ancient posts into the marsh. On one of these, crossing the main river channel to the southern bank, they came upon a post that was taller than the others, wound round with tattered scraps of dyed wool and wind-torn remains of offerings. Nema and Ribby stopped for a moment, their lips moving soundlessly as they invoked spirits unknown to Kirin and

Lad. The boys came from the Dobunnic lands where more stone was walked over than water. This was new to them.

Ribby realized that Kirin was watching. "I've crossed Savren once already. I made my vows then. I'll take no chances with the water gods today."

Kirin saw the value of that and, nervous now of the weight of Belin on weathered joints and planks, from then on made his respects often. They wound their way slowly but steadily from dry to damp then dry again, towards a low ridge up ahead. There was no mistaking the firmer ground there. The trees grew just a little taller, and the patches of grass grew more thinly but evenly. Nema stopped suddenly and put her hands on her hips. She gave a sigh and stretched her aching back. She looked at them for a moment, and then spoke quietly.

"I'll leave you here. Follow the direction of Uban's path for the rest of the day and stick to this ridge. You can't mistake it. There's a track, and the ground dips to either side for some way now. Soon you'll get a hint of Savren. She comes close, but not close enough yet to where you want to be. You'll find a hill that'll give you a view, where the Old Ones sit. Take your rest there. What isn't clear tonight will be plain in the morning. Remember, Terb's your man …"

Nema hesitated, as if she wanted to say more. The small group stood in the wind in uncomfortable silence, high flying birds circling and crying above them in the vast space. The importance of this moment weighed down on them all.

Then came a voice, sad but determined. "I ain't comin' with you." Lad looked hard at Kirin and Ribby's surprised faces, and then turned to Nema.

"I means, I wants to go back with you, if you'll let me. I can 'elp you." He spoke in earnest. "I'll build me a little stone room on yourn if you don' want me inside." His eyes filled with tears, and he rubbed roughly at his face with his arm.

Nema reached out with a hand on his shoulder. "Well," she admitted, "There's a thing to catch me out. I must be losing my edge." Then she grinned. "So – if I'm not as sharp as before, I'd better welcome any help on offer. Rest easy, Lad. There's nothing I'd like more.

The boy's face beamed and he reached out to clutch a fold of Nema's shawl, unable to speak in his gratitude. For Kirin and Ribby it now made such sense. Any trials ahead were best faced by the pair of them alone. They had set this in motion, they should bear the result. And Lad had had more than a fair share of suffering in his short life.

The hope and excitement of their earlier departure from the stone house blossomed again as they all said their goodbyes. The party divided. Nema and Lad set off to return to a familiar setting. Kirin and Ribby headed off with Kuno and Belin once more into the unknown, strengthened by friendship, with faith that the gods were on their side.

17

Following Nema's instructions was straightforward and they made good time along the track way. Kirin insisted that Ribby should ride Belin. They stopped once for food and water but did not say much to each other. It all seemed very quiet without their companions. In a way, they were both content to save energy and thought for the challenges ahead. Kuno settled back to his role of protector and guard, keeping one eye on his charges at all times and holding back from dashing off into the marshes after wild birds.

The track way was well used, muddy in places but mostly easy underfoot. They started to meet or overtake more travellers, who showed little interest in them, preoccupied as they were with their daily business. Strangers seemed expected on this important route along to the Savren passage. Kirin had wondered if this had been the river crossing used before by his family as they traded, but a curt response to his question from a tool peddler at a drinking hole told him that carts could not cross ahead. Ribby was silently very relieved. They were getting closer to the great river, and troubling memories were forcing themselves to the surface.

Twilight brought their efforts to an end for the day. They spotted some useful shelter at the base of higher ground. Bearded tendrils of creeper netted the undergrowth of a scrubby copse. They were fairly sure this must be the start of the hill that Nema had mentioned, but it had been a long day and neither Kirin nor Ribby had the will to go further. Evening had emptied the track of regular users. It made sense to avoid the attention of anyone out and about with less than honest intent after dark. They took their chance and left the rutted route way as it wound off towards the river through some trees.

Too tired to do much more, Kirin made sure Belin had everything he needed, throwing one of their rugs across his back. Then out of sight of prying eyes, he and Ribby wrapped against the autumnal chill and curled up with Kuno near the pony. Eyelids drooped and breathing steadied as the events of the day slipped from the present quietly into the past.

Ahead of the dawn, the chorus of birds started gradually as the sky lightened a little from the east. Jackdaws hacked in their roost some way over, and an inquisitive magpie hopped and cackled from nearby tree to bush and then to dewy grass. His luminous flash of white and dark caught the eye of Belin in the half light, who snuffled and shifted from one back leg to the other.

The sleepy travellers stirred in their damp homespun and pushed clingy hair from their cheeks. Ribby was the first to stand, easing stiff muscles as she looked about her. Kirin struggled to his feet, rubbing sore shoulders. Kuno stretched long limbs. The cold morning seemed to have come too soon today for all of them.

"There's enough light already to move on," Ribby considered. "There's little reason to sit around, and Belin needs water. We can stop and eat what's left later, when we've warmed up."

Kirin nodded. He felt the weight of this new day. They needed to face it quickly, head on and without too much thought. Packing their things, and visits into the copse to relieve night bladders, took no time at all. Soon Belin was untied and they were all on their way again, not back to the track but on up through stands of birch that rose with the ground ahead. It was time to see where they were.

With cold muscles complaining against the early exercise, Kirin and Ribby clambered up to the final stretch that brought them out into the open at the top of the hill. Then, at the very moment they lifted their heads, their pull of breath changed to loud gasps. For suddenly their view was transformed. Rich gold pierced through lines of low cloud behind them. Gilding tree tops and marshy swathes, the rising Uban flared the landscape ahead of them with the casual ease of a god that had the world at his mercy, as if offering a mystical feast at their feet.

Through the middle, glowing and molten as casting bronze, ran Savren. From north to south she marked her own line, pulling away from them into a vast curve and then back towards them, before widening and heading off into morning haze. And beyond, carved by her unrelenting power, were low red cliffs and fertile curves of brown that rose gently through threads of mist; land that rose to the forested ridges of Ribby's homeland.

They looked at each other, eyes wide, then back to the view.

Ribby was the first to break the spell cast by the golden light. "Nema was right! Our way is clear. See how the trackway down there leads like an arrow through the scrub. There's smoke and the top of a roof or two at the end, and more beyond the water." She peered and pointed towards the furthest reach of Savren's bend ahead.

"That must be the passage, then," said Kirin, very relieved.

Their destination was in sight. Kirin felt suddenly proud to be standing there with Kuno at his feet and Ribby and Belin at his side. He thought of one more member of their team that deserved to be included. He reached into his tunic and pulled out the knife, holding it up in the morning light so the creature could survey the scene with them.

"There, you wanted to see too, didn't you? Well, you've got us this far and mighty thanks are due. Can you keep the gods on our side for just a little longer?"

The bronze muzzle and eyes glinted at the view in a very self-satisfied way, Kirin felt. Smiling, he folded the hide back around the blade and returned it safely to its place above his belt. Then, with a rush of excitement and a whoop of joy, he charged off at top speed down the slope with Kuno barking at his heels and a laughing Ribby, leading Belin, close behind them.

18

Kirin dug his heels in, arms flailing to keep his balance. Something had caught his eye as he hurtled downhill. Kuno pranced back up to him and barked in disgust at the sudden end to their fun and games.

A raised and rounded line of turf had appeared on the higher ground. Nema had told them yesterday that the hill was known to the Old Ones; it was no surprise to find one of their markers left on the slopes. But there was something about this mound that had stopped him. He went over to take a closer look. There was definitely something wrong. He could see that the top had been dug into at some point; it had collapsed and was now as concave as a giant quern stone, pitted in places and uneven with animal burrows and bramble trails. Large stones had been pulled away and left flat to the ground, broken chunks just visible in the long grass.

Kirin was shocked. He could not believe it had been treated so shamefully. The place was now a damaged shell with any spirit life driven away. Ribby led Belin over to see what had distracted him. He turned to her, furious.

"I don't understand! How could the tribute lords have let this happen? Why have the gods not protected it?"

"Your leaders don't have the same power in these parts." said Ribby, sighing. "It's wilder around here, Kirin. You have been protected in your valleys." She took a deep breath. "Kirin, are you really ready for all of this? Some things are going to be strange for you from now on, as they become more familiar to me. Shall I go on by myself?" She bit her lip. The breeze lifted her long hair and stung the salt on her cheeks as she looked away, not wanting his answer. Belin nudged into her shoulder, impatient, concerned.

Kirin forgot his anger. He did not hesitate. "Ribby, of course we go on together! I'm going to get you home, I vow to Uban. Take no notice of me. Adventure I wanted and adventure I've got. I'm learning to expect surprises." He looked around him, searching for something cheering to reassure her. "Look! Bramble berries, pretty ripe I think. Our next meal was closer than we thought. See? Some surprises are going to be good ones!"

THE SMALL MAN took a step backwards, shifting a twisted leg a fraction and folding his wiry arms against his leather jerkin. "Hmm, let's be looking at you, proper."

He considered the children for a long moment, head on one side like a bird. His bright eyes added to the same impression: a barely tamed redbreast, perched lightly on thin legs and narrow feet that seemed as sharp as claws in their black pitched bindings.

"Yes, I'll take your story and run with it. Fomorik take me on the morrow if I'm wrong."

"Fomorik?" Kirin had to ask, although the man's stare annoyed him and put him on the defensive. Terb flung back his head and laughed. "So old Nema kept some things to herself, then? Don't blame her, no point in scaring you, with the gods on your side and all that. So you say."

He limped over and ran his hand down Belin's shoulder, looking the pony up and down as much as he had his owners. Belin shied a little and pulled at the halter in Ribby's hand. Kuno showed his teeth and growled, unsure of this person who seemed to have this moment completely under control.

"Fomorik, my dears," he continued, "is the god you'll be wanting to keep happy if your little venture is to have a happy ending.

God? Maybes I should say demon. Yes, demon does better."

He turned from Belin and cast a beady eye on Kuno, who backed away, ears down. Kirin and Ribby felt like doing the same.

"Oh, don't be scared of Terb, hound. I'm only doing me job. Got to weigh it all up, see. Story and load. Wrong weight, or wrong tale? Plenty of reasons why I could end up floating out to Fomorik and a watery end." He laughed again. It was not a comforting laugh.

"Anyway, as I says, I believes you. But you'll have to wait your turn. You'll see for yourselves." He waved a hand vaguely towards the ramshackle group of huts behind them, from which came chatter and trailing smoke and mouth-watering smells of cooking. "You've missed good water for another crossing today, see. Tide's on the way out. Good for the fisher folk and the eelers, bad for Terb's profit and your quick passage. Won't cross until tomorrow now. Never you mind, it'll give you time to decide how best to pay me and my woman for food and trouble."

He picked up the look that passed between Kirin and Ribby. "Ah, that's another thing that good old Nema forgot, then?" He chuckled.

Then he pointed to the beads and shiny stones threaded around Kirin's waist. "Well I won't be wanting any of these. But then someone here might, I'm supposing." He turned towards the water and his wooden boat, pulled up some way beyond them, then stopped to add over his shoulder. "If you're staying, put that horse in the shelter at the back. That's a good little horse, that is, we don't want anyone taking a fancy to it. Before me."

He limped off, whistling a tune into the wind.

Kirin looked again at Ribby, who shrugged. "We have no choice – this is the crossing," she said.

Kirin added doubtfully, "Perhaps we can promise him some sort of payment later."

Ribby let Belin go to graze by the side of the path and wandered further on to where the grassy bank fell away to the mud, at the edge of the wide expanse of rushing river.

Savren's character had changed in a very short time. It was a fascinating process, hypnotic and relentless. Slimy timbers from crumbled jetties and wrecked boats began to poke up from the receding water.

A man and a young boy appeared on the bank, wide wicker platters tied to their feet and bags in hand. Kirin watched in amazement as they carefully side-stepped out onto the newly exposed slime of mud and waddled their way over to a set of fluted baskets on wooden frames that were emerging as the water level lowered still further.

"What are they doing?" he shouted out to Ribby.

"They're checking the baskets for the day's catch," she called.

Towards the opposite bank the strength of Savren's flow was in no doubt. Things could be seen racing past, speeding on the bend. Leafy branches from a fall upstream turned and slowly tumbled, trapped in the current and destined for an uncertain end. And beyond that was the cliff of warm red sandstone, standing out in contrast to the flat levels of grass and scrub where they stood. The cut of rock sat there as tempting as a roasted haunch at a feast, close enough to see every vein, but out of reach for now.

At its foot, in front of a smoke-wreathed tumble of wooden buildings, were boats of all shapes and sizes pulled up on the bank, dark sails furled or flapping noisily in the wind. The thud and clang of iron working mixed with the cry of seabirds as they swooped over scraps thrown into the wind by women working at the water's edge. Children ran to and fro, squealing in their play. Down river, where larger boats were moored, dust rose intermittently and deep rumbling added to the wave of noise from across the water.

These sounds of industry were so different after the quiet of their journey, and surprisingly welcome. For a happy moment, both Kirin and Ribby saw themselves back amongst loved ones, back in familiar places where the fire that burned was their fire and the craftsmen that worked were their kin. Back where such smells and sounds meant home.

But hunger once again brought Kirin back to reality. Terb was still down at the high-water mark below them, at the edge of the now vast stretch of shiny mudflat. He finished making his boat secure, fastening it to a sturdy post with an iron chain from the bow. From the stern he threw out a small anchor into the silt behind.

He saw Kirin watching. Terb shouldered a long handled paddle and headed back up a narrow pathway worn into the grassy bank. "Can't be too careful, you knows!" he called. "Her water comes and goes with a mighty fierce pull."

Kirin nodded slowly. He had a closer look at the vessel as it sat there, listing on its bed of mud. It was short and wide bottomed, shallow at the middle, with raised bow. Kirin's stomach turned over at the thought of putting his trust into that odd, calculating little man. To step into that boat, and depend on another to get them across? It was not a comfortable image.

Then, like a hammer blow, another dreadful thought followed fast.

"Oh, no …" He turned pale. "Ribby!"

She saw his face and came over quickly. Kuno left his roaming and appeared suddenly at Kirin's side.

"Belin. There's no room for Belin. Look!" He pointed to the boat, and the truth of his words dawned on Ribby. She put her hand to her mouth and stared back at him, horrified.

"Oh, why did I not think?" said Kirin. "It's a foot passage, and we've brought him all this way! We should have left him with

Nema. It's impossible for him …"

"Indeed, my dears, indeed!" The wily tones of the ferryman broke into Kirin's words. He was standing right behind them.

"So it's lucky that I'm prepared to take the horse in good exchange for a passage of three," said the man. "Three, as I'm thinking you'll not be wanting to leave the hound as well, and the legs on that animal ain't going to tuck away to nothing, after all. Well, what d'you say?"

Kirin, deflated and unsure, stared at the ground. Ribby reached and squeezed Kirin's hand and stood close. She understood their plan was now going to cost him dearly.

Kirin looked across at Belin, cropping casually. Herbs and sedges rippled at his hooves with each wave of salt-laden wind that swept sideways across them. Terb waited for his answer, eyes narrowed. Kuno and Ribby waited too.

"What will you do with him?" Kirin asked eventually.

"Well, I ain't going to trade him as meat for the broth, am I?" Terb laughed. "A fine little mount like that? No, I shall find him a new home and a bit of profit for me along the way. You'll get your crossing and a return too. If you needs it. If you makes it."

This last comment hit hard. It dawned on Kirin that he had been so fixed on getting Ribby home that he had given no thought at all to his own journey back to Beindubn. He flushed with embarrassment, frustrated and angry with himself. All that childish excitement, sure that the gods might make this venture easy for him? Well, how wrong he had been. He had to grow up, and fast.

It was a young man, not a boy, who quietly walked over to Belin and untied their bags from his back. With an unspoken plea to Pona to watch over their friend, he took hold of the trailing halter and walked him back to Terb. He handed the leather strap over, not daring to look at the pony or Ribby.

Instead he looked at Terb directly, voice clear and firm. "You said there was food. Where do we get it?"

The ferryman pointed silently at the shack behind them, eyes glittering. Kirin shouldered the bags and put his other arm around Ribby's shoulders. With Kuno at his heels, he led the silent girl off towards the roughly planked door and she lifted the latch.

THE THICK WARM air that hit them inside smelt so good. It took a while to adjust to the dim light after the brightness of the open estuary sky outside, not helped by the haze of wood smoke blown back down the chimney above the hearth. Soon, however, they could see the extent of the long, low driftwood hut and its occupants.

Their entry, and the strong draught that howled in with them, had turned heads. Benches ran the full length of both side walls. Seated on one was a bent and weathered old man. He halted in his muttering to stare at Kirin and Ribby. Opposite him, three men stretched their legs into the space of beaten earth, beakers of brew in hand. Two of them had the same waterproofed leggings as Terb, and seemed to have a similar calculating regard for the new arrivals. The other, in more homespun tunic and trousers, kept a careful hand on a bulging sack of crab apples that he had wedged beside him on the low bench. He was the first to speak.

"Ah, more custom for the worthy Terb, I see. Hope he remembers to put his regulars first in line."

One of the others drained his cup, and raised it in signal. At the furthest end, a woman looked up from turning flatbreads on the hot stones of her cooking fire and smiled at the newcomers in a friendly way. "Don't you worry, my friend," he said confidently while the woman turned to a large jar behind her. "Terb doesn't upset the folk who keep him supplied with his needs, even if he treats us idly as entertainment."

The woman came over. Refilling the men's drinks, she looked

across at Kirin and Ribby who were hesitating inside the doorway.

"Come now," she said kindly, "Room for all here." She pointed to the bench by the old fellow, closer to the fire. They sat gratefully, too drained to speak, trying to ignore the squinting stare of their neighbour. Kuno tucked in under their legs and gazed out at the company steadily, his head on his front paws.

The woman's attention was distracted by the noisy appearance of Terb at the back between her stores and shelves. She rounded on him firmly. "Now then, keep your dirty wet feet away from my ground meal," she ordered. "You can do a lot of damage when you come in by that door, for sure. Come on, out of there!"

It was clear who was in charge of all things domestic in this arrangement. Kirin felt a lift of spirit at the sight of Terb taking the firm wag of her finger without complaint.

Terb glanced across at them. "You've met our young travellers then," he said.

"Yes, I have, and mighty tired they look too, poor things. There's a good feed in my pot for them as soon as you're out of the way."

"They've paid their dues, so I've no argument with that," he replied smugly.

"Nor would you have anyways," she retorted, "No lambs go hungry in my fold. Now, either sit with your drinking friends or go out and leave us in peace, for I can't resist those hungry dog eyes for a midge longer. I've feeding to do. Yours is later."

The woman soon had them juggling bowls of steaming soup and bread and pointed out the water pot and ladle in the corner. She gave Kuno a cooler version of the same, then left all three to attack their food. Outside, the ever-present wind pushed at the driftwood walls. Evening gusts rattled in the chimney as darkness approached. For Kirin and Ribby there was noise enough to isolate them in their thoughts. There seemed to be nothing to say.

Deep weariness and sadness at the loss of their four-legged friend dominated everything.

The old man bent next to them mistook their silence for nervousness. "Don't you worry none about the morrow, littl'uns," he said loudly, with a gap-toothed grin. Kirin was surprised to hear him making sense. For some while the leathery old man had done nothing but whisper to himself and occasionally chuckle at an unspoken thought. "Terb is a good man with a boat. Yes, he is. Yes, he is." he continued, nodding wisely. "Got the blood of the Venetes in him, that's why. Yes. Yes. If he doesn't know the ways of Savren, then no one does. You'll do fine with Terb, yes …"

"You talking about me, you mad old bag of bones?" Terb challenged across the room. He chose to join the men opposite with their brew.

The old man shrank back a little on his bench. "Oh, good things, good things." he replied quickly. "Telling of your skill. Telling of the Venetes."

The room, as usual, provided a captive audience, and Terb could not resist.

"Ah yes, my father's father. Came up from the ocean's spread, as has happened often through time on this great river." He gazed around at the faces turned to him in the lamplight. "Came with others like him, with their sea-faring skills and their tidy ships with the leather sails. Brought new ideas to these parts, they did. And a new blood line." He chuckled. "Not hard to see why they settled here, with the welcome they got from the womenfolk." He laughed again.

"Where did they come from?" asked the fruit trader.

"Long ways over the water, further than I know. Only Uban knows further," answered Terb.

Kirin found he was as eager as the others for the man to continue. This was what he wanted to hear. Even the whine of wind through the cracks behind him seemed to hold back for a moment to listen.

"No, my father told that his father had been in a great battle on the water, against a fearsome army. Romans they called themselves. Nearly took all their vessels, with shocking force. Some of his company escaped on a lucky wind and found Savren and her shelter. Here they stayed. So here I am," he finished, cheerfully. "Salt sea running through me, but happy to mix it with a little fresh water these days.

"Mind you, though," he added, voice dropping and bending forward a little. "There's warnings about, over the way." He nodded in the direction of the village on the opposite bank. "Talk is that we may not all be as safe as we think round here. The boys that pick up the goods, well they pick up the news too. They bring much that ain't cheery to hear from along the sea's edge. The tide could turn yet against our good living here. There's Roman men and ships in strangers' ports again right now, and not so far off. Trading and bargaining, with friendly smiles for now. But sharp teeth show in the end. They could do some harm turned against us, it's said, with loyalty to none but their own. May Fomorik continue to favour us in these parts."

"To be sure," murmured the men.

"No worries there. No." The old man had sat up again, and broke into the sombre mood created by Terb's musings. "No worries with Fomorik about. No. He can keep each to their own side of the ocean if he wants. See how he keeps Savren in her place."

"True enough," nodded Terb.

"What do you mean?" Kirin, restored somewhat by food and warmth, was caught up by the stories unfolding around him.

This time it was one of the other men that was keen to pass on a tale to the young pup in their midst. "You never heard of their fight? Well, you should be around here when it happens! There's no mistaking the winner when Savren and Fomorik decide to play. She sends her best efforts down river and he just turns her around and sends her waters right back, so he does. It's a fair wave when it comes, makes you watch in wonder at the power. Not one to be challenged, old Fomorik!"

"When does it happen?" asked Kirin.

"Well, there's those in the village that keeps mark of when the spirits are set to tease each other," Terb answered for the man. "But it ain't tomorrow, so don't get all frettled."

He stood up and looked down hopefully towards the firelight glow and the woman now sitting quietly knotting twine into a net. "With luck, my supper is to be had. You off out with your night traps?" He was speaking to the two local men, who nodded and started to stretch into action.

The fruit trader, rosy-cheeked from the heat and the strong brew, rose as well. "I'll be getting a bit of fresh air, and watering your willows at the same time," he mumbled, and followed the others out, banging the door clumsily.

"Well, it's an early start to ready for the tide in time," said Terb. "Old man, if it wasn't for your daughter there, I'd be sending you out for fish for salting. As it is, you can make your bed as you wish, that dog looks good enough padding for a weary head to lie on." The woman frowned in warning at Terb, but her father took it in good part as if he had heard it all before, and fussed busily with his cloak before finally settling in a corner.

Terb had nothing to say to Kirin and Ribby and they were glad of it. Their overwhelming need for sleep dragged at their eyelids and their limbs, and neither felt up to being mocked. But to their surprise, Terb reached up to a high shelf and pulled down a bundle of woollen weave, handing it without a fuss to Ribby. She smiled at him, but he was gone before she knew whether or not he had caught her thanks. In a few moments they were wrapped and warm, and quickly relieved by sleep from the heavy cares of the day.

105

19

With a powerful twisting motion the ferryman guided the wooden craft across the swollen surface of the great river.

Kirin knew he had to breathe, but it was hard with his throat caught tight and his stomach stiff with fear. He tried to concentrate on the lines of tallow and moss that marked the plank joints of the hull and to count the twisted yew withies, like great stiches through a wooden bag. Next to him, Ribby's knuckles were white as she clutched her wrap about her. Her eyes were closed and her lips moved in silent prayer. The fruit trader was hunched in the bow, still protecting his wares and staring fixedly at the line of river bank ahead that seemed in no hurry to get closer. Only Kuno seemed at ease, with head up and ears twitching, his nose testing the breeze.

With no ceremony at all, Terb had hustled them into the boat. After a few terse instructions he had pushed off from the shore, jumping on board almost too late, or so it seemed to Kirin. At this first image of being abandoned to float away out of control his insides seemed to leap up into his mouth, and there they had stayed, his pulse hammering. The wide open space of sky above was pressing down on them, while the shifting mass of water beneath pushed back. Out now in the middle of the river it was as if time was standing still. But Terb had strength and skill honed by years of experience. He had caught the tidal flow upstream just as it was slowing to its fullest, and with deft turns of the large wooden paddle at the rear kept the craft in a diagonal path towards the opposite bank, aiming for a landing place just above the settlement. He wasted no energy in reassuring his passengers, but neither did he tease them. Kirin realized he knew exactly what he was doing, and suddenly he knew they were going to make it. He breathed in deeply.

Ribby felt the change in him and opened her eyes, seeing as she did so the approaching bushes and gravel beach at the water's edge. She looked at Kirin with relief and he managed a grin back. There was no time for celebrating, though. A couple of travellers waiting for the return crossing had come into view, already picking up their bags and hailing the ferryman.

Terb spoke firmly as he flexed the paddle to bring the bow round. "Right, move quickly as we land. I wants you out of the way if I'm to catch the turn of the water. Savren wastes no time. Boy, sort your baggage and don't let the dog delay us."

With a scrunch they pushed up to the shingle and hands reached to help them all out. The fruit man, cheerful now that the worst part of his day was over, greeted the onlookers and shouldered his sack. With a nod to Terb, he strode off in the direction of the huts. Kirin and Ribby stood for a little, straightening themselves, trying to get their bearings after the shock of those tense minutes on the water.

"Having backward thoughts, eh?" The ferryman was back to his old taunting self. "Hah, too late for those! Die thrown and game in place. Be off now, it's those hills over there you're needing. I've got quick dealing to do and a turn of the tide to catch." He looked over to the men clambering into his boat. "Might see you, might not," he continued, peering at Kirin. "The god's luck with you. Whichever god you like! I'm off to shake hands with old Fomorik once more." He turned away.

"Terb!"

The man was startled to hear Ribby use his name. He stopped to look back at her.

"Find Belin a kind home. Please."

"Belin, is it? Hmm. No backwards thoughts, girl, like I said." He strode off and started to organize his passengers.

"He's right, Ribby," said Kirin. "Look how far we have come. We've made it across Savren now and we can't be far from finding your family." He raised his head towards the higher ground. "Any ideas?"

Ribby shook her head, a furrow between her brows.

"Come on, let's follow the apple man and see what lies beyond the huts. As long as we head upwards I don't suppose we can go wrong." Kirin picked up their bags and whistled to Kuno who had been distracted by a scatter of feathers at the high water mark. Ribby followed, looking about her carefully.

"There is something about this place," she said, as she caught up. "Something familiar." Her frown deepened as they approached the huts and smoke of the settlement. She took in the track that passed behind the buildings, marked by a solitary cart rocking between the ruts as it was driven north, raised well away from the riverbank. She saw eyes glance their way and work stop briefly as they took the main path through the village. The sight of children and a dog walking by without explanation was attracting notice. She felt cold creep into her veins.

"Kirin," she whispered, trying to keep her face down and her words between them only. "Kirin, we are making a mistake."

"Just keep walking," said Kirin steadily. "We are nearly through."

Their path took them past a group of men hanging around at the open entrance to a wood turner's shack. One man was fixing a length of wood to a rope-turned lathe. He seemed to be getting a great deal of noisy advice from the onlookers.

"Course, a fresh flint would do better than that ratted iron blade," one of the men was saying. "I picked up some good ones off that old scavenger from downstream when he tied up the other day. It would cost you, mind!" he laughed casually, as he looked away from the workshop and towards the children hurrying by.

At the sound of his voice Ribby could not help but take a sideways glance. Her eyes met his iron-hard stare. The laughter stopped abruptly. Ribby felt a sharp stab of panic under her ribs. Forcing her legs to work, she slipped ahead of Kirin as casually as she could manage.

"It's the man ... Who gave me to your ... Don't look, don't look!" She hissed sideways at him, head still down and desperate to avoid the man's gaze. Her breath rasped as she tried to take the steepening path ahead of them in a rush.

Kirin's eyes opened wide and his mind started to race. "Oh ... um ... Sister!" he declared loudly, waving vaguely ahead. "I think I can see Father waiting up at the trackway. We've made good time after all. Father!" he called to no one, striding up the slope.

But they hadn't realised that the man had slipped out of sight behind the huts. He emerged in a gap between buildings farther ahead and smoothly stepped in their way.

His slow grin spread as he stared at Ribby, ignoring Kirin. "So! My little fish returns upriver. Such a fine little fish, and leaping into my fingers again without even a tickle?"

She looked up at the huge man, fear and fury at war in her face. He shifted his body, making it very clear that if she tried to dodge past him, so much the worse for her. The other men were drifting nearer from behind. "Escaped from the net?" He laughed once more. "Well, you're back on my hook now! Come on little fish, looks like there's a second profit for me in your tail!" The man grabbed at Ribby as she tried to dive past anyway, and caught her firmly by the arm, pushing Kirin away to the ground. "Don't need no skinny eel like you, boy," he spat down at him. "I'm happy with this little catch!"

He turned downhill, dragging Ribby kicking and sobbing.

Kirin was horrified and very, very angry. He struggled to his feet, determined to launch himself at the kidnapper as he headed off towards his friends with his prize.

But Kuno got to him first. As if from nowhere, the dog skidded into view and sank his teeth into the man's thigh, momentum swinging his body with full force behind the man's knees. With a howl of pain the heavy man clutched his leg and stumbled badly, letting go of Ribby and rolling on down the slope in a cloud of dust and curses. Kuno followed him, barking and snarling in the man's face as he tumbled out of control. Ribby crouched in the dirt, dazed.

"Ribby!" yelled Kirin. He caught up with her and pulled her to her feet. "RUN!"

She focused her eyes and nodded, chest heaving. Twisting away, she started desperately up the slope. Kirin snatched their bags from the path and together they scrambled upwards, without daring to look behind. Across the rutted track they ran and up a dry gully into the trees, clambering higher with every step, chased by the echoes of Kuno's barking and the fear of cruel revenge from the village below.

20

"This is the place! This is where I came with my father!"

Ribby knew where she was. Kirin's plan had worked and relief washed through him. They had made it; the gods had wished it so and it had happened. Just as they made it onto the start of the high ridge that edged the forest Kuno trotted up from below, panting heavily. At the sight of their brave friend they knew for sure they were safe again, thanks to him. Ribby flung her arms around the dog and buried her face in his warm neck while Kirin grinned with delight and rubbed his sides.

Still breathing heavily from their climb to freedom, all three dropped down onto the stretch of thin soil and bracken at their feet. While they recovered they looked around them.

Savren's great valley floor was spread beneath them once more. Kirin was finally able to see the river from the opposite side, from those hills he had yearned to visit for so long. It was a spectacular view. The wide loop of water was nearer and clearer from this viewpoint than it had been yesterday at dawn. He could see Terb's tumble of buildings in the distance at the end of the causeway, a trickle of smoke from the roof at the river's edge marking where this eventful day had begun. Kirin thought of Belin, and of the friends made and left behind beyond the distant neck of Savren's vast meander. Those friends had got them there just as the landmarks had guided their progress. Now that he could see how far they had come he could hardly believe it.

Ribby pointed to the hazy line of hills in the distance. "So when I was here before you might have been over there?"

She laughed. "It seems so strange to think we knew nothing of each other then!" She handed him some bread and sheep's cheese. Terb had made a face when the woman tucked the food in their bags that morning but thought better of stopping her.

"It is possible," nodded Kirin. "I was staying at Elebyrig for some time, which must be over there, a little to the south." He took a big bite.

"Will you visit there again?"

The question made Kirin think. He would still have to make it home, and what sort of welcome would he find there? He wondered if he would ever be trusted again and allowed to leave Beindubn. He wondered if it would be Tirtos that decided. The bread suddenly seemed very dry. He reached for the water bag. "I hope so," he said carefully.

"Then when I want to greet you I will walk here to sit and send my good wishes across with the white birds," said Ribby. "The gods will deliver them to you, wherever you are, I know it."

"I'd like that," smiled Kirin.

But Uban was passing over and would soon be blocked by the tree line behind them. It was time to deal with the present. They needed to put as much distance between them and the river settlement before nightfall, perhaps even reach Ribby's kinsmen.

Kirin stood up, rubbing aching leg muscles. "How much further to your home, do you think?"

"It can't be far," said Ribby. "We keep high up like this as we head south. Land will guide us now, not water. We needn't drop lower until we are in sight of the camp. Oh Kirin, I will see my mother very soon!"

"Well, my job is over," he said. "You are the guide now, Ribby. Kuno and I are your trusting followers. Lead on, Sister, the end is in sight!" He bent in a sweeping bow of deference to Ribby, making her giggle and Kuno prance. Cheered at the prospect, they picked up their bags and headed off again.

It was fairly easy walking, and Kirin had time to notice differences between this side of Savren and the hills of his own. The high ridge they were following ran in line with others, separated by slashes of valley like the furrows of a newly turned field. The stone, where it was exposed, was not honey baked, but finely grained reddish brown. He recognized the trees they walked under but was surprised how undisturbed this useful woodland seemed.

"The families here keep to the valley sides, where we can cut the best stone," Ribby explained in answer to his questions. "We leave these upland woods to themselves. We have to show respect and know which part is for us. It avoids trouble from those who hate us, but mostly we like to keep the wood spirits happy. We take enough of the wood nearby already."

She turned to talk to Kuno, who was trotting steadily behind. "Keep a look out for the white doe," she said quietly to him, "for dusk is when she walks the forest. There are some who have seen her, and say she brings bad luck."

The dog pricked his ears up and came closer. Kirin remembered his knife, and checked where it was. He had experienced enough in the last few days to leave as little to chance now as possible.

As daylight dimmed Ribby was pleased to recognize more and more of their surroundings. Her pace quickened and she stopped talking. Suddenly, she dashed ahead of Kirin and Kuno to where pearl grey sky was still visible through the trees. There she halted, silhouetted ahead of them.

Kirin caught up with her and came out of the thick forest, joining her beneath the lighter open sky of the end of the ridge. The watershed they had been following had come to an end. Kirin could hear evening bird call rising from the shadows of steep valley sides directly opposite and below them. The daylight had long since left the depths of the sharp cut into the land that had appeared at their feet.

Ribby's mood had changed. She had slumped against a slender trunk, her cheek pressed into its scratchy bark. When she spoke, her voice was hollow with dismay. "There are no fires down there, Kirin."

"What do you mean?"

Ribby pointed over and down to their right, her other arm around the tree as if to stop herself toppling over the valley's edge. "We should see fires from here. There are no fires where there should be! No smoke, Kirin!"

Kirin could hear the panic rising in her voice. He peered into the gloom. It was true. There was no sign of a settlement to be seen, no reassuring noises of a village preparing for night. "Are you sure we are in the right place Ribby? It's hard to see clearly."

"I'm sure, I'm sure," she said, voice catching. "Something has happened." She pushed herself away from the tree. "I'm going down to see …"

"No." Kirin spoke firmly, trying to think clearly for them both. "Not now. We will go together, first thing tomorrow, when we can see more." He caught her arm. "Ribby, please wait until it's safer."

Ribby turned and looked at him, white-faced. Resigned, she lowered herself on to the stony outcrop and stared unblinking down into the valley, as if to force signs of life back into the dark. Kirin sat too and put his arm round her shoulders, Kuno at their backs. This was a cruel blow. In his head he had carried a picture of joyful cries and smiling faces on Ribby's return, of warm words of welcome. Instead they were faced with another cold and hungry night. And if the disappointment was bad for him, what must it be like for Ribby? Only returning light would help make sense of this.

As always, exhaustion gnawed at his confidence. It felt as though he was meant to wander homeless with Ribby forever. Was this journey never to end? He wondered what Nema had seen in the moonlight back at the stone house. He felt for his knife, but no answers came from the little creature as the last of the day departed.

21

Kicking aside burnt timber, Ribby and Kirin searched in the rubble for any clue to what had happened to her family. Ribby pulled a long and twisted piece of iron from the debris, its hook snagging on a tangle of deformed chain. "This hung above our cooking hearth," she said, flatly.

The camp had been abandoned. Everything within the bank of the small enclosure was ruined. The covers of the storage pits had been pulled off and the contents taken, the animals gone. Pieces of broken quern stone were scuffed into the dirt. There were no tools, no sledges. Where the mined stone had piled in heaps, only dust and rubble remained.

They wandered aimlessly around. The destruction must have happened some days ago, but the breeze still carried the stink of burning as it eddied around the abandoned settlement. Kuno pulled away as disturbed ash rose into the air and went up his nose.

Then Kirin spotted a stick, cast aside on the ground near the entrance. It had the charred remains of pitched moss at one end. "Someone fired this place," he called to Ribby, holding it up as she walked over. "It was no accident."

"No," said Ribby, "and I can make a fair guess who did it."

She hesitated, unwilling to put into words her worst fears. "Kirin, have we come all this way to find no one? Are they slaves now, or are they ... dead?" She felt beyond tears. Since arriving yesterday all she could feel was ice inside. A cold blade had hacked between her and her past. Was she never to return to her old life?

What could Kirin say that would help? The two of them stood

in silence and looked down from the little shelf of land, across the noisy meeting of the two streams in front of them. Kirin scanned the steep rise of woods opposite.

"We need to leave soon, that's certain anyway," Kirin said, finally. "Whoever did this could return. Where shall we go?"

Ribby shrugged. The spark of hope for the future that Kirin's support had rekindled, those few days ago, now seemed spent and cold. From here on her life had to be about surviving. Again. She pointed up the slope ahead. "That way for me," she said, flatly. "At the top there is an old track that leads to the worked valleys to the south. The families there are friendlier with my tribe. They may know something more about what happened, or give me shelter. If I earn it." She pointed back up the way they had scrambled down that morning. "It's that way for you, Kirin. We must part here. You have got me home, as you promised. It is not for you to protect me anymore. Go now." Her voice was dismissive.

Kirin was having none of that. "If this isn't your home anymore then I'm not leaving you here. What if you are found and taken again? No, Kuno and I are not going back yet. We have to keep going, together. There's no choice. Come on!" Without waiting for her, he tightened his hold on their bags and jumped across the narrow stream. He turned to face her, resolute.

Kuno pushed a wet nose into Ribby's hand and whimpered. She looked down at his devoted expression. There was no argument that would hold in the face of such loyalty. Ribby stroked his soft head and gave in.

"Oh Kuno, where would I be without you both?" she sighed.

In a moment the two of them had joined Kirin on the other bank, at the start of yet another exhausting climb up towards the sky.

22

The straight track through the woods was soft with leaves that slid slightly under their feet. Everything seemed so different, Kirin thought. Huge oaks on either side had replaced the clumps of beech and ash from yesterday. Each tree created circular spreads of packed bare earth as wide as the thick leaf canopies above them. Ancient knots in their bark grimaced at him without humour. Yes, these trees knew more than he did. They knew where they were and they knew he did not. Kirin had no plan, no destination in mind. He was just walking.

But he did not feel as if they were walking alone, and neither did Kuno. For a while they had both been picking up on tiny sounds, subtle and unexplained. Sometimes they seemed at hand but then suddenly from a distance, filtering through the still air under the trees. The dog had drawn closer, ears pricked, unsure of a response and as confused as Kirin, a soft growl ready in his throat but never let free. It was not a danger that the dog recognized. It disturbed him. Something seemed to be out there, keeping out of reach but keeping its eye on them. Kirin's skin prickled. He looked across at Ribby, who seemed oblivious as she plodded mechanically on, staring at nothing. He decided to speak up.

"Ribby, there's something watching us. It seems to be everywhere, but nowhere. I can't catch sight of it. Kuno senses it, too."

She looked up, dragging herself from her thoughts. She stopped in her tracks. "The Green Man!" she whispered. "It must be!" Her eyes grew round. "This is where he lives!"

Suddenly, she spun on her heels, looking wildly about her. And then, to Kirin's amazement, she pushed at him with all the strength she had left, startling Kuno into a defensive crouch.

"Go away, Kirin! Now! Don't let him get you and Kuno!" she hissed.

It was as if floodwaters had breached a dam in Ribby's head. She took off into the trees, yelling into the air and waving her fists in defiance and despair. "Come and get me then! Come and get me if you want me," she screamed at the top of her voice, "for I do not care anymore! Do you hear? I do not care!" Out of control, she caught her foot in some tree roots and fell headlong onto the earth, sobbing loudly.

"Ribby! ... Ribby!" yelled Kirin.

He and Kuno leaped forward, racing to help her, ready to fight off the unseen demon in the trees. But it was no demon watching and waiting his moment to pounce. As Kirin bent to help Ribby he saw movement in the greens and browns all around them. He watched, amazed, as leaves and dappled light reformed into human shape. From various hiding places near and far, young men and women appeared and walked warily towards them.

Kirin made himself stand tall, guarding Ribby and their bags with Kuno as she huddled on the ground. He held his breath, trying to hide his astonishment and afraid to show any sign of weakness.

The first to approach, a tall dark haired youth, stopped and looked them over from a short way away. The others fell in behind him, curiosity and interest rather than suspicion on their faces as they came closer to the bedraggled pair and their large dog. But before the first could speak, one of the others pushed through to the front.

"Ribby?" he said, staring down at the girl. "Is that you, Cousin?"

Ribby raised her head. Brushing dirt and damp hair away from her face, she looked up at the boy who had spoken. Unsmiling, disbelieving, she nodded cautiously.

"I heard him call her name!" said the boy excitedly to his companions, nodding at Kirin. "It's Bane's girl! The one who disappeared, remember, before the attack. The one they thought was gone! Where have you been, Ribby? Your mother has been wild with sorrow."

Her voice returned. "My mother … My mother is near? And my father?" She got to her feet, clutching Kirin's arm.

"We are all here, by the wood spirits' grace!" the boy beamed. "These people have given us protection." He stepped back and brought the young leader forward, smiling. "This is Turaius. He guards the high woods, with his friends. He looks for trouble from the river people. He was the one who warned us of an attack on the camp." He smiled proudly at his hero.

The young man nodded in greeting. "This is a welcome re-sult," he said. "We have been watching your approach. We needed to be sure of you."

"We heard something," said Kirin carefully. This was all happening too quickly for him to relax completely.

"Indeed?" said Turaius. "And what is *your* story, stranger? There's trouble between you and this girl? She wanted you gone." He folded his arms, ready for an explanation.

Kirin opened his mouth to speak, but Ribby spoke first.

"This is Kirin. He is my friend. Take no notice of me, I was crazed. He deserves… well, the highest tribute. Without him I would be lost."

Kirin smiled at her and at last she was able to smile again. Tension melted away and Kuno's tail began to wag from side to side.

"Then come," declared Turaius. "Shelter is not much further. Let's call everyone to the stone and give the good news!"

He set off in an easy stride, as others ran ahead. The boy and girl did their best to keep up, and Kuno stayed faithfully at their side. Light-headed from exhaustion and this sudden change in their fortune, they felt as if they were sleepwalking through a dream.

It was not long before they reached a clearing next to a trickle of stream. Thankfully, Kirin and Ribby dropped their bags and bent to scoop the cold fresh water. Drinking deep, it flooded through them like a potion, clearing their heads and restoring a little of their sense. As they stood again, they saw Turaius was brushing aside some fallen leaves, revealing a flat boulder in the sparse turf of the clearing. Between the pattern of grey and yellow lichen, it was marked with rounded scoops in the stone.

One of the girls dragged out a heavy length of oak from some ground cover. With two hands she held the thick staff of wood above the stone for the briefest of moments, then brought its rounded end down with a mighty thump into one of the cups.

Kirin felt the thud in his chest as much as he heard it. The strike repeated itself, endlessly, as the deep reverberations echoed out into the forest, bouncing off trees and scattering birds.

Turaius smiled across at their shocked faces. "Wait," he said, and turned back to gaze into the trees. They did not have to wait long.

People of all ages appeared from the trees, just as before, but this time in a hurry. Kirin and Ribby watched as they emerged into the clearing, chattering and wondering.

Turaius was quick to set everyone's minds at rest. "No danger here, friends," he called out. "None at all."

He looked about at the faces. "Where are Bane and Kerdos?"

Ribby hugged herself tightly, hardly daring to breathe.

"Here," replied a voice. "Who needs us?" Voices turned into people as a man and woman eased their way through the growing crowd to the front. They stopped, disbelieving, when they saw who was standing with Turaius.

"Kirin," said Ribby, leading her friend slowly towards them. "Kirin, this is my mother, Bane, and my father, Kerdos." Her trembling smile spread wide, her tears only a blink away. "Mother, this is Kirin. He has brought me home to you."

23

The happy reunion that Kirin had imagined was nothing compared to the shared joy in the forest that afternoon.

Once Ribby's parents had grasped that she was no apparition sent to torment them, they fell at her feet crying and laughing in a family embrace that looked never to end, and it was not long before Kirin was included. Kuno would have been engulfed too, had he not managed to slip politely backwards from under Kerdos's enthusiastic hug. His tail swept the floor as he watched. He was very happy, for these people smelt to him of wood fires, of dinner and bones and of a sheltered bed. But mostly they smelt of safety. Kuno was ready for that, and his friends were too.

On a wave of chatter, they were whisked off by the forest dwellers to their shelters. This time it was not a ditched enclosure but a huddle of dwellings and fences, built against the flanks of the trees. The houses were low on the ground – merely woven branches and creepers propped over earthen hollows and covered with dead leaves. Sturdy, yet easy to dismantle at any sign of trouble. They also blended brilliantly into the protection of the background.

Here, Kirin, Ribby and Kuno were finally able to sit and eat and listen and tell a little of their tale. The other families withdrew quietly to give Ribby and her parents a chance to talk, to make sense of everything that had happened since they were last together.

Turaius and his friends went back to their forest patrol, but not before the young leader had taken Kirin aside.

"I know nothing of your plans," he said, "but I could use fresh eyes and ears like yours. You have seen things I have not, and I think can sense things that others may not. There is much to do here in the woods if we are to keep safe. There are many who would drive us away. Will you join us and help?"

Kirin was heady with food and water and felt as though he never wanted to make a serious decision ever again. He looked over at Ribby, in the arms of her mother. A part of him wished he could hand himself over to this family right now and never have to take responsibility again. But he was being spoken to as an adult, not a boy, and Turaius deserved an adult answer.

"I will talk to Ribby," Kirin answered slowly, "but I think I want to try to get home, and I think it must be soon. Before I lose the will ..." He swallowed hard. He did not want to think about the enormity of what he had just decided.

"As you wish," accepted Turaius. "I will find you tomorrow and we will talk some more. Sleep well tonight. Maybe the gods will be on my side and advise you to stay." He smiled, and followed the others.

"Turaius needs you," observed Kerdos, as Kirin joined Ribby's family and Kuno again. Kirin nodded.

"Well we want you, too," said Bane. "You have a home with us as long as you need it, though the gods have decided it is to be wandering one." She frowned. "Ribby has told us of such dreadful things. Oh, it is marvellous what you have done for us, Kirin, and I will love you as my own. Stay, please, and be a brother to Ribby."

But sleepy as she was, Ribby spoke up. "Kirin has little sisters back at home, Mother. They will need him more than I." She looked again at Kirin, a little anxiously, not wanting to get this wrong. "You want to go home, don't you." It was not a question. Kirin nodded, unable to speak. "I know you do, for that is the right thing, and you always do the right thing. But let's not think of this now, for my belly is full and my head is addled."

"Quite right, there's time for that tomorrow," agreed Kerdos. "Today we are a family again, and a greater one than before. When Uban says his farewells this eve he will leave the overworld a better place than he found it." He reached for Kirin's hand and shook it warmly, raising his beaker high with the other. Emotion caught in his throat, but he managed to continue. "Once more the gods have shown their hand and marked us with favour when all seemed lost. And for that I, Kerdos, newly of the woods, offer them my humble thanks." He bowed his head in respect and drank deeply. The rest of his family silently joined him in tribute.

TURAIUS APPEARED OUT of the trees early the next morning and brought two other young men with him as escort. He showed no surprise when Kirin said he had not changed his mind and asked for all the details about his route home. When he realized how far Kirin and Ribby had travelled, and learned a little of their trials along the way, he could not hide his astonishment. He was especially interested when Kirin told him of their near capture down at the river.

"I know of that man. He is dangerous; one of many who keep too close an eye on the affairs of people who live along the river. Very little happens without their approval. We forest people have to keep our distance from such men. You did well to escape him."

"It was Kuno who fought him off," said Kirin, proudly. Hearing his name, the dog sat up tall and shook his ears cheerfully.

"Then I should have asked him to join our band as well," laughed Turaius. "We could use such a weapon! Now, tell me, do you have to go back the same way? It would be good to avoid that river crossing. There are other passages upstream."

"I think I have to," said Kirin. "I only know that way, and I have already paid. That's if I can get to it without being spotted, and that's if I can trust the ferryman. He may decide there is more profit in handing me on to others." Kirin remembered the calculating look in Terb's eye.

"Well, the first part of your return we can help you with," Turaius said. "We can get you within sight of the crossing but from there you will have to manage. We must stay hidden. We live like wood spirits and pretend so to strangers; the river people have no idea how close we really are. If we were discovered it could be the end of us."

Kirin nodded. "I am thankful for any help, Turaius."

"Then so be it," decided the young man. "When shall we leave?"

Kirin's stomach turned. He knew these next few moments were going to be hard. One step at a time, he thought to himself, just one step at a time. He looked over his shoulder. "I must say goodbye," he said.

Turaius understood. "Find us when you are ready."

Ribby was over at her family's shelter. As Kirin approached he hardly recognized her. She was scrubbed clean, with long shining hair falling freely over her shoulders. She smiled brightly at him and Kuno, determined to make this as easy for them as possible. He was so grateful.

"We are going now, Ribby."

"Yes. I understand, Kirin … You know I will always remember you, don't you?" she said. "And Kuno." She stroked the dog gently as she spoke. "And Belin, and the stones on your special belt, and … and … oh, everything, Kirin. How could I ever forget any of this?" Her tears started to fall.

Kirin felt for those belt stones, smooth and cool on the rough leather thong at his waist. Tucked above, the knife suddenly made its presence known again, unbidden but insistent. Kirin reached and pulled it out. He unwrapped it. A shaft of sunshine speared through the leaves above and caught at the blade. Kirin was in no doubt of what the creature wanted.

"Take this," said Kirin. "It wants to be with you, and I want you to have it. Then I will always be with you, through its company. While you have it you will be safe."

She reached out for it slowly. "I will keep it close forever," whispered Ribby.

Suddenly Kirin felt happy, not sad. The sun was shining and she was home at last. With the knife creature's help he had done his best for Ribby and he felt proud. And now he could leave her among friends, with the best future he could provide. A smile spread across his face and so Ribby had to smile too.

"Say farewell to your parents for me. Turaius is waiting and it's best we leave now," he said. "Come, Kuno," he called, shouldering his bag.

Together they turned and headed off to join their forest companions, on the move again. Ribby watched until they disappeared from sight. Wiping her eyes, she bent and entered the shadowed privacy of the woodland shelter, clutching Kirin's gift tightly to her heart.

24

Turaius had to leave Kirin and Kuno where the trees thinned out. He had insisted on accompanying them as far as possible, using the hidden ways and animal runs that only an outlaw would know. The rest of his team had already fallen back at the orders of their leader. If they were seen, the alarm might be raised, and to be spotted now would mean a hasty and nervy retreat back to the high woods. And Kirin knew enough to judge that getting down to the passage now was a good idea.

The roofs of the village were below. Beyond, he could see that Savren's waters were reaching their lowest level, making the far side more brown than silver. All was quiet beneath them in the middle of the day. The river people were leaving Savren to herself for a while as she rushed southwards through the narrow channel, and had turned to their huts and their workshops until the currents eased. There were no noises rising from the track that led down to the village. It was a good time to cut across country to Terb's landing place without being challenged and to find a good place to hide. One step at a time, Kirin reminded himself, one step at a time.

He turned to Turaius, suddenly very nervous.

Turaius understood. "Farewell, my friend."

"The gods' blessings on you all," Kirin got out. Swallowing hard, he stepped out into the faint thread of a deer track that headed away downhill.

"Come and visit us sometime," called Turaius softly. "You can call us with the stone. We won't be far." He melted back into the undergrowth.

There was no time to waste. Running, crouching, Kirin and Kuno made their way from one patch of protective cover and shadow to another, steadily dropping down to the level of the village. He couldn't use the trackway for fear of being ambushed again. It was rough going. When they were too low to glimpse the course of the river above the terrain, Kirin kept his eye on Uban for direction, just visible through the thin cloud packed high above by the chill wind. That same wind, funnelled upriver, now brought the smoke and smells from the nearby village. It was reassuring to know they were heading in the right direction, but the feeling that they could be discovered at any moment wracked stretched nerves. After a damp scramble through a maze of reeds, Kirin was very glad to come out onto the riverbank and recognize the gravel landing place only a stone's throw ahead. He quickly ducked behind an old, split willow and pulled Kuno to him. He took a moment to steady himself before risking a careful look over the top of a twisted branch. There was no one in sight and he had a clear view of the approach from the village.

"Now we wait," he said to Kuno, settling back, "But waiting for good or bad, Brother, I can't tell you."

It was true. Now they had got to this point, Kirin had no idea whether he was doing the right thing. His fate would be in the hands of Savren and her crafty boatman, and he did not like that. All morning he had deliberated as he walked, bothered by the memory of the look in Terb's eye. He guessed that the ferryman would have heard of their narrow escape after their crossing. News travelled like an arrow. Was he in league with that bully? Would he take the chance to impress by handing him over? He sighed out loud, and Kuno fixed him with a concerned stare. But it would be a risky decision to set off for another crossing; he knew no one upriver. And how would he barter his passage? No, he had to make contact with Terb and then leave it to the last moment to decide whether to put himself at his mercy. It all depended on who else might be using the crossing, he decided. If he suspected anything at all he would make a run for it.

He ached to get back to Elebyrig. Bulva and Tass would know how things stood at Beindubn. The thought that Tirtos might have spread more lies, calling the tune with the families and belittling his father, made Kirin feel sick. Perhaps Tirtos had even managed to take charge. Oh, how he missed Ribby's calm common sense. Shivering, he held Kuno closer to him. He had to fight the fear that was placing its cold fingers around his throat. Waiting around when you would rather be moving always did him no good at all, he decided miserably. He tried to empty his mind of everything except the sounds of the wind and water and the soft warmth of Kuno's side. Kuno did his best to comfort him with his nose snuffled into his neck.

After a long while Kirin was aware of a subtle change in the sounds around. He looked up carefully to see that the silver-grey shimmer of water had swelled wide, ripples of wave replaced shiny mud on the inside of the river's curve. If Terb had any custom this afternoon he would be looking to come across any time now, before Savren turned. No one on this side of the river had appeared at the landing place to hail the passage back, he was relieved to see. He took a deep breath and moved his hand to feel for his little knife, for luck, before he remembered it was no longer there. His gift to Ribby. He peered into the wind, eyes watering for many reasons.

He realised he could see movement and people further down on the opposite bank. It was not long before he could make out that Terb was launching his boat. He had passengers then. He hoped against hope that it would be someone just passing through, with no interest in a boy and his dog. Someone who did not remember him from the other day. He sent up a plea to any god with the will to listen.

Little by little the dark shape of the ferry approached. Kirin could see Terb standing in the stern, legs rammed against the wooden struts, steering hard with his paddle as he harnessed the strength of the flow. Surely there was the outline of one, or maybe two, other people. They were seated in the belly of the boat, hunched against the cutting cold out there in the open. Kirin strained his eyes to see more. He would have to come out of his hiding very soon; it would not do to miss his chance. If only the wind would drop enough to let him see properly. He wiped his eyes, frustrated and unsure, his heart hammering in his chest.

When he looked again Terb had got much more than halfway and was approaching fast on ripples of foam, heading straight for the landing. Outlines turned into texture and detail and Kirin could now see more of the passengers. What he saw brought a bitter sting of disappointment and a jolt of fear. It was not two people making the crossing but the bent back view of one, and a large one at that. With sinking heart, Kirin thought back to the last time he had seen such a wide spread of shoulders in dark jerkin, with muscles bunched for action and none of it well-intentioned. He was about to come up against Ribby's kidnapper once more, and what was just as frightening, in the company of Terb. He would never escape the two of them. His luck could not have turned more for the worse, and at such a vital time.

Kirin shrank back into his hiding place and tried to pull Kuno back down, who had perked up, ears twitching, to see the approaching men for himself.

"No, Kuno!" he whispered in his ear. "Not this time, leave him be!"

But Kuno took no notice. His whole body stiffened and his nose quivered. To Kirin's horror, just as the boat lurched with a scrape of gravel onto the narrow beach and Terb jumped out to secure it, the hound gathered himself and sprang from behind the willow tree out into the open. Barking feverishly, he sped across the shingle in great strides and leapt at Terb's large passenger just as he was putting feet to land. There was an almighty splash as both dog and man tumbled into the shallows.

There was nothing the boy could do. Kirin closed his eyes in despair and sunk as low as he could in his hiding place, waiting for the dreadful howl of anger, resigned to the fact that his luck had now finally run out.

"Whaaat …? KUNO!"

The bellow was not of anger or pain but of great surprise, and despite the noisy barking was one that Kirin knew. Shocked, he knelt up and peered once more over the willow leaves.

"Father?" he gasped.

Yes, it was Colios, straightening himself onto dry land and shaking river water from his beard as he tried to hold off Kuno's excited bounces. Seconds later, he was landed on again. This time it was his son.

Terb was as surprised as father and son but not as speechless. "This is all very interesting," he said loudly, above Kuno's delighted whimpering. Colios had scooped Kirin up in an enormous hug, the boy's feet swinging wildly. "Yes, all very entertaining, but I've a turn of the tide to catch." He folded his arms and tapped a foot in mock impatience.

Colios came back down to earth and put Kirin down also.

"Kirin! I can't believe it! I've followed hints and half-sightings … and here you are! Pona be praised!" he boomed. "Oh, the worry you've given me, boy! Taking off like that, without waiting for me to return?"

He looked beyond Kirin to where he had come hurtling out of hiding. "The girl?" he asked. "Is she here, too?"

"No, Father," Kirin replied proudly, "I got her home! I found her family, she is safe." He was conscious of the ferryman listening, and his father's loud voice was probably reaching some distance despite the brisk wind. He looked warily up and down the riverbank and towards the huddle of buildings to the south. "Can I explain everything later, Father?"

Colios nodded slowly. "Have you reason to stay here, my boy, or can we make a quick return with this fellow? You're right, there's much to ask, but maybe not yet." He glanced over to Terb, who rolled his eyes, trying to look bored. "Before anything else though, Kirin, I need to know you are well." He checked him over. "Hmm, damp and cold, but then aren't we all, thanks to that dog of yours," he chuckled. "No worries about *him* of course, I can tell he's got fire enough still in his belly. So, leave or stay?"

Kirin had no doubts. "Leave," he said, happily.

With a sniff, and a shove on the planking, Terb caught enough water under the bow to turn it outwards again onto the lapping edge of the water. "Get yourselves in, then," he sighed.

Kirin retrieved his bag and then scrambled in after his father. Kuno followed, bounding in with tail wagging in their faces. Terb eased the boat to, and with just the right effort sent it smoothly into the turning current and jumped into the stern.

25

This time, Kirin was perfectly content to enjoy the boat ride. How wonderful it was to be with his father again and to see the soft hills of his homeland getting clearer with every twist of the paddle. There was so much to say and so much to ask, but he was conscious of the wind that would whip any conversation back to Terb's sharp ears. How dreadful it would be to betray the forest dwellers after all this. Colios wrapped his arms around his son and kept him close while the boat rocked its unsteady way back.

Once they were on dry land Kirin remembered there was one thing he needed to say quickly, and it made him uncomfortable. Colios had strong views about his ponies and their value.

"Father, I had to give up Belin to the ferryman to pay for our passage."

"Belin?" Colios did not understand.

"Your mount, we called him Belin. He was a fine pony and a good friend. It was not a fair exchange but I had no choice. I'm sorry."

"Oh, Kirin," Colios pulled his son to him. "Kirin, my boy, nothing matters to me now except getting you to Elebyrig tonight, then home safely tomorrow. And I hope you are not getting in a worry about that young worm Tirtos. He was so stupid. He's been packed off to the scoundrels in Calleba for good. If that's the kind of company he wants to keep then he can stay there. There's a new wind blowing in those southern parts that I don't want to reach our hills." For a moment Colios frowned at a thought but Kirin did not notice. Tirtos had left Beindubn, that's all he needed to know right now.

His father returned to a smile, for his son, and said, "As for the pony, what's done is done. Another is here, stabled for my return. Unless our ferryman intends to take more advantage where none is due …" He turned as he spoke, raising his voice to make sure Terb could hear as he passed them by, paddle on his shoulder.

Terb just grinned. "A man has to make a living, as best he can. You'll be wanting that mount already, then," he called back, and disappeared behind his hut.

When he emerged he was leading not one pony, but two.

"Had a feeling you might be back," he said. "You looked like a boy who knew what he was doing." He shoved Belin's halter into Kirin's hands as the pony nuzzled and snuffled at the boy. For once the ferryman looked a little awkward. "There's some strange folk over there that I have to keep with, but I know right from wrong. I wish you well. Wouldn't be sorry to see you again, boy," he finished gruffly.

"The gods' thanks, Terb!" replied Kirin, astonished. The little man shrugged off a quick smile, then turned away and limped back to the hut without a backward glance.

"Then that's that," said Colios, his long legs dangling down the sides of his sturdy pony. He was up and anxious to get on their way. "Looks to me like – Belin, did you say? – has found his proper rider. And with Tirtos gone I'm going to be needing more help from you both, young man. Elebyrig next, though. I won't be sorry to get dry, and lay my head down after today's excitement."

He glanced up at the sky and down the track that led away from the river, as Kirin swung on to Belin and straightened his bag over his shoulder. "We should get there in time for a good meal from Bulva and Tass before dark. And it's time to tell all, my son. There's many a question needing an answer, if I'm to get that easy sleep tonight. Ready to go?"

At Kirin's nod he turned his pony's head in the direction of the distant hills, and clicked his tongue to urge it on.

"Kuno!" called Kirin, doing the same. "We're leaving! Home soon!"

Kuno left Savren's edge and raced up after them. Once again life was as it should be. His two favourite people were in the same place, and this time he had heard the word *home*.

PART TWO

AD 30

1

Howls of fury and shouts of jubilation rose into the smoky fog that hung above the jostling crowd. The victor stretched its bloodied neck and flapped its wings, adding its own screeching crow to the surge of noise. Its broken opponent fluttered for a final time and lay still.

To the man pressed back into the shadows, the fighting birds were of no interest. Mercurius had already ignored his prayers on this cold wet night. The few stolen coins he had started with had long been handed over. Now the hubbub of winnings being paid or argued over was no longer entertaining, it was getting in the way. For a single word had caught his full attention just as the bird had closed in for the death blow.

Beindubn. That was the word. No doubting it. A name he had heard often enough while waiting on his master. He pressed his ear closer to the slatted partition behind. His eavesdropping went unnoticed by those pushing and shoving around him.

It was a local voice speaking, loud and slurred by too much brew and too much confidence. "Ah, there's plenty more of that fine work to be had, I promise you. And a good bargain to be made if I've judged it right. The Beindubn boys get quality ores and have a good eye. And now the old mother and son are in charge, and they no smarter than the man was. Out there on the edge of everything they are, ignorant as babes. Make it worth my while and I'll act for you. That fruit is ready and ripe for the picking, I know it!"

Another voice responded. No drink-fuelled bravado here, just control and calm. It was a voice smoothed by travel and deal-making in places much further afield. The contempt in his voice was obvious. "Yes, well, it's good enough I suppose. It's fine for this filthy town and the money grabbing matrons of uncultured men. But I have customers who can pick from the best. Our citizens are in touch with every corner of our great empire and the quality it can offer. You would have to get me a very good deal indeed …"

That was all the silent listener got. One of the gamblers stumbled drunkenly, almost landing in his lap. He sneered as a greasy money bag was waved gleefully in his face. He shoved the man on towards the low doorway. Then he sat for a moment and thought carefully about what he had just heard.

The conversation was like many others to be heard in the drinking dens and shanty pleasure houses of Calleba any night you chose. But this one held information that had real value; value to his master that could end up with coins back in his own pocket in gratitude. He grinned to himself. Mercurius had been on his side after all tonight. Gathering his thin cloak around him, he rose and headed for the doorway himself. Outside, he ducked down the alley and braved the mud and open drains of his short walk home through the lanes. For once, the dirt and distractions of night time Calleba went unheeded.

2

"Kirin? Kirin, come and see!"

Kirin smiled to himself as he strode towards the roundhouse, wondering what Kele had discovered now. She was always finding something interesting in her wanderings around the woods and valleys of Beindubn. And Kirin was always the first to be shown. He was happy to pause in his busy day for his sisters. Galete, her twin, had little patience with baby birds in a nest or interesting patterns on a leaf. She had her own demands at times, but it was usually for help out of some dare that had gone wrong or to hold her bow as she re-strung it.

He loved his sisters. At first they appeared so different, but he knew the bond between them was unbreakable. Both should have set up with their own partners and homesteads by now, but neither seemed in a hurry to leave each other or the family home. This had been the gods' blessing for him during his father's illness and death, and now his mother's increasing weakness. The people of Beindubn had looked to him and Cuamena to pick up the leadership after the death of his father. Kirin had never shied from responsibility, even as a boy, but it could weigh heavily at times. To have their support meant everything.

Kele took his arm at the door and pointed up to a shelf just inside the entrance. Through the swirl of dust motes in a shaft of morning sun, a bright eye blinked back at them.

"You see? That's where the bad bird has been hiding. And I thought her lost last night when we closed the door. Can you get her down without frightening her? I'm still a bit wary of that beak."

"I don't think she would hurt much," laughed Kirin. He reached up for the hen, took her firmly around the middle, and placed her on the ground between them. The bird fluffed her glossy feathers in mild complaint then scuttled out into the bright spring morning to join her companion scratching in the dirt for spilled grain. He then held up a smooth white egg that had rolled along the shelf from her and grinned at his sister.

Kele sighed at the sight. "Oh Kirin, I really don't think these new birds are very clever. They lay their eggs in the strangest of places. And now we know they must both be girls, there's no chance of breeding more between them. The trader must have thought us fools."

"Yes, I'm afraid he caught us there," he agreed ruefully. "But we know better now, and haven't lost a great deal in the bargain. We'll get a male off him this summer – that's if he brings one, I've heard they are still hard to get hold of. The man is worth keeping happy anyway. His contacts at Calleba like our bronze work and he's a reliable outlet to the south for the iron. Letting him think he has the upper hand will do no harm. It will bring him back for more. And for now there are eggs enough for Mother; Cuda be thanked that she enjoys those at least."

The two strolled out together across the enclosure. "Where is she, anyway?" asked Kirin, looking for Cuamena over outside the weaving shed. With the strengthening of the sun it had become her favourite place again to sit and work with her spindles and threads, wrapped snugly in her own wool shawls.

"She said she was off to find Galete down at the river. I think she wanted to see the fishing stick in action. She finds it better to keep busy than sit for long now, Kirin. Whatever is eating at her is not going away. She makes light of it but I'm worried."

Kirin nodded. 'Then we must make these days the best we can for her, that's for sure.' He turned and gave Kele a hefty hug that pinned her arms and lifted her off her feet for a moment. She had little resistance and could only squeak in surprise. He grinned at her then set off for the old enclosure gateway, putting as much cheer in his voice as he could, calling over his shoulder. "Samos and the boys are finishing the ditch filling and hut clearing down by the horse pastures today. She was going to give me a pin for the ceremony. I'll go and hunt her out!"

Kele smiled and waved, still breathless. Her brother had inherited the strength of their father Colios, tempered by the lighter build of their mother and with the common sense of both. He was in charge of the estate now. She felt their lives were in safe hands. But despite the fun and brotherly teasing, she always sensed a loneliness about him. He had never brought a young woman into the family, despite plenty of interest from the tribes around and about. She felt a little guilty that she was glad about that. While he was content to lead the family by himself, she and Galete felt they could stay close to help him. She watched with deep affection as he passed through the gap in the fencing and out of sight.

Wriggling their woolly tails in pretend alarm, the lambs sprang up and off the bank of the holding pen as Kirin passed by. They skipped off ahead along the track and then, like dancing butterflies, scampered back to leap up onto their vantage point once more. Their mothers paid much less attention to him, lifting their heads from the new grass for just a moment, used to people coming and going from the enclosure up on the higher part of the Beindubn plateau.

As he walked, he swept the landscape with his usual critical eye, always checking, always thinking, always planning for the next improvement. He preferred not to ride about the estate. He liked to feel the land beneath his feet. His father had been the same, and used to say that the way he looked on a pony did little for his dignity, and even less for the poor laden animal. Kirin was happy to ride when he had far to go, but day to day he loved to experience the same view that the animals they managed enjoyed. And there was another reason, one that he would only admit to himself. Once he had allowed his pony and his dog to become close companions; they had become very dear to him. His sorrow when they died was a burden he did not want to carry again.

The future, that was most important to him now. Developing the settlement down where the rivers met was working out well. It was the perfect site to extend the terraces for the forges and bloom ovens, and new stone culverts to channel the springs would help drain everything properly. Their latest effort to level the tumble-down cattle yard, with its ditch and bank above the grazing pasture, gave them fresh options. Breeding pens for the ponies or south facing grain fields? Kirin planned to make a final decision with Samos and Cuamena. In his experience land used for animals first grew more grain. They would decide soon.

As he walked he passed in sight of the new dairy yard. That had been a good decision too. Its position was much more useful, now placed in the centre of their land with an easy slope northwards and down to river water. He lifted his hand in greeting to the women busy over there around the milk shed, and to the children playing tag around the hayricks.

Healthy business had created healthy people. He was very pleased that the families of Beindubn were happy for him to be leader after Colios died. He could not manage without their support; he and his friend Samos worked hard to build the teamwork that was so important. They watched and encouraged everyone, directing their skills as they became old enough. The youngest knew that the sheep, cattle, pigs and ponies depended on them and their daily duties. Sharp eyes and nimble fingers of all ages were ideal for the delicate metal work in the good light of long summer days. Those with strength and stamina managed the ploughing and harvesting of the farming season then made light of the ore crushing, iron forging and die stamping in the darker days. Each season, trade had increased and they all benefited. Their goods spread out to distant places, and in exchange came new ideas and tools to try as well as profit.

The latest example of this was giving his sister some difficulty, as Kirin discovered soon enough down at the riverbank. Cuamena was indeed there, and warned Kirin with a look as he approached. It was not wise to tease Galete when things were not going her way, not unless you wanted to heap trouble upon yourself.

"Don't ask me how I'm getting on!" she challenged, as he sat down beside them.

"How long have you been here, then?" he enquired carefully.

"Too long, I believe," scowled Galete. "There's better sport than this found with a dull spear and a lame pony to ride. I swear the bigger ones swim by and laugh, and the little ones aren't worth the trouble."

She raised the wand of bound withies and line and swung the lead weights clear of the water. With a huff she laid it all on the bank, the bark float and metal hook trailing soft strands of wet green.

"See?" she exclaimed. "When Arbin and Tala do this they usually catch more than a tangle! Did you see the teeth on the last one they brought home? I can't take this stick back to them without something to show for it."

Cuamena bravely tried a suggestion. "I think you are too close to the watering place, Galete. Perhaps move to a spot further upstream where the water cuts deeper on the bend? I've often seen the largest ones hovering there on the shallow side. Such lords of the river, they seem, just waiting for the tinies to swim into their mouths. What a life; food delivered by the water spirits with as little effort as possible." She started to gather her shawls about her. "Perhaps they are not meant to be eaten. In my day we feared to upset the gods."

Kirin jumped up to help as she struggled to her feet. "Now Mother, has Uban not shown enough approval for you yet? If we look after his land he will look after us. Come on, I will give you my arm up the hill to the top track. The gods' luck be with you, Sister. I think this is to test you more than the fish."

Galete sighed as she stood herself, hitching her damp skirt higher under her belt and gathering her basket and fishing stick. "I'll have one more try upstream then. These creatures are the spawn of Volkos. They are certainly not pretty. If they did not taste so good, I'd not bother. I'll see you both later then, after better success I hope." She trudged off up the riverbank.

Cuamena and her son slowly made their way up, Kirin picking out the gentler slope of the sheep tracks and avoiding the muddy scar caused by the regular watering of the cattle and oxen.

"Where's the stick I cut for you, Mother?"

"The walking stick?" Despite her shortness of breath Cuamena managed some disgust in her voice. "There's plenty of time before I need it, son. It's a sad day if I can't take my usual walks without that. Now tell me, how is the work getting on down at the south valley?"

Kirin was quick to recognize her change of subject. Cuamena was a Dobunnic woman to the core, determined and proud. "That's why I came to find you. I'm heading that way. Samos intends to close the ditch today and you promised me a pin for it."

"I remembered, son. I have it here." She pulled at the thong of her leather purse and handed him a small brooch. "It could be mended I know, but it has a better job to do now. I would come with you for the ceremony, but I'll save that walk down to there for another day. My spinning is waiting."

"Well, we will need to decide on the best use for the cleared terrace soon," said Kirin, tucking the brooch into his own belt bag. "It doesn't have to be for the farm of course. That old roundhouse up on the top leaks more wind and rain with each season. I'm not sure more patching is worth the work. We could build a stone home for us down there, with thick new thatch and a sheltered view across the fields and the ponies in the water meadow. Would you like that?"

Cuamena smiled and patted his arm. "You must not worry about me, son. I know how many plans you've got for the south valley. I'm happy up here on the top. I can feel Colios with me still, and the fresh air gives me life. These valleys can hold a lot of mist till Uban is high, and the smoke and smells from the furnaces are only going to get worse if your plans work out. Not the place for me."

She had a point, Kirin conceded. Balancing progress against problem was often awkward. He and the elders were going to have to consider where any new homes for growing families would be best placed. The ditches and banks down there would soon need improving. They were going to have to shield more than the ponies and crop fields from curious passers-by who followed the river out of the hills. There was much to think about, and do.

They parted company where the tracks forked, and Kirin strode on down the hillside. The view quickly changed. At first spring-green treetops led his eye across to the distant horizon, but soon he was amongst the copses and clearings of the cultivated farm. The faint call of birds of prey high above him was replaced by chirrup and flash of feather in and out of the bushes, and after that only one sound dominated. All he could hear as he emerged above the water meadows was the thump and clatter of the men moving the final heaps of broken stone and earth.

"Ah, Kirin, there you are. Hold it, boys!" Samos stretched and wiped the sweat from his face with a dirty forearm. "It's nearly finished, as you can see. Most of the stone is too ice-cracked to use for building again but it'll pack in well as drainage in these old ditches and pits. And we have enough loaded on the ox cart to complete the foundations for the new smelting terrace. The boys have done well." Praise from their father did not happen often, and Tala and Arbin made a face in surprise.

Kirin spotted their sideways looks to each other. "Good! We will soon have you supervising work teams of your own, lads. Alisne's brood are growing fast, she thinks the eldest at least is ready for the fieldwork this year. Galete will welcome more competition this sowing season."

Samos laughed. "Ha! Galete or me, who would you want to answer to? I'm not sure which one they would prefer!"

Kirin decided to save the young men from that. "Well, you boys can catch your breath while you take the stone across. Your father and I need to close this work down with the usual honours." He put his arm around Samos's shoulders and steered him over to the remaining mound that banked the edge of the old enclosure. Fast drying soil and rubble was already dribbling from its open side into the end of the perimeter ditch.

He took Cuamena's brooch from his bag and held it high to the bright sky. Samos raised his hand also, and the two stood in silence for a moment. Then Kirin spoke. "Take this, Uban, and with it our thanks. We ask that this cut into the dark be healed and our overland remain healthy. We give thanks for your trust in us. Let us remain in your light forever."

"Let us remain in your light forever," repeated Samos quietly. Kirin dropped the pin into the ditch and his friend followed it with a handful of earth and stones. They stepped back.

"Good. It will be short work after the midday bread to get this closed," said Samos. "Come and see the progress on the yard."

The new development was already in sight, ahead on the hillside. There were still bushes to be cleared, and a flat bridge across spring water improved. Cuamena had her concerns about it all but Kirin believed the planned layered terraces were going to be worth all the effort. The cluster of thatched stone huts already in place would be easy to maintain, and there was good access to the traders' trackway beyond the gate in the boundary bank. He went with Samos along to Arbin and Tala. They had put a brake on the ox cart with a couple of logs at the wheels and were looking down into the wide foundation cut, waiting for orders.

"I think you are right, Samos," said Kirin, as they joined the young men. They all wandered along the edge considering the depth of the foundation ditches. "That cart load should be enough. If Kinbe and his ploughmen have finished the upper field they can join you later here and help get it filled...."

"And you can use this to close it!" declared a loud voice behind them.

A dark stained bundle flew past and landed with a thud in the trench in front of them. To their horror a mass of human hair rolled out to a stop and a face grimaced up at them. The other men wheeled round, their hands to their knives in a flash. But for a moment Kirin could not move. The sight of the severed head at their feet was bad enough, the sound of that voice worse. Slowly he turned to face the man he had hoped to never see again.

His uncle's eyes were challenging and cold. His forced smile was for the benefit of others, not Kirin. Taking the advantage, Tirtos held out his arms both as gesture of greeting and to show he had no weapon at his side.

"The old ways are sometimes the best, nephew. Your grandfather would have approved. He will have closed many a cut with another bloody one!"

Samos was hesitating, looking at Kirin for explanation, his

knife wavering. Tirtos chuckled confidently and carried on. "Kirin, isn't it? Son of Colios, and finally looks like it too. You didn't hold much promise as a skinny boy."

He turned to Tala and Arbin, who were also wondering how to behave. "Well, I won't expect him to be glad to see me, boys. We've had our differences in the past. But I'm back now. My brother is gone. There's a blood right waiting for me. Is that not so?" The eyes returned to fix on Kirin.

"Kirin?" Samos felt at a disadvantage, and did not like it.

Kirin was finding it hard to control his anger. "How did you know about Father?" he hissed.

"Oh, you're not as far from Calleba as you think. And I'm a man with connections. Connections that'll come in very useful for us here, I think." He gazed casually around the new construction and the dug trenches. "Hmm, I'm impressed," he patronized, nodding. "You seem to have a few ideas. With my wider experience this could work." He turned from the men and wandered along the trench edge himself, pretending to inspect the work.

Kirin was horrified at his nerve. With a yell of fury he shot after Tirtos and grabbed at him. Time had brought them to the same height but Tirtos was ready. He had learned much on the streets of Calleba during his exile from Beindubn. Despite his weight he whisked around and caught Kirin's wrist with the grip of a practiced fighter.

"Mind yourself!" He breathed heat and stale brew into Kirin's face, squeezing hard. "Do you want to gamble with your luck like the fellow in the ditch over there? You thought I would never claim my place at Beindubn? Then you are more of a country sop than I was told. Colios is gone now. You lost me my living before, you won't do it again. Do you understand?"

He released Kirin with a shove, and faced the men who were advancing on him. "You can stand back! Your loyalty has been for the wrong man. If you dishonour our bloodline then you dishonour yourselves. Now, get some earth on that miserable head of maggots before it crawls back out. And send some help to the gate. I have a wife and child there, and my brother's family to find and greet."

"OH HUSBAND! THANK the gods!" called out the young woman, as the unwilling welcome party trailed down after Tirtos to the entrance yard inside the gate. The watch boy abandoned the ponies to rush up to Kirin. "He said your name, and the baby was crying, so I opened the gate for the cart. Did I do wrong?"

Kirin sighed and answered as gently as he could. "Is the gate secured again?" The boy nodded. "Then go to Alisne and get your bread. Take a breath, boy. After that, return to your post." The boy stared around at the scene and then rushed off to his mother.

Tirtos was helping his wife and her bundle of shawl and child down from her pony. Feet on the ground, she shifted the complaining baby and pouted up at him. "Is this the place, Tirtos? I do hope so. My poor bones won't take more travelling today, and Kenet needs fresh wrappings."

"No fretting, wife." Tirtos was in no mood for fuss. "This is indeed the place. Eburia my sweetness, meet Kirin, youngest son of Colios. He is happy to welcome you, are you not, Kirin?" He turned to Kirin, one eyebrow raised in warning.

The short walk down to the gate had given Kirin a chance to collect himself a little. He realised this was a nightmare he was going to let happen for now, until he had spoken with Cuamena. Ignoring his uncle's sneer, he conformed to Dobunnic tradition, and forced a formal welcome to these new members of the Beindubn family. "Pona's blessings on your safe arrival," he said, and bowed slightly to the young woman. "My mother and sisters are a short ride away still, but we will soon be able to offer food and shelter."

Eburia instantly forgot her discomfort and brightened at his good manners. "Oh Tirtos!" she declared. "You told me to expect little of what I know, but here already is a handsome man who knows how to speak to ladies. He would not be so out of place at our dining table, you know. Although I do feel that I prefer a smooth faced man like you, my husband. There seems to be much hair on the face generally as far as I can see." She smiled bountifully at the men, who shuffled slightly and rubbed their chins.

Kirin realized how young she was. He felt some sympathy for her, plucked from Calleba and landing like this amongst strangers with strange ways. From somewhere deep came the echo of events past and best forgotten. He stepped up and continued, "So if you could mount for a final time I will lead the way. The cart should manage the track. Give me the child to carry, if you wish." He held out his arms and Eburia gave an affected little squeal.

"My bones are aching so! That would be a kindness indeed. Look, husband! I see now why you were in such a rush about this place. I should have trusted that you knew best, as always. Yes, I think that this is a kind place and we are all going to be very happy."

Tirtos frowned as he helped her back onto her pony and then took the halter to lead the laden cart. Kirin smiled to himself just a little as he set off at the head of the strange procession. It was not the best smelling child in his arms, but for now it had helped him regain a little advantage in this unexpected game.

WORD HAD SOON spread. By the time they reached the top a straggle of onlookers had attached themselves to the group. This did not include Samos and his sons. They had returned to deal with the gruesome ditch offering and wait for some sort of direction from Kirin. They were as thrown by the events of the day as their leader. They had a vague recollection of a half-brother to Colios but in the passing of years that had become irrelevant to their busy lives. One thing was sure, however. The deposit of that festering trophy showed the new arrival was a man to be careful around. They would make sure everyone was clear about that.

Eburia's enthusiasm for her new surroundings dimmed as they approached the roundhouse and work sheds in the enclosure, all of which had seen better days. On the way up Tirtos had been taking in everything with a silent satisfaction, oblivious to his wife's stream of excited commentary. But now a fresh breeze from the west was beating down the blue haze of woodsmoke from the patched thatch straight into their faces. She coughed loudly, her chatter trickled to a halt and she bit her lip in disappointment. Tirtos fixed his face for greeting.

They drew to a stop. Cuamena and the twins had thrown back the wooden doors and were standing waiting, watching, unsure of how to proceed. Kirin realized that Alisne and her children must have run like hares with the news. At the same time the child in his arms gave a wriggle and a wail, and Eburia summoned some energy for her audience.

"My baby needs me. Get me down, if this is where we are to stay. Tirtos? Tirtos!"

"Be quiet!" From between his teeth the words struck like a slap. Eburia winced and paled. Tirtos wanted no distractions during his next scene. He jumped from his pony and went straight into action. He rushed up to Cuamena, took her hands in his and knelt at her feet.

"Sister, sister! The gods be praised that I should see you again! When I heard that Colios had left this world for the other, I was afraid for you. Cuda has led me here once more, for your hearth has always been the true home for me. I had to leave it through my own stupidity, I know. Can you forgive an older and wiser man and welcome him again?" He bent his head.

In the silence that followed, Galete caught Kirin's eye. None of Cuamena's children had a right to speak before she did, although every fibre in Kirin's body wanted to scream out in warning. Galete has realized this is a dangerous moment for us, he thought. Patience, he said to himself. This is not the time. He jiggled the child with the pent-up energy of a hazel trap, until Kele came and quietly took the baby from him.

Cuamena had lost none of her good sense, and easily recognized the shallowness of this display. But she was tired. All her life she had taught Dobunnic values to others. She could not now ignore them herself. And there was one thing that could not be dismissed easily by any elder of an ancient family, and that was a child from the same bloodline.

"Stand up, Tirtos," she sighed, and added wearily as he rose, "I recognize you as brother and equal under Uban's gaze, and welcome you with his blessing." She looked across at the pale girl on the pony. "Now help your wife down. As a kinswoman and mother I offer respect to her. And bring that poor child in out of this wind."

Tirtos rushed to do as Cuamena asked. Galete sidled over to her brother and spoke low.

"Why are you allowing all this, Kirin?" She could not hide her surprise at how he was letting Tirtos charm his way into their day. "I remember the stories, and now I see for myself. He is no good. We should stop Mother before it goes any further." She made a move towards them, but Kirin held her back.

"No, Galete. They would be wasted words right now. First let her do her duty and we will see the outcome."

They watched as Eburia, flushed with relief and desperate to impress, showered thanks on Cuamena. She snatched the child from Kele and held him out for inspection as Cuamena led her, still chattering, through the door. "My name is Eburia and this is Kenet. He is such a good boy. I know you are going to love him!"

With a triumphant look at Kirin, Tirtos dusted his knees and straightened the cloak around his shoulders. He strode after the women.

"Of this I am sure, Galete," Kirin muttered. "You and I need to watch that snake to find out the strength of his venom."

At the door they nearly bumped into Kele coming out again. "I'm to fetch the pannier. We need the babe's cloths!" Kele was excited. "He is so plump and healthy, Kirin, and he can crawl. His mother put him on the ground and he went straight to his knees. He lost his wet wrappings. So sweet!"

"Hmm, I bet there are sweeter smells on the midden," said Galete. "It seems the man has an unlikely weapon with him. And my sister is the first to fall by it."

Inside, the child had taken over. Cuamena had already poured warm water into a bowl and had started to wash the little boy, while Eburia sat cooing and twiddling her fingers in his face to distract him. Kele was soon back with the bag and starting to fuss with the contents, while Tirtos sat back on the sheepskins and let it all happen, a quiet smile on his face.

Kirin decided it was time for a few questions, although he was sure he already knew the answers. "So Tirtos, are you expecting to stay here for long? What about your mother's estate at Comelris? I'm sure they could do with advice from a travelled man." He could not keep the sarcasm out of his voice, and Cuamena looked up quickly.

It was then he discovered that he and Galete were going to have to tread a difficult path out of this mess. Cuamena's response was not what he wanted to hear.

"Leave your uncle to rest, Kirin," she said. "He is here now, so the gods must wish it. What was done in the past must stay in the past. This baby carries the blood of Grandfather Tovisac just as you do, and I am glad to be still on this earth to welcome him."

Galete caught her breath in the shadows, and Kirin fought against sick dismay. He stood up and walked out.

EBURIA FINISHED FEEDING Kenet and dumped him back on a shawl beside her while she re-tied her shift. She peered through the dim light at the different mounds tucked into their bedding over on the far side of the roundhouse. She sighed. If she was going to have to put up with this nowhere place, then she had to try and find some benefit in it for her. After a moment a plan came to mind. She reached under Kenet's wrappings and pinched him firmly on his plump little leg. His wail made everyone stir.

"Hush now, my baby!" she declared. Then even louder, "Oh Kenet, am I not enough for you? Do you want your new friends? Oh, husband, I'm too tired …"

"Bring him to me," called Cuamena, from across the way. "You need your sleep. I'll be glad to have him."

Eburia lost no time in passing the boy over, and after disturbing everyone even more with loud thanks, scuttled back to bed and tucked in next to Tirtos. He sniggered sleepily. She relaxed, confident for now in his approval. She decided to push her luck a little further.

"Tirtos, must we stay here?" she whispered. "It's all so horrid. No table for my lovely dishes. Such rough homespun …"

He turned towards her and silenced her with a finger to her mouth. "Trust me," he answered, "it will be worth it. Calleba is finished for us, for now anyway. By the time I'm tracked down I'll have made enough to satisfy any low-life debt hound. We can leave this midden then and get back to civilization."

Eburia needed more. She dropped her voice even lower, trying to hold back a giggle. "What about – you know – Cam?"

"That worthless slave? Well, his head did me a favour even if his work was never up to much. Nobody follows me and gets away with it. Nobody ..." His voice started to rise and Eburia stiffened beside him nervously. She quickly diverted him, her breathing quick in his ear. "Did they see it? That stupid gawp on his green face. I took a look, you know."

"Oh, you did, did you?" Tirtos was amused now. "Well!" He slid his arm around her waist.

"What a suitable little wife you are turning out to be, my dear," he whispered, pulling her closer. "I think this is all going to work out very nicely for both of us."

3

If Kirin had overheard that conversation in the dark he would not have been surprised. There had to be many reasons why Tirtos would brave coming back to Beindubn after twenty years in disgrace. He guessed that introducing his son to the family would not have been high on the list. Cuamena's quick acceptance of them had probably surprised Tirtos as much as Kirin, and given him such pleasure. Her words had put Tirtos back above her son and daughters in seniority, and there was nothing Kirin could do about it. And now he had to watch Tirtos making the most of it. It was infuriating.

Fearful respect for Tirtos from the young men was no problem at all. His performance with the severed head at the ditch closing had seen to that. The older men and women were cautious at first. They were loyal to Kirin, they were happy to defer to his opinion and wanted to see if this new arrival would affect them. The younger women and children melted like beeswax to his charm. Tirtos would ride around the estate dressed in his finest clothes, dropping a teasing comment here, a twinkle in the eye there. But behind the mask of good humour his eyes would be sharp, considering and weighing up any advantage. He was cultivating admiration with one aim in mind: unquestioning loyalty from them all.

Tirtos soon worked out a plan. He persuaded everyone that he should supervise the metal working, leaving the farming and woods management to Kirin and Galete. Kirin had to admit that this suited him, mostly because it meant their paths crossed as little as possible. But like Galete, he soon found the best workers were pulled out of their usual tasks on the fields to help his uncle down at the new furnaces and workshops. The promise of greater and quicker profit was hard to resist. Tirtos refused to wait for the return of the Beindubn trading team from Elebyrig with their summer haul of ores, and declared there was enough left from the last season to start making whatever they needed.

"With some drop in quality, of course. Not a problem. Just good business … And who would know?" he persuaded. "The tribute lords sit on their rumps far away and leave the hard work to us. As long as the coins do their job for us Dobunni they don't care how they are made. The clink of metal, that's what makes things happen beyond this valley. Enough piddling about with pigs for promises, isn't it time you and your families started to share in the good things of life?"

Nobody could argue with that.

Kirin survived by working harder than ever, rain or shine. Often he would wrap bread and meat and stay away from the main settlement for all the daylight hours. When he did return to the roundhouse he would find Eburia and Kenet the centre of attention, with Cuamena pointing out every new development of the little boy. Eburia was thrilled to have Kele to order around as a servant. All her thoughts of moving from this primitive lodging had disappeared. Why be responsible for meals and chores? How ridiculous she had been.

At first Kirin tried to convince Kele that she was making life too easy for them. He would suggest that she leave her cooking pots and join him for an afternoon out in the woods, to plan the coppicing or clear the springheads of leaves and twigs. But Kele had the most generous heart of them all, and had decided that she felt sorry for Eburia, despite her bossiness. She wondered how she had ended up with a man so much older. Perhaps, she thought, someone had not shown enough care for this girl in the past.

Maybe Cuda had a purpose of her own when she had sent Eburia to Beindubn. So Kele had decided to honour her favourite goddess by setting a good example. She could see that the household work was too much for her mother now, so Kele would always refuse Kirin's invitations and return to her quern stone or water carrying.

He eventually gave up, and decided that if everyone else was content with the new arrangements, then he would have to be. A sort of calm settled on life at Beindubn again, but it was a different one than before. And it was too fragile to last for long.

It was Eburia that lost her patience first, and it was with her husband.

Her day started much later than Kirin's, and even later than her husband and her son. Kirin had taken himself off on a pony early in the morning, Tirtos had already left the roundhouse, refusing Kele's offer of warm water for his shave, only snatching some honey bread to break his fast. Kele noticed he was not so fussy about fashion now there were no slaves to wait on him in the morning. Kenet was where he always was, as close to Cuamena as possible. The two of them were over at her bedding, where the little boy was learning to pull himself up at Cuamena's knees and sidestep from her to a roof post and back again, encouraged by her warm praise. Eburia was content as she fastened her tunic and pulled a comb through her long hair. Not needed here, then. She took a scoop of crab apple tea from the iron pot at the side of the fire and sat quietly, wondering what to do with her day. Kele had given up asking for help, thank the gods. Eburia's calculated uselessness at basic tasks had guaranteed that. Hadn't she done her duty with chapped hands and an aching back as a girl? Catching the eye of Tirtos at her father's drinking house had taken her from the worst of it. Those days were over. She did not want to think about those days.

"Eburia, come and watch Kenet!" Cuamena had finally noticed her. "I swear he is nearly walking on his own. Come on, my fine boy, show your mother." Eburia wandered over dutifully, and cooed and praised his small steps to everyone's satisfaction.

"Are you happy to mind him for a while, Aunt?" She had taken to calling Cuamena this because she wasn't sure how they were actually related and it sounded suitably respectful. Cuamena liked it. Eburia knew what the answer would be.

"Of course, of course, child. He is happy with me. Aren't you Kenet?" She tickled the boy under the chin. "You fed him earlier, did you not? If he complains he can chew on a honey-water rag. It'll help his teeth, too. Kele, did you put some fresh water to heat for the boy?" Eburia took her chance to escape.

Outside the two chickens scattered as she swung her cloak around her shoulders. From where they had been scratching came a glint of metal. She bent to look, and recognized something instantly. It was Tirtos's ring, his most favoured. She picked it up and stroked the carved flat surface of its precious stone, enjoying its delicate feel against her fingertips. It was of a beautiful young man, standing and posing; one of the Roman gods. Tirtos had come back with the ring after one of his trips down to the coastal ports, full of confidence about alliances he had made and the promise of deals across the water. He had worn it ever since, and impressed many at Calleba. It must have slipped from his finger. She wondered if he had realized. She sighed a little at the reminder of pretty things and the pretty words of the life she had worked her way into, before all of this.

Eburia decided to find him and return it quickly, and hopefully earn a little praise. She set off along the main track, heading for the south valley.

But Tirtos had long since left the metal workshops and was pursuing other interests, which Eburia soon discovered. As she came in sight of the ditches and banks of the cattle yard she noticed her husband's pony cropping freely. She turned down towards the thatched roofs and skipped along the path, anxious to please him with her find. As she approached she heard his voice from inside the milk shed, and a girlish giggle.

"Tirtos?" she called. For a moment there was silence, and then he appeared in the low doorway. "What do you want?" he growled.

Eburia put her hand to her bag, ready to explain, her excitement fading fast at his stern expression. "I—" But her words dried up, for one of the milking girls had appeared behind her husband. The girl slowly and possessively put her hand up on to Tirtos's shoulder. Eburia could only stare.

"Well?" Tirtos could not care less at being caught at his old tricks.

Eburia tried to save some dignity. "It was … Oh, nothing that can't wait, husband. I can see you are busy." Her tone was icy.

She turned on her heels and stalked back up towards the track, raging inside at having to put up with such disrespect. Again. So things were going to be no different here. How dare he, how dare he! Fuming, unthinking, with a yell she threw Tirtos's ring as far as she could.

But catching her sob, she gasped in horror at what she had done. Panicking, she looked back over to the yard but no one appeared to have seen her outburst. She ran over to where she guessed the ring had landed. Feverishly she scrabbled in the grass, praying desperately to any god she could think of, crying hot tears. Against all the odds, she spotted it. But as she picked it up she realized it had lost its carving.

Wiping her face, she got to her feet, trying to focus. This would not do. She had to find the stone, and quickly. Carefully she paced the grass, looking for a sparkle other than the last of the morning dew, covering the ground between there and the path over and over again. But now a boy moving pigs was driving them up towards her. He was looking over with interest at her odd behaviour. It would not do to attract unwanted attention.

Eburia was a survivor. She knew she had no options beyond life with Tirtos, and her son gave her an importance that other girls could only pretend at until their novelty wore off. And there were ways to deflect Tirtos's anger; she had learned from experience. Slipping the ring carefully back into her pouch, she headed back to the roundhouse with a plan forming.

Inside Kenet was having his morning sleep next to a dozing Cuamena, and Kele was not to be seen. Eburia went back out to sit and pretend to work at some bits of leather, a half-hearted attempt at shoes for Kenet. The sunlight rose to its height through the clouds.

She did not have to wait for Tirtos for long. He trotted across the enclosure towards her, and jumped down from the pony, mildly defensive and ready for a tedious rant from his wife. But her voice when she spoke was calm.

"Husband, do you realise you have lost your carved ring?"

It took him a moment to take in this unexpected greeting, then his hand went to the space on his finger and he rubbed the smooth, pale strip of skin marking the loss. Before he could answer, Eburia rose and moved closely to him. Her eyes widened. "Well, I have bad news. It is found, but it is broken, and I think I know who is at fault ... and who tried to hide it!" She held up the ring and Tirtos saw the damage for himself. His face darkened and he snatched at it.

"Well! By Volkos, I'm not putting up with this!"

Eburia beckoned him closer, and dropped her voice.

"I've been watching Kele. I've seen her poking through our things when she thinks no one is looking." She had his full attention now, so she layered on some detail. "I can't blame her, her life must be so dull and our things from Calleba so interesting. She must have picked up your ring and then damaged it, and was scared. She hid it under Kenet's weave, in his cot! What a stupid girl! I found it of course, checking on my little dear, you can't be too careful when the spring season brings out those biting bugs and you know how I hate to see the little red marks on his …"

Her over-long story had worked, boring him quickly. Tirtos turned to the doorway, jamming the ring on his finger. An annoying morning had just got much worse and someone was going to suffer for it.

Kele appeared, carrying a heavy storage pot. She stopped, alarmed by the look on Tirtos's face. She was right to be worried. The full force of his temper exploded in her direction.

"You!" he yelled. "Can't you keep your fingers to yourself? Haven't you got enough to occupy your empty head once you've finished fussing over that old woman?" He marched over to her and shook the ring in her face, and in her shock she let the pot slip. With a crash it smashed on the ground, spilling grain in all directions.

"I don't know what you are talking about!" she gasped, dropping to her knees and trying to scoop some of the grain towards her.

"Lies!" hissed Eburia to her husband. But he needed no encouragement to vent his fury. It was a relief to stop pretending.

"And look!" he scorned, "She can't even get the chores right! Ha! No wonder you're still hanging round waiting on a worthless brother and no home of your own!" He stamped and kicked the grain up into Kele's face, out of control. She burst into tears, completely confused, cowering beneath this tirade.

Galete flew across the yard, pushing Eburia to one side and reaching for her knife.

"Leave my sister alone!" she yelled.

The sting of sharp iron caught Tirtos under the chin from behind, and for a fraction of a moment he stiffened. But she was no match for the strength of his anger. He shoved her backwards, knocking her knife arm upward. He followed that with a blow across the face that knocked her sideways to the ground. There was a terrible silence.

"Enough!" Cuamena's command swirled around them with the dust, as she stood propped against the door frame. She was exhausted and disgusted by what she had just witnessed. Wearily, she turned back into the roundhouse, just as Kenet started to wail. "I have had enough."

4

"I've been a fool, my son. I've followed tradition over common sense. I allowed Tirtos back into the family and it has led to this. Colios would be ashamed of my judgement. I'm so sorry."

Head bowed, Cuamena held Kirin's hands in hers. She did not want to let him go, afraid of what he might do.

It had taken all of Samos's strength and reason to restrain him when he met Kirin at the ford earlier. "For there will be a killing, friend, and if it is you lying there what will happen to the girls then? And the families, how will they react? That man has smiled his way into Beindubn. They all think Tirtos wears Colios's shoes, and Cuamena hasn't argued with that. They will follow the strongest, as usual. Too much at stake not to. Fighting leads to empty bellies," he had said. The truth of Samos's words had hit home.

Now, with blood ringing in his ears, Kirin had to force himself to sit with them in the shadowed valley below the roundhouse and try to make sense of what had happened, though no one could really say what had triggered it all. Galete was clutching a wet rag to her swollen cheek, silent with shame at what she felt was such an easy defeat. Kele was crumpled beside her, holding her other hand, now beyond tears. And Cuamena, well, now she looked every one of her years.

Samos was there, holding the ponies that Cuamena had ordered. Once she heard that Kirin had been found, and been persuaded to talk to his mother before wreaking revenge, she had wasted no time. The animals were loaded and shuffling for action.

"You must all leave, and leave today," she continued. "Go to Elebyrig, and stay there, for Cuda's sake. This is no longer a safe place for any of you. I thought this could all work, and it still could for me. I'm tired, my children. I just want to wait here for Colios to collect me, but you could all start again. You love it at Elebyrig, you always have done."

Kele buried her head in her mother's lap. "We cannot leave you! I cannot leave you!" she sobbed. Galete could not speak. Cuamena's resolve could not be shaken. She grasped her shoulders firmly and sat her up.

"Now, my child, listen hard. Alisne will help me. I'm no threat to your uncle and Eburia will give me no trouble, she will want her child minder. Truth is, I'm happy to watch over that little boy till Uban calls me."

She looked hard at Kirin, and hammered her final nail in.

"Son, I do not expect you to refuse me. You saved another girl many years ago from that man. It's time to save your sisters."

5

"Stop, stop! I can't laugh any more, Mog. My sides hurt!" Kele complained in vain. Her cousin, who had given up trying to finish Galete's obstacle course whilst sitting backwards on the pony, was now trying to vault over the long-suffering creature. The animal, ears pricked with an uncanny sense of comic timing, would shy sideways at the very last moment, leaving Mog to tumble grass-stained and breathless on the ground and the audience rolling in laughter.

In the weeks since their arrival at Elebyrig, Kirin had felt his worries shift a little from his shoulders. Sitting here now, watching his sisters relax with Aunt Tass and Uncle Bulva as they cheered Mog's antics, he felt more content than he had in a long while. Whether it was the fresh wind that drove up from beneath, sweeping through his thoughts like a brush drives cobwebs, or that loved stretch of open sky that meant freedom, Kirin could not say. He was sure now; they had been right to do as Cuamena ordered.

Mog, of course, had been ready to return with Kirin to Beindubn instantly, on the attack, but wise old Bulva pointed out the sense in Cuamena's wishes.

"Cuamena's last task is to leave her family safe. As safe as she can. She doesn't care for herself, her work is nearly done. She knows her loved ones are secure. There's no better feeling than that." He looked across at Tass, who nodded in agreement.

So Kirin, Galete and Kele had begun to settle into purposeful, busy days at Elebyrig. Mog was very glad to have more family around to take responsibility for the farm and their trade. Most of the routine work was getting too much for Bulva and Tass, and it was all getting in the way of Mog's real interests. Their cousin much preferred to be out and about, building up a network of friends and useful contacts that stretched from their vantage point high at the hills' edge down across the Savren flood plain.

"We need to stay strong together," Mog explained to any who would listen. "Tirtos is one of the new breed, mixing with the big traders and their Roman allies. It's easy to get drawn in by their talk of a better life. I hear of it all the time down at the river. They laugh at our traditions and think we are simple, but they forget we run with the blood of fighters. The better life they promise will only be for them. We need to be ready in case they step too far. Some maggots may need stamping on soon."

"I don't think Tirtos needed anyone whispering in his ear to do the things he has," Kirin said. "He decided the path he would walk long ago."

"Yes, but that doesn't change the fact he isn't a lone voice. There are many who seek to divide us."

In the bright sunshine it was hard to believe that the Dobunnic settlements could ever be under threat, but Kirin accepted that Mog might be right. Life had changed so dramatically without warning back at Beindubn. His uncle's brutish confidence was a sign perhaps of something more insidious heading their way. Galete's response was less careful. She was hungry for action and desperate to feel in control after their flight from home. Mog, only two years older but so confident, spoke straight to her passionate nature and inspired her with these ideas. The two became inseparable, often riding off at first light on some scheme or other, leaving Kele and Kirin to the day-to-day routines that kept people and animals fed and healthy.

There was one evening when Mog and Galete returned to Elebyrig with an invitation for them all. After some negotiation they had succeeded in convincing the local leaders and their families that a shared festival would be a great way to bind their alliance. For the first time they had agreed to a combined mid-summer Fire Gathering, the ceremony that honoured Uban's might at its strongest. This was an important occasion in the Dobunnic year, held to fend off the slow slide into winter and warn off pests and disease. Lives depended on a successful harvest to come.

Mog was so excited. "Do you see what this means? Our work is starting to make a difference. Others are accepting that we need a show of unity; that there's more than profit at stake – that we need to look to the future together!"

"You all have to come," enthused Galete. "It's going to be up-river at the trading point near Savren's cart ferry and the long ford. So, not too far Tass, for you and Bulva, just a day's ride up the valley. Everyone is going to bring meat and bread and brew for the feasting. There will be goods to exchange, and a chance to show off the best produce around. Can you imagine how fine the fire will be, with so many there to add to it?"

Kele looked unsure. She had not yet felt like going far from the roundhouse. It was starting to become a habit bred from anxiety, Kirin knew. This was a chance to do something about it. "Well, I think it would be good for all of us to go, Kele," he said. "We need to stand alongside Mog and Galete and have some fun at the same time. We deserve it."

"Yes, it's a good idea," agreed Tass, "but one for you youngsters, I think. Bulva, shall you and I stay here and have our own fire? My ears get to buzz like a waggle bee these days when there's too much noise."

Bulva agreed. "But Kele, you should get out and have an adventure. Cuamena sent you here to be free, remember that. We'll come to no harm for a day or two." Bulva was conscious of Kirin's grateful look as he patted Kele encouragingly on the shoulder.

Kele smiled in return and shrugged her agreement. It was settled, and for the next few days there was little conversation that did not involve plans and preparations for the trip.

USUALLY IT WAS a good idea to spend a warm night outside the smoky old roundhouse, in the fresher air, but at mid-summer Uban's light seemed to hardly leave the overground before it returned from the other side. Kirin saw the fingers of shadow stretch to meet as he lay there, annoyingly wakeful, then part with pink edged trails in what seemed like a moment. It didn't feel like it, but he must have got some sleep, he realized, for his head juggled with broken images from poorly-remembered dreams.

As his eyes focused on the morning, he found himself clutching a handful of dewy grass as if he never wanted to let it go. Flexing his stiff fingers, he struggled to his feet and collected up his bedding. In the washhouse he scrubbed some shine back into his long brown hair and cropped beard. A final dousing from top to toe with a bucket of cold water flushed away the last of his sleepiness after his strange short night. He tied his hair back and put on clean clothes under his leather jerkin, fixing his knife sheath and pouch comfortably from his belt. It was the day of the Fire Gathering. His sisters expected the effort.

The others were ready in good time too, and they were soon able to ride off together with a loaded pack pony in tow. The view, at the start of the steep track to the valley floor, seemed on this morning to heighten Kirin's senses even more than usual. It was both familiar and fascinating, altering with each careful step of his mount. Savren led his eye north between leafy rises of wood and settlement clearings of field and pasture. Beyond the river Kirin could make out the ridge of forest and shadow but very little else. He had given up looking for more years ago.

Maybe it was the quiet calm and the rhythmic step of their

mounts as they gently rocked their way downwards that did it, but without warning Kirin's dream came to him again. He remembered he had been trying to open his fingers in his sleep, knowing he was holding something but unable to see. He remembered feeling interested and surprised at his frozen fingers, quizzical and amused, not distressed. Now, on this bright morning, he suddenly felt energy flooding through his right hand. Clutching the reins with his left, he uncurled his fingers slowly and stared at his warm palm. He knew what his dream had placed there, even if now in daylight it had disappeared. It had been a knife, a small knife with a handle like a strange dark-eyed creature. A friend from his past had just jumped back into his present.

When Kirin looked up again at the landscape ahead it was with the eyes and excitement of the ten year old boy. He sat up straighter. The energy that opened his hand seemed to be running through him, invigorating and enlivening, as though it was not a short night he had woken from but the sleep of years. The gods must be plotting and scheming, he thought. They had sent him a message that his life was not his own to manage. He had to be ready for whatever challenge they were lining up for him.

He realized Mog was looking at him sideways.

"How goes it with you, Kirin? You look as though Volkos is after your last breath. Too much of a shock to come down from the hills at last?"

Kirin laughed. "I go well, Cousin. I go very well. And I'm not such a stranger to these parts, as you well know!"

"Ah yes, the tale of the boy and the slave girl, that story entertained us all for many a while. Although the warnings that came with it from Tass were fearsome. I'm surprised you were ever allowed back to Elebyrig. Colios must have kept you in his sight for seasons round."

"Oh, I managed a few trips before the work at Beindubn took

over." Kirin stared wistfully across to the western horizon of forest. "I used to dream of going back to find the friends I made, but it was never possible." He grinned again at Mog. "But maybe I will meet some of them today. Do you know of a man called Turaius, from the forest?"

"I don't think so. And if he comes from much beyond Savren he's not likely to be at our gathering. I've done my best and passed the word around of course, but the Siluros folk usually keep to their mountains and hideaways. They have no need of us. It's the valley and riverside folk you'll mostly see today, those with need of first defence. Savren is an open door to unwelcome visitors."

"And has always been so." Galete joined in, trotting closer to her brother. She and Kele had been listening quietly while negotiating the slope one after the other, but the track way was starting to flatten and widen and they were able to ride alongside each other.

"So Galete, you have woken up too!" teased Mog. "We know why, of course. Not long before we meet the others now. I believe one of them matters to you more than most."

Galete flushed. Kirin realized his sister had more than one interest in the outcome of the day. Chatting together happily, they picked up a little speed and headed along the track through the trees with the sun behind them.

GALETE'S ADMIRER WAS good company. Tilek was the same age as Mog. He came from a large farm on the valley floor between the hills and the river. The friends had planned their route to pass his home so he could join them along the way. His family was there to welcome them, and invited them to a short break with warm bread and brew. They were obviously very fond of Galete, and pleased to welcome her sister and brother as well.

Mog already seemed like one of the family and was soon up

messing about with the younger children, juggling stones and pulling faces. It was Tilek who had the sense to shoo them all away and bring his friend back to the purpose of the day. "Get on your pony, fool. The children have their water carrying to do. Uban will scurry towards winter before we know it, if you don't shift yourself!"

With Mog rounded up, and with the addition of a couple of kinswomen on ponies packed with cheeses to barter at the market, the party set off again. Kirin was impressed by the size and prosperity of Tilek's farm, and there was even more to interest him as they progressed along the track. It was as though Savren's wild floodplain was slowly being tamed. In the years since he had followed Nema step by step through the marshes a great deal of work had been done. Streams had been channelled into order as they meandered across to join the main river. The tracks they were using that day passed through reclaimed patches of useful farming land. They were defined and firm, not likely to suck the unwary down into the wet darkness. Amongst the chattering and laughing as they trotted along, Kirin enjoyed all the sights and sounds, warming in the memories of his boyhood adventure. Deep in his duties at Beindubn he had found it hard to believe it had ever happened, but here every glimpse of the hills on either side sparked a recollection of those few days.

At Uban's height they crossed water on a wooden causeway. Kirin knew this had to be his river, their river, now banked and constrained for its last stretch to Savren. This must be the river that had led him and Ribby back then. And there on his right, through the midday haze, he could make out the clefts in the hill line that marked the end of the Dobunnic valleys. He had travelled to Savren's cart crossing from Beindubn many times since but never from the south. He looked at the nearer slopes and wondered about Lad. There was no time now, but he knew which route he was going to take back to Elebyrig. Nema would have passed on to Cuda's care by now, but if his old friend was still around it would be good to see him.

With the excitement of the evening to come, it was impossible for Kirin to get buried in the past for too long.

Since time began, it had been the custom for each family to keep watch over a flame through the longest nights in the darkest days of winter. Nobody would dare risk displeasing Uban, that most powerful of gods, when your survival depended on his returning warmth and light. And it was just as vital to honour him at the height of his summer strength. The coming harvest was at the mercy of Volkos and his wicked tricks of pestilence and storm. Uban needed due tribute to keep him on the side of his people on the overground. The killing cold of dark days had to be kept away for as long as possible.

And today, it looked as though Mog's suggestion to unite everyone for this was going to be a great success.

As they got closer towards the festival there were many people travelling in the same direction, either on foot or with laden pack ponies. Every bend brought new groups into sight, and Mog's enthusiasm and cheerful greetings brought smiles and nods from all they met or overtook. By the time they reached the site agreed on for the Fire Gathering it had already become a busy scene.

It was on a cleared terrace, wide enough and high enough to be free of flooding. Over time an open space had developed at the junction of important and well-used trackways. These converged from every direction to meet at the first reliable point of Savren's crossing. There were other ways to get across Savren to the north, but her course was fickle there and altered with the season. You could take your chances with fords and marsh in dry weather, but a valuable load needed a secure route. Here her channel was clear to see even as the water level rose and fell. A large timber raft was held in place by a system of ropes that crossed from one bank to the other, operated by the same family through each generation. Once the bloody days of neighbour against neighbour had passed, it had become accepted that the crossing could be used by anyone with something to barter. Kirin's family had always used it for their waggons and ponies. It was needed by all, and could keep up with demand even at the busiest times.

As a popular meeting point it was becoming a lively settlement. Around the edge of the clearing were the thatched huts of the local boatmen and traders. Today they were almost hidden behind clusters of people intent on a deal, bargaining loudly at trestles and cloths spread with pots and iron tools, breads, vegetables, cheese and berries. After some negotiation, Tilek's kinswomen were able to squeeze a spot for themselves and start unpacking, quickly absorbed behind the milling customers. At the centre of the swathe of mud and grass, which led down to the wooden ferry moorings, a pile of faggots and coppicing for the fire was already taller than a man and being added to by every new arrival.

With a quick apology, Mog, Galete and Tilek handed all the reins to Kirin and Kele, before hurrying off to find out which of the leaders had arrived already.

"It seems our main job today is to be pony handlers," Kirin said to Kele. "Let's head along towards the ford and find fodder for them before it all disappears. They can get to the water more easily there, too. And then it's time to see whether some of our dried meats are fair exchange for a cheese …"

A lively afternoon turned into a noisy evening. Bartering was done and a great deal of brew had been drunk. Kele and Kirin had hardly seen the others. Tucked away in one of the large workshops for most of the day, the heads of the families were taking the rare chance to share views and opinions, just as Mog had hoped. They lazed on the grass, watching the competition and banter around them. Everyone else was intent on making the most of a day free from work and out of sight of their elders. Most of it was good humoured, luckily, despite flushed faces and wavering steps. Galete escaped for a while from the meeting and found her brother and sister.

"By the gods, this is better than that hut," she observed crossly, as she plumped down on the ground next to them. "The air back in there is thicker than barley pottage, and some have their wits drowned in it. I don't know how Mog isn't driven to madness. I'll give due respect if the end of today finds them all still speaking to each other. Any of your bread left, Kele?"

"Some." Kele handed it over. "What's to happen now? It'll soon be time for the fire, won't it? Uban is dropping fast, don't let them miss the moment with all this talk." A murmur of expectation was growing. The main reason for the day was beginning to take shape.

"The fire's to be started as Uban goes underground," she explained as she chewed. "Mog and Tilek have asked the elders to head a procession from the brew house to the fire, with the rest of us to follow. The families have each chosen someone. They are going to light it together, and then pass the flame from one torch to another. Those who wish can throw their torches to the flames and make their own tribute to Uban." Galete jumped up, her usual enthusiasm restored by a bit of food. "Come on, let's collect ours now."

By the time they returned from the ponies, tallow torches in hand, a respectful hush had fallen over the clearing as the procession arrived. The three of them joined the crowd at the back and waited quietly like the others, shoulder to shoulder.

Uban was a clear disc of fire now, carving down gradually through the golden-edged strips of cloud. Partly hidden at times, then set free to float, the sun was relentless in its descent, expanding in front of them. Around the clearing and beyond, evening birdsong began. It grew and grew into a treetop anthem. To Kirin it seemed that the approaching dusk behind them had a voice of its own, infinitely wide and infinitely beautiful.

The last sliver of gold shimmered out of sight behind the hills, to the sighs of the assembled worshippers. The sky above them held on to its light as long as it could, mottling in orange, then ragged red and grey, then …

A spark turned into a flame and a crackle. The fire was alight. Straining to see over everyone's heads, Kirin saw a wave of small flames spread towards them, as torches flared and people turned to light those waiting behind. Finally it was their turn. With their flames sputtering into life they walked slowly towards the blaze to pay their tribute. Kirin followed his sisters in throwing his torch as near to the fire as he could, not easily done now through the wall of heat and smoke reaching across the clearing. He turned away to find a place to sit in the growing circle of onlookers, looking for a gap between faces flickering red in the firelight against the black shadows behind.

A face, a thud in his chest, nearly a stumble. Time stopped while his mind registered what his eyes were telling him. One of those flickering faces was looking straight at him, with surprised eyes and lips moving in his name.

Light and dark formed a smoky tunnel ahead. He forced his feet along it and towards that face at the end. Like a child learning to walk, he had to concentrate only on that. Somehow he stayed upright. Somehow he reached her.

"You recognized me, then,' she said. 'It's been a long time …"

Ribby's smile was the same, her eyes the same. Kirin could only nod, throat dry. She nodded to the young man seated next to her to move along. He did so without a question.

"Sit by me, Kirin?"

Kirin lowered into the space. This was Ribby, wasn't it? She had used his name. But she was so different. A woman, assured and calm. Of course, how stupid he was; as if all those years would not have changed her. She reached out and brushed his beard gently with her finger tips, then pulled her hand back, suddenly less confident.

"Say something, please," she managed.

But Kirin had no words. He took her hand in his and brought it to his lips. The missing piece of his life, that he thought lost forever, had fallen back into place.

6

Tired and grumpy, people wandered around gathering up their things and preparing for their journey home. The smoky remains of the fire stung heavy eyes and dry mouths. The festival atmosphere of the evening before had disappeared with the flakes of ash to the sky.

But Kirin and Ribby noticed nothing of this. To them everything was perfect. The few hours of darkness had given them all the time they needed. Questions had been asked and answers given. Some things had not needed to be said at all, as the bond of their youth became a bond of their hearts. Eventually they had fallen asleep, wrapped in Kirin's cloak.

Mog was the first to find them as they sat on the riverbank and watched the water rippling by. There was happiness in Kirin's face that Mog had never seen before.

Looking from one to the other, surprised to find him in such company, Mog was unusually hesitant. "Kirin? I wondered where you were …"

But then laughed outright. "And need not have bothered, I can see! So you have introduced yourself to Elder Rianbe without my help. Uban's greetings, my lady, though I'm not sure the god has guided you right. It was a welcome surprise to see you yesterday, but you have ended up in the company of my dull cousin here!"

But this Ribby could hold her own with the likes of Mog. She wagged her finger and pretended to be cross. "I suppose Uban's greetings are due back, you pest, but how is it you have kept me apart from Kirin for all this time? While taking the best of Siluros hospitality when you turn up, shame on you!" She stood up and pulled Kirin to his feet. "Take care not to upset me and this 'dull cousin' of yours, Mog!" She flung her arms around Kirin in mock protection, smiling broadly at Mog's expression.

Kirin hugged her back. "The boy and the slave girl, Mog? Remember? I think that story has a happy ending at last."

Mog was finding all this hard to grasp. "But this is Rianbe, of the far forest. Widow of Kalte… Elder of the Siluros. The slave girl?"

"My lady!" The next to find them was a group of Siluros, harassed and tetchy. "Rianbe, we were worried. We couldn't find you." They faced up to Mog and Kirin, ready for a fight.

Ribby was quick to take charge, raising her hand. "Be at ease. There is no trouble." They pulled back unwillingly.

"You must recognise Mog of the Dobunni?" she continued. "Well, Kirin is from the same family. We are old friends. You all know of my life before Kalte. This is the man that was the boy."

She ignored their muttering and pulled at the drawstring of the leather bag hanging from her waist. "This was his gift," she declared, "and now I return it. With this goes me, for good or ill. Be ready for change. I will not be returning to the forest, I am going to stay with Kirin."

In the silence that followed, few could ignore the light that bounced off the blade, or perhaps was it from the eyes, of the knife creature as she placed it back in Kirin's hand.

In the end, Ribby had to accept that her companions were not to be calmed without a good deal more explaining, and went off with them to soothe the situation. To have gone to the meeting was unusual enough for her tribe, but then to leave one of their elders behind with a stranger? Kirin promised to wait where he was. He watched her go, moving and talking with that same gentle purposefulness he remembered from the past. He had to leave her to this, but his stomach gnawed with impatience and worry that she might be talked out of her decision. He paced up and down the bank, to the amusement of Mog, until at last she reappeared on her own, leading her pony.

After that it was easier, at first anyway. No one from his family could argue, or wanted to. Kele was so happy at the new look on her brother's face and was fascinated by the story as he told it. Ribby stood close to him, blushing with all the attention, and a little in shock at how her life was changing again so quickly. Galete could hardly believe that Rianbe of the Siluros was the Ribby of family legend. She was very keen to take the credit for drawing her and her followers out of their hidden valleys to the Fire Gathering.

"With such a surprising result!" she exclaimed, "We have a new sister!"

Mog and Tilek found it all very entertaining and were soon making jokes at Kirin's expense. "Felled like a tree," Mog grinned, "and no soft landing. Who would have thought such a slight wind could do so much damage."

"Enough talking!" announced Galete. "We must get back to Elebyrig and tell Tass and Bulva all the news. Rianbe, they will be so happy to welcome you into our family."

But Kirin and Ribby looked at each other, and Kirin spoke steadily.

"We are going to head back towards Beindubn. There is unfinished business waiting there. Please do not be upset. We talked it through in the night and have decided to put our future in the hands of the gods. They have led us to this day, and we can't ignore them."

Galete shook her head and was about to protest, but Kirin silenced her.

"Galete, I can't rest without knowing how Mother is. We are

not going to challenge Tirtos; Uban knows Ribby is always to be protected from him. But I'm not going to let him take everything from us anymore. I want to see Cuamena."

He took Ribby's hand and held it to him. "I am stronger with Ribby by my side, she says she is stronger with me. We are going to find somewhere to stay out of his sight. We've been good at that in the past," he smiled.

Kele had to speak. "Kirin, can't you see how we will worry? Can't you come to Elebyrig and plan properly. Think through your ideas? Stay a little longer while we get to know Rianbe?"

Galete looked at the ground, willing tears to stay hidden. She let Tilek put his arm around her shoulders.

Kirin moved to comfort Kele. "Oh Sister, what are the use of plans when the gods have their own ideas? This seems hard today, but Ribby and I are excited! And we are not going across the river. We will stay in contact. Just give us some time now to find our path."

Ribby stayed quiet. It was not her place to reassure Kirin's family. After all, it was her reappearance in Kirin's life that had caused this upset. Mog saw her face and realised the awkward position she was in. There was an easy solution.

"May I travel with you both, just for a day or two, Kirin, until you have more idea of how things stand? Then I can report back to Elebyrig and set everyone's minds at rest." The twins looked happier at this.

"Good idea," said Kirin. "You may be surprised at our first stop, though. We will go with you towards Tilek's farm, but then we have an old friend to find. We can't start our future without looking for him at least."

"Lad," smiled Ribby. "Dear Lad. This is not going to seem right unless we try to see him too."

7

The path from the village up to the old quarry was little more than a sheep track through the short grass of the slope, until they rode closer. Then a spider's web of trodden mud and muck reached out towards them from the gap in the outcrop of stone. The smell of pigs grew very strong.

"Someone must still be working here," said Kirin.

"I'm glad we're not walking," muttered Mog," I put on my new boots for the Fire Gathering."

The quarry floor was a muddle of pens and shelters that almost hid the old stone house at the back. Cracked tiles slid from patched roofs and wooden posts propped up makeshift gates in a maze of low walls. Piles of clean hay were toppling down to the mud and were getting trodden into the dirt and pig muck. Kirin was a farmer, used to a bit of dirt, but even he was not sure he wanted to dismount into this mess.

In the midst of it all a man rose up in one of the pens, with his back to them, talking away. "Thass it, my ol' mother. You done me proud. I think they babes is big enough to be out wanderin' with the others pretty soon. You'm a good girl."

He nodded to himself with satisfaction, and then turned to the gate. He caught sight of the three visitors on horseback and stood still, blinking into the bright light.

"What you'm wantin'?"

The fringe of hair had receded way back from a weathered forehead but his full and tangled beard made up for that. His eyes peered out as defiantly to strangers as ever. He sniffed and rubbed his nose on his sleeve. Kirin chuckled, so happy. There were some things that Nema had not been able to change then.

Ribby encouraged her pony forward.

"Lad! It's us!" she called. "It's Ribby." Ignoring the mess, she slid off her pony and went to him slowly, hands outstretched.

Lad smiled a slow smile that grew broader with each moment. He cleared the gate and stepped to meet her. He took her hands and seemed about to hug her, then drew back shyly.

"Nah, don' you get too close to me, Ribby. I aint fit for touchin', not by someone as lovely as you. Why, you'm a fine sight, after all these seasons round. An' that can't be Kirin, can it, up there on his hoss like a lord?"

"Yes indeed, old friend." called Kirin, as he jumped down. "But it's you that is the fine sight!" And despite the dirt, Lad found the air squeezed from him in a hug from them both.

TO RIBBY'S RELIEF, inside the old stone house things seemed to be pretty much as they had been in Nema's day.

"I keeps it like she told me," said Lad, when he saw Ribby looking around. "It makes me think she's still around some place. I misses her, Ribby," he added sadly. "She was mother and father both to me. I would a' been nothin', without her, I knows it. She got me started on the piggin' an all. I was so glad in my heart when I could watch over her till the end. She was Cuda here on this overground, I'm sure …"

He jumped up, remembering. "Her things! You'm here, and can have them. Oh, I'm that pleased!"

He went behind the curtain, brought out some bundles of cloth and placed them carefully in Ribby's lap. The weight gave Ribby a clue before she unwrapped them. Yes, there were Nema's bronze bowls and, such a happy sight, the highly polished disk with the looping handle, as beautiful as before.

"She told me to guard it, to keep it till t'was clear where it should go. She never said that might be to you, but 'tis so right!! It needs to belong to a woman. I shouldn't have any of it. Oh, Nema is goin' to rest easy tonight, and so'm I. Since she passed, I ain't wanted to go too far from the stone house in case some vermin gets in and nabs it all. Me and my pigs have worn out hereabouts. We can go a bit further in our rootin' about now!"

Mog and Kirin caught the end of this as they appeared in the door after settling the ponies.

"Well, that is a beauty. I've not seen one before, though I've heard tell of their power." Mog's eyes opened wide at the sight of the scrying mirror, and went to touch it. Lad leaned in the way.

"No offence, friend," he said firmly. "I'd rather it settle and get to know its new mistress if you don' mind. Ribby can mind who can hold it when she is ready."

Mog backed off quickly, a bit put out, already surprised at Kirin's obvious devotion to this rough, untidy man. But then so many surprising things had happened this day. Was it only one day?

Kirin knew what was needed. "Lad, are you happy for us to stay here tonight? We are all pretty tired. We will get out of your way tomorrow."

Lad realised that he might have spoiled things a little. He rubbed his beard, embarrassed. "Oh, don' mind me. I bin on my own too long. You can get very set when there's nobody but a hog to argify with. Don' you rush off, I begs you. I ain't felt this good in a very long while." He smiled at them all, and his eyes welled up. "Don' let my rough talkin' send you away. I got food …" He couldn't say more.

Ribby stood, still gazing at the bronze treasures in her arms, a little overawed by her new responsibility. But Lad's discomfort broke the spell they seemed to cast. She placed the bundle gently down on the seat and moved to reassure him. "That would be very welcome, Lad. Let's eat and sleep. And then in the new day we can tell you our plans. What do you think?"

"I think that now you all is 'ere, then I'm good. An' Nema is good. An' Cuda is smilin' on us," said Lad steadily. He turned to his shelves, to see what could be done for rumbling stomachs before the long day came to an end.

8

Mog lay back on the grass with Kirin and Ribby, making the most of the fresh air. They had all slept well, but it was good to get out of that quarry for a while.

Lad was up before them, watering and feeding the sow and her youngsters, throwing scraps and hay into another pen for the others. He was not finished with his work when the others got up; he wanted to stoke the fire and make a soup for them.

"I ain't walking me pigs today. I wants to make everything proper for you. You go an' walk they ponies for grass while I sees to a few things."

It had given them a chance to talk.

"I'm bothered about Lad," said Ribby. "He is lonely without Nema."

"I could take him to Elebyrig," suggested Mog. "Or see you camped near Beindubn and come back to get him? But what about his pigs? And I'm not sure he would trust me."

"We have nothing sure right now to promise him, except friendship," said Kirin.

"Then let's offer that," said Ribby. "Offer ourselves as a family, with the chance of a new start, whatever that turns out to be. We could come back for him later, as Mog says."

Kirin nodded, considering. "Maybe he would set us going today anyway. His knowledge of the woods behind would get us faster on to the upland. It would save an extra day's ride wandering towards Elebyrig before we can pick up the drovers' tracks."

Ribby stood and stretched. "Well, I was about to suggest we go and talk to him now, but look – he's changed his mind and decided to walk them after all."

As they stood, they could see Lad striding away from the quarry, chivvying his sow and his hogs before him with a piercing whistle and a slap to the thigh.

"Well, he looks happy enough right now," observed Kirin. "Maybe we have been worrying for nothing. He has lived on his own for most of his life." He put his arm round Ribby and held her close. "I want everyone to be as content as I am today, with you by my side, Ribby. I can't imagine being without you again."

Ribby reached up to Kirin and kissed him. "I'm content too," she murmured. "Whatever is in store we can face it together now."

"Oh, the gods rescue me from all this cooing!" sighed Mog, heading for the ponies. "I'm hungry. D'you think Lad's broth can be braved, or will we be straining husks through our teeth?"

LAD WAS NOT a worrying man. He never had been. He had had a tough life so far, sometimes short of food, often short of company. He usually found his next meal, thanks to his skill with a slingshot. Usually he stayed healthy. Most important of all, he had always recognised what was right for him and when things were wrong. And that morning, at his cooking, he had come to a decision. He was not driving the pigs to the woods, he was heading for the village. There they had everything he needed, and he knew how to get it.

The hard bargaining took some time, but the village elders and Lad parted on good terms. They all felt they had made a fair deal. Lad's tuneful whistle was as cheerful as ever as he trotted back into the quarry on a rather sleepy looking pony, empty wicker panniers bouncing behind him, and a heavy bag of stores across his back.

His visitors looked up in amazement. Lad laughed at the expression on their faces.

"There, now I looks like a lord on a hoss! I'm comin' with you. There's no need to be here no more. The village has my hogs and glad of it, and I'm goin' to bring the litter."

He jumped down and tied the pony, then eased the bag down carefully. "They's big enough to leave their mother, and we could do with a start to our next home. Four littluns ain't goin to be much trouble. What d'you say about that?"

Four squealing piglets as travel companions? The thought silenced all three of his audience for a moment, but Kirin recovered first.

"Nothing to say, but welcome!" he laughed.

"Oh, Lad, that works out so well!" said Ribby. "We have been wondering what would persuade you to join us."

"How shall you carry them?" asked Mog. That smelly duty was one to be avoided. This trip was turning out to be quite a story for the winter evenings. New boots were already as stained as old. There should be the revenge of Volkos on a few heads if the new jerkin went the same way!

"Two in each o' they baskets." Lad had thought things through. "On a bit o' dry grass. I shall let they heads poke out a bit so they can see where we's goin'. Where are we headin' first off? You ain't goin' to take Ribby to danger are you? Your old 'ome weren't the best place for her before, and surely ain't now if that man is there."

"We need to head up and on to the top. I'm hoping you know the easiest way up through the woods to open land. Then we will get across the hills and as close to Beindubn as we dare. Lad, this could work so well ..." Kirin was full of enthusiasm for the days ahead. Somehow being together again made everything possible. "Mog will leave us when we have news of my mother."

"To have you with us is a blessing from Cuda. And from Nema, I'm sure," said Ribby.

"Then let's get sortid. There's a few things 'ere that could be useful fer us," nodded Lad. "Make sure you tuck Nema's things safe out a sight in yer bag, Ribby. You got to guard that mirror fer a lifetime. Pick anythin' else worth the carry. They villagers will be pickin' over this ol' house the moment we get into the woods."

9

It was impossible for any of them to stop smiling. To be together, under a wide sky, swaying with the regular motion of the ponies and breathing clean air felt like a gift from the gods. Ribby and Kirin kept catching each other's glances, still amazed at their luck in finding each other once more; Lad jogged along, head high and eyes bright. He knew his lonely days were a thing of the past, and that Nema's legacy was now in the hands of the right person. And Mog had to smile at how this unlikely group, and their rustling passengers, must appear to the few travellers they met or overtook. Soon Lad had them back on familiar territory and Kirin knew exactly which valley they should head for. The distance and hours seemed as nothing, in the quiet happiness of the afternoon.

Without hesitation Kirin led them off the higher ground and down to their first destination. It was a small farmstead that would not have existed when his grandfather was young. Back then, families needed to live in sight of a refuge, ready to rush back up through the gates of the hillfort when the alarm sounded. This one nestled comfortably where a valley widened briefly, separated by a ridge of hill from Beindubn, spread on a slope in the afternoon heat.

Their arrival at a ford, and the antics of the brown piglets as they scampered with joy in the shallow stream, freed at last from their hot and bumpy ride, drew children from the farm down to watch. The children soon drew the adults and cautious greetings were made.

But Kirin was in a hurry to follow his plan. He left his pony with Mog and Lad, and left Ribby to do what she was so good at.

He knew her sure way of talking and reassuring the locals would give him the time he needed. Eyebrows were raised at the visitor's haste in heading up towards Beindubn land on foot. There was certainly something familiar about him, but he did not allow them too long a look.

Now he turned from the view of one valley and trudged on over for the next. His pony would have made for a quick getaway but a very obvious arrival. Walking was best. There was still enough day left to maybe find workers in the fields and a bit of information. He had to wipe the sweat from his brow. He was overheated and nervous.

The gods favoured him. To his huge relief the only person he saw in the distance was his friend Samos. He was very easy to recognise, his arms folded in his usual stance as he studied the green wheat wilting slightly in the fields. Beyond him the hillside dipped to the water meadows and up to the new thatched buildings on the terraces. For a moment Kirin's heart gave a jolt, but he had no time to give to emotion.

"Samos!" he called.

"Kirin! Well now, Pona's blessings on you!" Samos beamed in surprise and welcome as he strode over, then looked nervously around him. "Not sure this is the best place for you, man, but oh, it's good to see you!" He took Kirin's hand and pumped it up and down heartily. "Are the twins with you?" He looked past him and around.

"No, they are at Elebyrig. They are safe, and happy."

"I'm thankful for that. It was the right thing to do, leaving when you did, Kirin." He gestured across to the workshops. "Your uncle has Beindubn in a firm grip. Don't consider coming back, man. He fair skips around the place now he is the master and none to argue with him."

"Mother? How is she? It's her that I'm here for. I … well, we …

are going to settle somewhere new. I'm not sure where but I can't leave her here any longer. What news?"

Samos's face shadowed. "She died, Kirin. Not long past. The Elebyrig folks know. I sent a messenger. I thought that was why you were here ..."

Kirin studied the grass in silence for a moment, shaking his head. "I was travelling. The twins will know then, by now." His throat caught. Then he straightened. "What happened?"

"She died as she was sleeping, Kirin. She had got much weaker and very thin. She made the best of it after you got away, and she did love that little boy. Tirtos kept his patience; didn't dare to do otherwise with Alisne watching over her. Your mother is happy with Colios now."

He shuffled a little, uncomfortable. "They moved fast. Alisne and I did what we could. They buried her the same evening." There was so much he couldn't tell Kirin. He would never describe to anyone the shameful way Cuamena's body had been bundled into that cut.

In his pain, Kirin did not pick up on any awkwardness. Sorrow tied his tongue. The two men stood together quietly in the heat at the edge of the Beindubn fields while Kirin recovered himself.

"Then I am done with this place." he said finally. "There is nothing for me. We are going to start again, here on the hills. Somewhere we can keep Tirtos and his pitiful little wife in my range, but where he can't see us."

"We?" Samos was glad to change the subject.

"Ribby – my oldest friend, and friend no longer. More than a friend. Everything I need." He managed a smile. "And Lad, rough and strong as stone. With his hogs. There's a lot I could tell you with more time, Samos."

"Then you sound well set up to me," smiled Samos. He paused for a moment. "Kirin, would you let me know when you have the place in mind? My sons have swallowed that man's stories and bribes. They weaken the metal for him and turn out cheap rubbish. The farming has no pride in it; meat for his fancy table and honey to fatten him up, that's all he is after. Can I join you when you are ready? They will be glad I'm gone; we have argued enough. Volkos has his hold on my boys for now, but I'm their father till the end. I'd like to stay nearby, like you. They might need me yet."

Kirin was pleased. That would work so well. "Start preparing, Samos. See what tools can be spared and maybe hide them up here. We will need all the help we can get. Take a walk this way when Hatane is harvest full. You might find me here, and no time to be lost." He hugged Samos briefly and thumped him on the back in farewell. "See you soon, my friend. Very soon, I hope."

He turned his back on the Beindubn valley. Soon he was striding back downhill to the farmstead, swatting at the midges in the humid haze of sundown. His mind was working hard. Cuamena was free at last from pain and sadness on this overground; he had to be glad for her, despite his sorrow at not seeing her once more. Thank the gods he had chanced to meet Samos. There was much to tell Ribby.

10

The next morning it was obvious that they could not stay longer. The mother had realised who Kirin was. She was not going to be persuaded otherwise. A sticky night and the oppressive heat so early had not helped her mood.

"I've heard enough of that man over the hill. We don't want him turning up here and us getting the worst of his temper. It's a terrible sight, I've heard. I feel sorry, I do, but there's no place here for enemies of him. I have my farm and my family to protect."

The eldest daughter looked more disappointed than anyone. Her mother caught her eye and relented a little.

"Oh, I could find a place for this Lad and his hogs. He's not from here. We can always do with fresh breeding stock." Mog sniggered and got a glare from the woman.

Lad looked from Mog to Kirin, confused. "Um, I think 'tis best I stays with my friends. Fer now, anyways. I could be needin' you meself later. Same reason."

The girl smiled and collected the beakers from them, giving Lad a coy look as she took his.

Ribby decided it was time to rescue him, for now. "Well, Cuda's blessings on you all," she said. "We thank you for the night's rest. We will not give you more trouble."

"Yes, we must be on our way." Kirin glanced over his shoulder at the sky. "The clouds are gathering fast and heavy. We'll need shelter if the gods decide to play with them and us. Lad, I'll help you with your baskets." There were quick decisions to be made. He knew they had to leave but they had no fixed plans as yet. And this storm brewing was a threat in itself.

The woman then felt awkward about sending them away so soon, and she called for the children to help collect the piglets from their temporary pen. With much squeaking and wriggling, Lad's cargo was loaded and the ponies were brought forward. The four companions slung on their bags and cloak rolls and mounted. With a nod of farewell, Kirin turned his pony to the ford and the slope opposite. At the last moment, the older girl rushed forward with a large cloth wrap of dried meat and thrust it at Lad. They could still hear the woman telling her off as they trotted away.

Once up and out of the valley they soon found the drovers' track again along the top. Kirin wondered if life was like this for everyone; working in constant circles, familiar places revisited like the turning of a wheel. Each time there had been changes: different companions, different plans, different seasons. Over to their left was the Old Ones' mound, his and Kuno's playground of old, the one with the stone standing high. Dear, dear Kuno. That was where his life had become bound with Ribby's, as he watched Tirtos getting her back in the cart. He glanced across at the woman riding quietly at his side, thoughtful and composed. She trusted him and she loved him. The wheel of time went round, thought Kirin, and seemed to get better for him with each turn.

Not the weather though. The heavy clouds towards Beindubn were now glowering blue and black, thrown into contrast by the hot yellow haze over their line of hill. The thunderstorm was building. It forced a decision.

He reined in the pony and turned to the others. "So, north or south? Back towards Comelris we would be in touch with you, Mog. Northwards takes us along the top. A little higher, windier. We need shelter soon, though."

"Wait a bit," said Mog. "I've been watching that storm; I think we may be in luck. I think it's going to miss us."

Sure enough, the blackened clouds seemed to be churning north, rolling along the eastern horizon, thickening and deepening. They watched, fascinated, as the gods stirred the heavens like a cauldron of boiling tar. The wind picked up against their backs, rushing in towards it, cold.

"Blowin' up fer rain. Glad I ain't under that," commented Lad. "Goin' to fire soon!"

But the gods held back. The pressure seemed to grow and grow, with no relief. The storm drew towards them, then back, then on; a huge prowling lizard in the sky. They watched, open-mouthed, as it seemed to swing around their point on the hilltop, creeping slowly on northward. The ponies shied and whickered in the wind. Ribby shivered. She moved her pony closer and took Kirin's hand.

Then at the creature's head, far in the distance, a sudden strike of lightning flashed down through the dark, like the slash of a knife. Then another, exactly the same. Then another, the same place. They steadied their mounts and held their breath, waiting, waiting ... The layered claps of thunder that followed shook them to the core and echoed from horizon to horizon, until finally losing their strength and dying away.

It was over. The black clouds broke up and melted away in front of them. The heat, the haze, was all gone. And with them went any indecision. Kirin and Ribby looked at each other and announced, as one, "We go there!"

11

Following the contours of the upper plateau further northward turned out to be a straightforward ride that afternoon. The drovers' track was still clear for most of the way. It had been used by generations of traders and travellers, gently undulating along the top. The land gradually grew higher and more exposed. The few stands of trees that stood out above the scrubby undergrowth on either side formed strange wind-curved shapes against the sky. The grass here was stubborn, determined stuff, patched with tiny flowers and herbs. But it was soft to the hooves of the ponies and they made good time.

"Are you sure you wants to be up along here? This ain't the best land for hidin' or piggin'," remarked Lad.

"We must be getting to the hills' edge soon." Mog recognised the gleam of light under the cloud bank to their left. "I know there are old forts like Elebyrig that mark the scarp edge along. They were left a long time ago so I've never had reason to come so far. If you want somewhere out of the way you've picked the right place. Who would farm here with a choice? Savren's plain is much more welcoming, Kirin."

"A little further, I think …" said Kirin.

"We will know," added Ribby. She was sure.

A short while later they trotted around the brow of a hill and the view opened up. "Cuda's breath," said Lad. "Don' think we can get much higher …"

Ahead of them the ground levelled to the left and right, open land that stretched briefly towards trees at the hills' edge. To their right, the afternoon light picked out the stony layers of a steep cliff hanging above a valley cut.

"There," said Mog, pointing. "At the top … do you see the ditches? That's one of the old forts."

They started down the slope, leaving the drovers' track as it headed off through the trees at the edge. As the ground grew rougher, the ponies had to pick their way more carefully round ridges and bumps in the undergrowth. Brambles and nettles disguised mounds and low tumbled stone. It was not such easy riding now. Lad's cargo squeaked loudly in disgust at the change.

Then …

"Ouch!" Kirin's yelp halted them all and silenced the piglets.

Tutting, he pulled at his beaded belt and put his hand under his tunic. His frown slowly changed to a grin. He pulled out the bundle that had been tucked at his ribs since they had left the Fire Gathering together. The blade of the knife had worked its way out through the cloth, making its presence felt. He unwrapped it completely, holding it up for Ribby to see.

"Well, this must be it, Ribby. Our sharp friend has made his point. I think this must be where the lightning struck. "

He looked around, seeing the disused fields for what they were. "This was a farm once. There will be useful material to hand, if we look hard enough."

Mog was doubtful. "Are you sure? It's windy. It's going to be mighty cold in winter."

"No, he's right," said Ribby, excited. She recognised the hope in Kirin's eyes. "Tirtos will never reach this far. Why would he?"

She took the knife from Kirin and gently rubbed the creature's muzzle. "So be it," she smiled. "Our new home. No more wandering."

"Well I hopes that ol' knife is goin' to give us a bit more than a scratch now an' then," said Lad, jumping down and reaching for the panniers. He cast a knowing eye at the rough land around them and the poor bit of shelter over by some bushes. "Goin' to need his advice pretty reg'lar to make the best o' this. Ribby, where do you an' ee reckon fer a fire?"

OVER THE FOLLOWING months, something had to have been on their side, for time and weather turned out to be kind to them. Slowly but surely their farmstead developed and grew.

There was a place at the edge of the cliff, not far from their new roundhouse, that was their favourite place to sit when hard work could be left for a short while. Here a small landslide must have pulled away once, taking a sapling or two and clearing the view to the west as far as was possible to see. In clear weather they never tired of it. The flat plain stretched into the distance below, around and beyond scattered islands of hills. A mound of higher ground viewed to the north from Savren's banks, so long ago, had turned out to be the end of a short series of hills that lay away in the distance now, looking as content and still as a sleeping giant resting a weary head. To the south, hazy ridges marked the start of Ribby's homeland.

Ribby, Kirin and Samos swung their heels over the stone edge. Ribby smiled at a memory and took Kirin's hand.

"Do you remember how I vowed to send you greetings with the birds, across Savren? I never dreamed that we would find each other again. We were just children."

"The gods look after those who work hard," said Samos. "You two seem to have pleased them, for sure. And with Uban's grace I'm rescued too."

Mog had long since returned to Elebyrig, but returned regularly. Often Galete, Tilek and Kele came too, and their visits were vital. In the early days they would not have managed without the extra grain and dried meat in their baskets. Lad was tireless and as cheerful as ever, clearing and felling with Kirin, trimming the wood for their new roundhouse and fences. But the arrival of Samos one night had made a big difference. His strength and knowledge took the pressure off all of them. Lad was freer now to think beyond keeping themselves and his pigs alive. Tonight, he was where he often ended up these days, gazing shyly into the eyes of a certain eldest daughter back at the farm by the ford. Kirin and Ribby couldn't have been happier for him.

Calm had settled over their small farmstead. Kirin squeezed Ribby's hand in return. Sometimes he couldn't believe how things had worked out either. They watched Uban dip to the horizon.

"Tomorrow another new day, and another free one," he said. "This is good place to be, don't you think?"

There was no arguing with that.

PART THREE

AD46

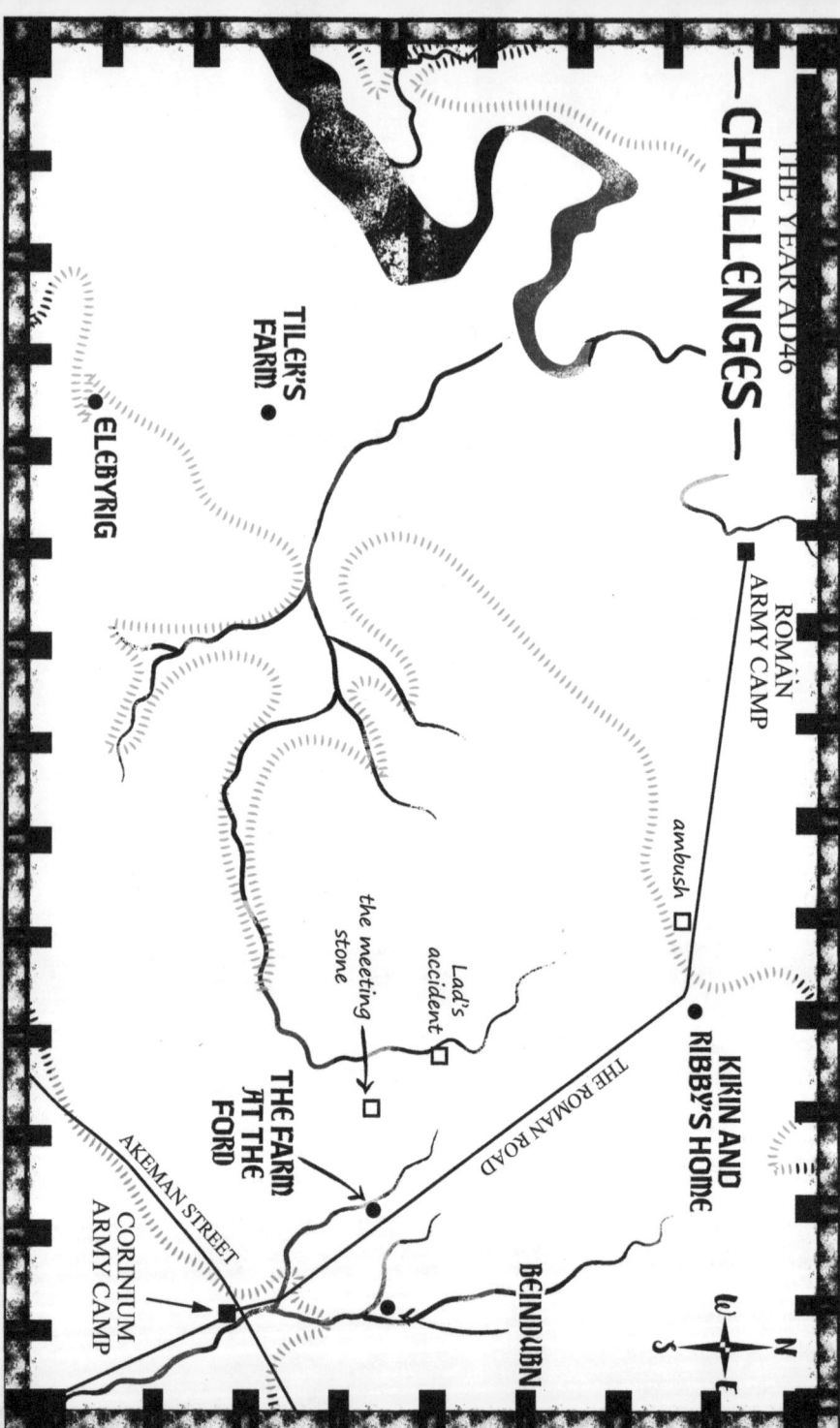

1

"Turn back, turn back!" hissed Galete to herself, as if she could make the soldiers ahead of her do as she wished, just by the power of her thoughts. Ahead of her, they stood quietly in tight formation, awaiting orders, armed and ready. The mounted escort had pulled their horses up and one officer was consulting with another on foot. Despite the drizzle, the sound of metal on metal drifted back to her as a horse shook its head and harness. Galete understood its impatience in the cold and wet.

Soon she would find out. Recently the army patrols had been extended downhill, but not every time. Galete prayed that this time they would turn and head back down the long straight track to their camp to the south. Today's plans would depend on it. But she was out of luck. The stop was only temporary. Orders were given and the foot soldiers marched forwards as one, the dull light catching on helmets and chest armour, moisture deepening the colours of their shields. Their solid threatening presence was a sight that she was becoming used to. A sight she hated with a passion.

Everything that they had been warned about, so long ago, had come to pass. Assurances of peace and benefits for all, trade and support with neighbours from across the water, this had indeed proved to be a calculated mask. A mask hiding the ruthlessness of an invading force. The Dobunnic families had heard enough about the suppression of those in the path of the Roman weaponry and determination. Galete had been as sure as any of her companions as they talked long into the night, around many fires. They had determination of their own. Their lands and lives were under extreme threat. The very real prospect now of slavery under these Romans turned ice to fire in their bellies. So they were not going to give in. They were going to fight back.

She wriggled back through the dripping bushes and drew upright as she got to her brother. She shook her head.

"They are going on. We need to tell Mog."

Kirin held out her pony's reins. "You, or I?" There was no time to lose.

"I'll go."

Galete didn't hesitate. She knew her brother should get back to the warmth of the fire; his knees were giving him trouble today in this damp. And if anyone knew the best shortcuts down through the trees it was her. She flung herself on the pony and slapped its rump, wheeling its head towards the woods and the steep drop beyond. It would be a reckless dash but she had no choice.

Kirin turned and led his pony back along the path, through the bushes and stunted trees. Only those in the know could see it was more than a deer trail. The wind drove the rain behind him as hard as ever, but he kept his cloak wrapped tightly around him and hardly noticed. His thoughts were with his sister. Soon he came out into a clearing, and to the first of their huts and fencing. He tethered his pony in its shelter and went on to the roundhouse.

Ribby looked up from her work as he entered, throwing off his cloak. He came up to the fire and rubbed his hands in the warmth.

"They've gone on down," he said. Ribby didn't need to ask more. "Galete has gone to tell Mog. They will have to keep their waggon out of sight until later now. They may not have time to reach everyone today."

"Hmm, the new camp on the near bank of the Savren crossing is going to stay, then. If they can feed and rest the patrols there overnight, it means they are getting organised."

"Samos has heard the camp to the south – the one they've named Corinium – is growing daily. Now they're out checking all the travellers that cross the river there. And they've got soldiers out improving the trackways all the time." It was a worrying development.

"I still can't accept how they have just walked on to our land!" Ribby threw down her knife in disgust. It was rare to see her angry. "Leader after leader just waving them in, smiling. Smiling at the bags of coin they are handed. That army is growing roots here, Kirin, and we are going to get tripped up in them."

"Not if we are careful," said Kirin. "They think they are in control. Maybe their confidence could be their undoing. After all, no soldier has been sent off the track to check us out yet. If Mog and Tilek can deliver those weapons and build up their network we may be able to give these soldiers trouble. And don't forget," he continued, "News of the tribute lord Caratacos has impressed Mog. Caratacos may have retreated to the Siluros people for now, but Mog says the man has faced the Romans in battle, and survived, so must have learned much about the way they fight. It's a different world beyond Savren, as we well know. There may be more people there willing to make a stand. It's worth finding out. We need all the help there is." He sighed, and drew Ribby to him for comfort. "We must do our best to stay strong."

Ribby turned her cheek against his woollen tunic.

"But I know," Kirin admitted quietly, "that right now, it is not looking so good."

2

"Well, that all looks very good," breathed Tirtos heavily, as he leaned back in his seat. He flicked at the empty glass in front of him with a fat finger and his rings clanged against it harshly. "More wine, Eburia!" he shouted. "Kenet, fetch your mother. Our glasses are empty."

Before the young man could respond, the Roman officer gathered his tablets together and reached for his helmet.

"Not for me," said Marcus Claudius Petronius. The legionary's work, as beneficiarius, was done here this morning. He had spent long enough with this awful man, who seemed to think he was one of them. How could he? It was pitiful. He was just an overweight and overblown peasant. The Latin he spoke had been learned on the streets, not schooled like a true Roman. It was galling to have to deal with these locals on a daily basis. But he had secured a month's supply of cheese and horse feed, and the promise of a slave or two for the kitchen work was a bonus. He stood up.

"I must get back. We have more cavalry arriving today. Camp Corinium is expanding daily. There will be messages for me from Governor Plautius. He answers to Great Claudius himself." With any luck, if he continued to oil the wheels of this Roman advance so successfully, Plautius might have many rewards in mind for him. He deserved to move on from these plodding valleys to central command. But right now it didn't do any harm to remind this pig whose side he should be on. He leaned forward and tapped the coins on the table, fixed Tirtos with a straight look, and strode out through the latched door.

The false smile on Tirtos's face stayed for a while in the silence that followed. A suppressed cough from his son wiped it off. He turned his bulk a little and raised an eyebrow at Kenet. "How much of that did you get?"

The youth left his stool at the fire and slumped onto the empty chair. He reached forward and took a dried plum from the dish on the table. Tirtos slapped it out of his hand. "I said ... How much did you follow of that?"

Kenet shrugged as he rubbed his hand under the table. The truth was, not a great deal, apart from the money. Coins were easy, the language not so. His father made it worse, always shouting and making him feel stupid. And it wasn't as if the old bully was any better than him when it came to scribing the stuff. Kenet doubted that the miserable git knew what Petronius had written any more than he would, so why should he work up a sweat making sense of the scratching? He sat in surly silence, just waiting to be allowed to leave. There were friends to be met and dice to be thrown behind the dairy.

Tirtos was not in the mood for a fight, for once. He shook his head in disgust. "Eburia?" he spat.

This time his wife appeared quickly. Kenet's mood lifted at the sight of his mother. She was twisting her long hair in her fingers, eyes sparkling.

Tirtos was not so pleased at the sight of her. She looked even younger and more beautiful today and he guessed her flushed cheeks had plenty to do with the two soldiers who had been waiting outside to escort Petronius back to the camp.

"There you are," he grunted, eyes suspicious as ever as he looked her up and down. "Wash these glasses and put them away. You do it, don't let the girl near them. She is even more likely to break them than you. And next time, don't keep me waiting like that in front of Petronius. He's the one we need to impress, not those thick sticks that come with him."

Eburia's eyes lost their sparkle. Every day a little sting, every day a carefully placed insult. Sometimes worse. Designed to control. She should be used to it by now, she thought.

The usual urge to defy flashed into her mind, but she abandoned it as quickly as it formed. She knew better than to aggravate him more. Now was not the time. "As you say, husband." She rushed to collect the glasses, head down. "Did your business go well today?"

"Well enough, I suppose. Alisne won't be too happy to hand over a couple of her daughter's litter for kitchen work at the camp, but it'll mean fewer to feed. She'll thank me one day. This lot could pack up and move on at any time, and we need to profit when we can. Clear off now, I'm tired. And take your son with you. That's what wearies me most, looking at the great lump."

Eburia glanced nervously at Kenet but his face gave nothing away. So with a too-bright smile, and clutching the precious glassware, she gabbled on about nothing in particular and ushered him out in the direction of the bakehouse. Another day, another diversion. It was exhausting.

None of this was lost on Kenet. He was keeping his own score, and keeping it to himself. Being Tirtos's son had worked to his advantage. To start with, no one beyond the old man dared argue with him, so hard work was easy to avoid. His mother was always ready with a treat or a little indulgence behind his father's back. All in all, his seventeen summers at Beindubn had been fairly satisfactory. But his father's treatment of his mother was getting harder and harder to ignore.

One day, he decided, as Eburia sat him next to the oven and ordered the girl to bring him a beaker of the best honey mead, we will be free of him. I will build her the best house in the land and we will impress any Roman who comes our way. Let the old turd think he's top of the pile for now, he mused, but I have plans.

3

"Tis good, Father, very good!" The girl put her arms around Lad's neck from behind and squeezed him tight as he sat at his workbench.

Lad put down his chisel and patted his daughter's hand.

"You likes it then? I'm pleased! Tis better than me first, I think. Got the size of 'er right." He had been working on the carving for some time and it was starting to take shape.

"Tell me the Nema story again, Father."

Serun loved it when she had him to herself. She was going to help her mother bathe little Kirin down at the ford, but she could hear that Tarn and Anba had finished their chores and had run down to join in. And from the yelling it sounded like even young Cam had decided to get wet for once.

"Ah, you don't need the telling right now, my lovely. I reckon you know's it better than me, the times you've heard it."

Serun sighed and let go. She slid round to join Lad on the bench while he continued to carve away at the piece. For some time he had been preparing a little shrine to set up in the wall of their hut. The memory of Nema had become entwined in his mind with images of Cuda. To him they were one and the same now. For had not the goddess herself decided to save him from his lonely childhood? Nema was Cuda, come to walk on the overground amongst tiny people like him and send him his friends Kirin and Ribby. Who knows what would have happened to him? And now he was here, making a good living at the farm on the ford with Melis.

And the children had followed, fending off old age, keeping

him as fit as ever. First was Serun, kind and thoughtful, then Tarn who loved the work with the hogs now as much as his father did. Anba followed, all smiles, who found the funny side of anything she did. Then Cam and little Kirin arrived in turn, both noisy and wilful and leading them all a fine dance through these happy days.

He reached his arm round Serun and gave her a cuddle. His daughter was growing fast; she was a young woman really. But there should be no rush to leave childhood behind. He pushed the piece of golden limestone away from him.

"Tell you what, let's collect they damp hoodlums from yer mother and get the beddin' out early. Nothin as good as wrappin' up tight, with warm milk and a long story, while Uban goes on down."

He had a reason for settling his lively family as early as possible this evening. Tonight Hatane shone full, which meant it was the night for slipping off quietly to meet up with Kirin at the Old Ones' stone.

LAD WAS SURPRISED to find Mog sitting with Kirin in the moon shadow cast by the standing stone. It was good to meet up again. They had all shared much hard work and laughter getting that old farm going again for Kirin and Ribby in the early days. But then Lad had moved in with Melis and now their paths rarely crossed.

Life had changed for Mog too since those days. Elebyrig had lost its importance after Bulva and Tass died. There was no longer the horse trade westward, Tirtos had seen to that. Although the remaining families up by the old hillfort continued to make a good living, it did not seem like home. After Galete and Tilek bound hands together, and Kele moved in with them, the obvious thing for Mog was to follow them down to Tilek's farm. And now, the Dobunnic settlements on the valley floor, like Tilek and Galete's, were perfectly placed as bases for hit-and-run action against the invaders' advance. Which was why they were there in the moonlight.

Mog grinned at Lad's raised eyebrows and held up a hand in greeting.

Kirin got to the point quickly. "Lad, you've heard how things are going with these soldiers. Their camp to the south is getting bigger. The locals have to call it Corinium, and get trouble if they don't. And their patrols are going further. It's getting harder and harder to keep out of their way. They're controlling and demanding a share of goods at every road crossing and ford or ferry. They are threatening the farmers if they don't hand over their stores. They think their worthless coins will make all the difference."

"They are calling it protection," chipped in Mog. "Protection from what? They are the only ones we need protection from. Lad, the warnings can't be ignored. They've marched towards our lands harvesting the fittest for their slaves and all the food for their stomachs!"

"I hears what you say," said Lad carefully. "But me an' Melis ain't had no real trouble. I sees them stomping along that high way they're making above our place. They goes right past. We just gets on with things."

"That high way is making things very easy for them, Lad. Easy to move their men, easy to drain the Dobunnic life blood from these hills. The new camp at the end of it, at Savren, is set to stay," said Mog, and added "Don't worry, they'll get to you in the end. None of us will be free. They are after the big farms first, the local elders and leaders. They want the ones with influence, right now."

Lad had to chuckle. "Well, we ain't got none of that."

"But you have!" said Kirin. "You are in the perfect position to help us. Listen, Mog here has been planning with the Siluros, who have helped Caratacos hide in the mountains."

"Caratacos? Who's 'ee when 'ees at 'ome?"

"He's the only leader talking any sense right now," said Mog. "He and his brother made a good try at fighting back at these Romans. It was a fierce battle, I'm told. Our warriors and chariot fighters were a wonder to be seen. But his brother was killed and he pulled back with those who survived. He says that another face-to-face attack isn't going to do any good right now. He says we have to sting them on the rump, like horseflies in summer. They'd be so busy scratching their behinds they'd drop their shields, sort of!" Mog chuckled at the thought.

"Which is where you can join in," said Kirin. "We need to know when supplies are heading up the high way for the new Savren camp. If Mog and Tilek can be sure they are on the road, then they can prepare a large ambush in good time. They've had plenty of volunteers from the farms. And they have the weapons in place now."

"You would get the message to Kirin and Ribby, for them to pass it on to the next," added Mog.

"The supply convoys are slower than the patrols. It's a long haul for the waggons up to us, and then the quick descent downhill is tricky. We've been watching them," said Kirin. "The soldiers on escort duty get distracted and have to stop often. We could do a lot of damage with a well-timed raid."

"We need to rattle them, take their supplies and make them think," said Mog. "It's going to be our turn now. They've been having it all their own way. That has to stop. We need to draw some Roman blood in return." Mog was no longer smiling.

Lad was thoughtful. "So you'm thinkin' I could beat them to it, up to your place?"

"You could, with the pony we've brought you," said Kirin. "Mog's picked you out a strong mare. It's tethered over there with ours right now. You've been without one too long anyway. What do you say?"

"Then yes, with four legs under me it could be done," considered Lad. "The way you've come down to this stone is easy goin',ain't it."

"It is," said Kirin, "But the Roman high way cuts right across the drovers' way. It heads straight for the edge of the hills and the steep drop. You would need to choose your moment to come out of the trees to cross it. We had no trouble at night, but it would be harder in the day."

"Hmm ... I could get Tarn an' Anba to walk the hogs up in the woods nearby, an' then one could run and tell when there's a bit of action on the road. They needn't know too much of it all. Melis will need to know more, though. This is a serious thing you'm askin' from her. She's used to me nippin' off to meet you reg'lar, and don't see no harm, but ..."

"Tell her the freedom of her children is at stake," said Kirin, grimly. "Tell her we have no choice."

"I think she will say I should see that for meself." Lad was thoughtful. "Kirin, how's about me an' you headin' down to 'ave a better look at this Corinium camp? Right now, I mean. Get the measure of 'em. Tis a quiet night, an' clear enough."

Kirin shook his head. "This is still as close to Beindubn as I dare. The locals are using the high way as much as the soldiers now. I daren't risk being recognised. If Tirtos get a sniff that I'm still about these parts, then we are in trouble. Even more is at stake now."

"Kirin's right, Lad," said Mog. "I'm afraid this part of the plan falls on you."

"And me family," pointed out Lad.

"Yes," said Kirin, quietly. "And your family. It's a lot for us to ask, I know."

But Lad raised his head and grinned.

"Well, I trust you, Kirin, always 'ave an' always will. If you says that's what we do then we does it. But give me a day before you expects anythin'. I'm goin' to head for that camp now and see what's what." He stood up, then reached to help Kirin to his feet, too. "Three old rebels, plannin' against an army?" he laughed. "Don't know what the world is comin' to!"

"Old?" grumbled Mog, leaping up quickly. "You can leave me out of that. Uban knows I'm as frisky as a spring calf compared with you two old heifers."

"Well, may Uban grant his blessings on us all now, old or not," said Kirin. "We are going to need all the help we can get. I will see you soon then, friend, if the gods continue to be kind."

4

Once Lad was through the trees and up on to the high road above his farm, he realised it was going to be an easy trek, even without the pony. He had left his new mount tied up safely behind his pig pens, hoping that horse snuffling was little different from a hog on a quiet night.

"That bit of explainin' can wait for the rest," he had decided.

On both sides of the track the undergrowth and trees had been cleared back very recently. There was enough light to see where shallow quarries had been started for road stone to level the middle. He was surprised at the trouble these Romans were taking. "Like they means to stay," he muttered to himself.

He was glad they didn't work at night, and there seemed to be no patrols. His walk took him southwards at a good speed. The track was now remarkably straight, and its ups and downs gradually dipped downhill, picked out ahead of him like the path of an arrow. With the dawn, he could make out others joining the track ahead from either side. Men and women carried goods or led ponies with small loaded carts, all heading down from the hills. "Headin' to what?" Lad wondered.

He didn't have too long before finding out. As the land started to pull away on either side he realised that in the distance he could make out structures and activity. A settlement was ahead, wreathed in wood smoke, and dotted with pin pricks of flare or fire; but not one with the familiar skyline of roundhouse or thatch. He picked up his pace, more alert now, and more self-conscious. Now he wished he was carrying a bag, a bundle of firewood, anything to give him reason to be there. The track was tempting and easy, but it meant he and the other travellers could be seen from a distance. Here was purpose and planning, he realised. Here was control.

Soon the road brought him down to a wide marshy stretch where rivers and streams came together. To his right he could see his own valley opening up. To his left was a similar view, and he realised it must be where the Beindubn river emerged to meet and join with his own. The track was now smoothly surfaced with stone all over and raised up above the rushes and tangle of undergrowth. There would be no flooding from spring rains here, Lad could see. Ahead, a stretch of dark fence on a bank emerged from the mist, with a raised watchtower above. And in that tower his first sight of soldiers, guarding the scene below.

There was a lot going on. The day had hardly started but there was already a small crowd in front of an open gate. The trickle of locals had become stalled there, joined by others arriving from tracks to the left and right. Lad could see the helmets of soldiers moving amongst them, checking and questioning. Now he was nervous. He had no good answers to satisfy their questions, he was sure. He moved to the side of the causeway and crouched, pretending to re-tie his leg bindings. Glancing up quickly he could see that the track to the right continued away from the soldiers' entrance and headed off again between the defences and higher ground. Some travellers were being allowed to carry on their journey, and some traders were allowed through the gate.

"Might as well finish the job, nows I'm 'ere."

As casually as he could he looked around him and was glad to see there was no one close behind. Hoping the guards ahead would be distracted by the crowd, he dropped off the edge of the road into a patch of tall rushes. He landed with a squelch and a cold wet shock to his feet. Luckily, his next step took him to firmer ground. Keeping his head down he wove his way off to the right, parting the bushes and tall grasses as carefully as he could, making his way to some trees in the distance.

"Where there's trees there ain't no water, I 'opes," he reasoned out loud.

He had to deal with a couple of small streams that crossed his path, but eventually he picked his way up into the tree line and more protection. He sat for a short while to get his breath back.

"Getting' too old fer all this," he sighed, shaking his head.

There was no point in waiting any longer. He was getting cold. There was more to see and he needed to see it. The chance had to be taken.

"I 'opes ol' Kirin is grateful," he grinned to himself. "Melis will say I'm a mad fool!"

He scrambled to his feet and carefully crept through the shadows towards the light at the edge of the wood until his way, and the light, became blocked. He realised he was at the base of a large mound. It rose among the trees in front of him, tangled with bushes and stunted trees, wreathed in trails of half-dead climbing plants. A mound of the Old Ones, he guessed, sitting there hidden and silent on the last of the higher ground. Carefully he picked his way up the sides, grabbing at the ropes of vegetation to help, until he got to the top.

And there, suddenly exposed, he had to drop down amongst the creepers.

Beneath him, the trees had been felled and bushes cleared back, right up to the base of the old mound. The track he had spotted earlier ran through this cleared area, heading off to his right past tree stumps and wood piles. Lad could see travellers rushing off along it, probably relieved they could carry on their journey, heading away from this place as fast as they could. And he could see why. Spreading before him was the strangest settlement he had ever seen.

It was a village of brown cloth or leather, stretching across the terrace of land that levelled out above the reed beds and marshes that surrounded it. The pointed fence on top of the bank turned from the track just before him, and he could see it was unfinished. Only the earth bank and the deep ditch with it carried on southwards. Lad could see more towers, placed at intervals, marking where the bank continued and turned once again to finally enclose the village completely.

The tops of their shelters were visible from his viewpoint. They were set up in rows, some large, some smaller, the sides and roofs flapping and rippling in the breeze. Morning light reflected off weapon stacks and signs stuck high on wooden poles. Everywhere, he could see or sense movement. People were milling about carrying, fetching, each absorbed in some duty or other.

"Like they little bitey crawlies movin' their eggs," muttered Lad.

In the middle he could see a space where waggons were being unloaded. Orders were being shouted. Horses whinnied from tethered lines. Animals and birds called from wicker pens. Smoke and steam from cooking fires waved across the site, dulling the noise and confusing the eye. It was as if these Romans had landed from another world; as if Volkos had planted them to cause trouble for his own amusement.

As he watched, a gate halfway down the bank opened. A group of soldiers marched smartly across the ditch on wooden planks, followed by a horse and cart. They turned along the side of the camp, then cut away and headed for the felling area and the wood piles directly beneath Lad on the mound.

"Time to go, boy," whispered Lad. He realised he was shivering, and it wasn't just his wet feet. The cold wind that blew with the morning had brought with it a cold dose of reality. He understood Kirin's mission now, and he understood the part he and his family had to play.

5

Kirin was sure it would work, and it did. Lad had no problem in reaching him with the news well ahead of the Roman supply convoy. Kirin's prompt ride down, zigzagging through the woodland, meant that the message was well on its way along their spy network before the waggons and escort of soldiers had made it even halfway along their journey. It was exciting, and very satisfying.

"This is what I have missed!" Kirin was jubilant when he returned.

He slapped Lad on the back. "We have kept our heads down, stayed out of trouble. Now we fight back! It's a good feeling."

"So Tilek's friend was ready. Excellent!" Ribby handed him a beaker of warm ale. "Pona's blessings on them all now. Let's hope they come out of this day unharmed."

She could not help worrying; all the people she loved were caught up in this. But like Kirin, she wanted to kick back at these invaders. Fear had turned to anger, but her anger also grew from a deeper seed. Tirtos, sitting comfortably at Beindubn, had always been in the back of her thoughts. His presence there had seemed to threaten everything they did, hanging like deadly smoke above their lives and sitting unwelcome in her memory for such a long time. She was tired of feeling like a victim. Challenging the Romans like this helped make up for the years of hiding.

"I ride next time," she said, firmly.

Kirin didn't argue. Their partnership was as secure and as equal as ever. It had been hard at times but their love for each other had never dimmed. Their small farm had survived, and even prospered, up there in the wind and rain. It had become a safe haven for others, too. Waifs and strays, wandering past, found a home in exchange for hard work and loyalty. Ruins and the roughest of pasture had been replaced by a collection of small roundhouses and workable land.

Lad was enjoying the warmth of fire and friendship but knew he could not stay long.

"I'd better be on me way," he sighed. "Me ol' sow is likely to pop with her babes any time now an' I can't expect Melis to cope with that an' little Kirin. He's trouble, he is!" The look on his face showed that whatever trouble the little lad caused, Lad was more proud than bothered. "An' there was me thinkin' that if I named 'im after a great man some of it would rub off!"

"Greatness is for the gods, not for us," Kirin laughed. "Let the boy live free without that weight on his shoulders!"

"Aye," said Samos, entering the roundhouse and catching their conversation. "Live in a land where he has a bit of choice. There's a lot depending on what happens down there in the valley today."

6

Tilek blew the horn for the attack. They charged out of the trees from both sides, some on foot, some mounted. All were screaming, with long swords flailing.

The soldiers driving the carts and waggons were caught completely by surprise, pulled down from their benches as they reached for their weapons. Their cavalry escort, horses rearing and thrashing in the confusion, tried to order some sort of defence. But the Romans were outnumbered, betrayed by their complacency. Within minutes, dead and dying lay scattered on the roadside. Bewildered, the pack mules and surviving horses shied and turned in circles, eyes bulging in fear.

Mog and Tilek jumped down from their mounts and leapt to each other. They hugged in relief, streaked with blood and sweat.

Tilek turned to his fighters. Slumped, injured, all exhausted, but all alive.

"D'you see, men?" he yelled. He clenched his fist and punched the air. "There's no armour thick enough to resist us! We have right on our side!" He caught his breath and whistled loudly towards the woods.

"We are not yet done!" he shouted. "We take no prisoners. Do what you have to. Get what you can off the bodies and then pull the carts into the woods."

Galete and her band rushed from the trees with stretchers of sapling and hide. "Our wounded can walk, Uban be praised!" he called to them. "Strip the waggons and rescue the animals. Quickly!"

A MAN AND woman came striding along the track, heads down, heavy baskets on their backs. They pulled up short at the bloody scene before them and looked at each other in horror.

"This is not for us to know," the man said, shaking his head. "We have not seen this." The woman nodded, frightened. The two of them shifted their burdens a little and set off in haste past the abandoned waggons and bodies on the ground. Behind them not a bird sang and the wind blew cold as they rushed on towards the Savren crossing and the Roman camp ahead. They would not forget that sight in a very long time, but they would not tell.

And so it continued. Mog and Tilek knew so much about that wide river plain, and the Romans knew so little. The Dobunnic fighters could travel fast and light, using the old and hidden ways. Bloodletting had been their ancestors' way, and now it was theirs. Sometimes Mog would stand, gasping for breath, sword weighing stained and heavy, and watch and wonder. Watch as more dead soldiers were rolled over, arrows pulled free or knives retrieved. Wonder how long this killing would have to go on. They would limp back home to Kele and her quiet care, back to Tilek's farm and the families there. They felt proud to be standing up for them and their freedom, but it was hard to get the taste of blood from their mouths these days.

To some it was fun. Back at the farm near the ford, the younger ones loved their new game. The children had made a shelter up in the woods, with a good view down the road. They would come running down in excitement when they spotted anything interesting. Lad would leave his work and stride up the slope to see for himself. The slower and larger the convoy, the more likely he would get his pony and head for Kirin and Ribby to pass on the information.

In their turn, the warriors in the valley would choose random sites and random times to make their attack on the supply lines. They found places to ambush the Roman cavalry scouts and messengers. They made sudden mounted raids on the Savren army camp at night, firing burning arrows over the high fence as they rode past, setting fire to hay stores and shelters. They did everything they could to wear the invaders down; to make them go back to where they came from.

7

Outside the Beindubn gate it was a nervous wait at the ford. But patience was rewarded by the arrival of the trader with a loaded pony and a knowing eye. A stranger in these parts, no interest in a back story, passing through. A careful question was answered carefully. A phial was dug out from the pannier and passed over quickly.

Later a quiet moment created opportunity. The gods were generous today. As the liquid dripped slowly into the flask of wine, deep breathing steadied the hand to get the count right. It would not do to make a mistake at this stage. Slow but sure, that was the best way to solve this problem, the trader had said, quickly tucking the payment out of sight.

Time to make him suffer for a change.

Gently the flask was swirled and the green from the woodland flower – which in life was so content to live in the shade – in death blended happily into the dark red, primed for its work.

8

Marcus Claudius Petronius was in a filthy mood. "Do something or we will!"

He had been sent out from the camp with one message to deliver. He needed to ram it home. There was to be no negotiating here. He could not let these country idiots get in the way of his promotion. Especially this idiot.

Tirtos shifted uncomfortably. He was weary, his insides hurt, and worst of all he was at a disadvantage; he did not know what Petronius was shouting about. The officer had come barging in on his breakfast, and was now pacing up and down, red faced and threatening. Eburia fluttered helplessly in the background, scared that someone was daring to speak to her husband in this way.

"These bands of barbarians are a drain on our time, our manpower, and our denarii," spat the Roman. "I don't know what they think they are doing! As if their pitiful attempts to undermine our mighty Empire are going to make much difference. They will get swatted like flies, and stamped underfoot!"

Tirtos realised that his ignorance was going to work for him, at least for a while. He raised a plump hand and gestured the legionary to a seat.

"With the greatest respect, my friend, calm yourself. I need you to explain." And say it simply, thought Tirtos. His Latin could not keep up with this outburst. He reached for another glass and gestured with his wine flask. A peace offering.

Petronius stopped and looked at him, eyes narrowed and suspicious. After a moment, he took off his helmet and sat heavily at Tirtos's table, dismissing the offer with a wave of his hand.

"Our convoys are being attacked on the way to the new camp at Glevum. We are losing goods and men. Are you saying that you know nothing about it?"

Tirtos was able to look Petronius in the eye as he answered. "Believe me, my friend. This is news to me." *And shouldn't be,* thought Tirtos.

"You call me friend, but the word means nothing." Petronius was not to be put off. "It's your 'friends' that are behind this, I have no doubt. Your tribe, your workers. Who else could it be? The road passes above your land. Someone is spying. The barbarians seem one step ahead, they pick and choose. But we have to send extra men in escort with every patrol, every mule."

He did not admit the number of dead to Tirtos, or the struggle of their despatch riders to keep reliable contact between the Corinium and Glevum camps. It was all too embarrassing. His legion was used to getting its own way.

"I see." Tirtos was thoughtful, and worried. There were still many deals to be made with this army. There was a lot at stake, a lot of wealth to be picked from this Roman money tree yet. Who would want to go back to fiddling about with worthless clatters of bent coin and clumsy jewellery?

So Petronius's next words hit its mark. "If you are not able to sort this, then we will for you. We will take over your estate and put someone else in place, someone who can control your worthless scum. If this does not stop, well …" Petronius subtly moved his hand to the short flat sword hanging at his side. "Your day here may be done very soon."

Tirtos was well aware of Eburia's gasp. He needed to take control of this conversation, and quickly. He pushed his seat back and heaved himself up, careful smile in place.

"Leave it with me," he said smoothly. "They must be a few rebels who do not realise when they are well off. It is clear to anyone of sound mind that your army and governor are bringing advantages beyond their dreams. I will help you all out, Petronius. I will find them for you and, well, 'bring them around' to our way of thinking."

Petronius was not happy with the idea that his great Empire was in need of help, but decided to let it go for now. Tirtos noticed his hesitation and took the lead.

"Come, now, I'm sure you have much important work to be getting on with," he said confidently and headed for the door. He left the legionary no alternative but to pick up his helmet and follow him outside to his horse and escort.

Eburia took a deep breath and sank on to his chair. Her husband was back in charge, confident and in control, so she and her son were safe from any beatings today.

AS SOON AS the soldiers had disappeared through the Beindubn gates, Tirtos yelled for Arbin. He was out along the water meadows, checking the ponies, so it was a while before the message got to him. The delay did nothing to calm Tirtos down.

"There you are, finally. We have a problem. Well, you do …"

Arbin did not react. He was used to his master's moods, though these days they seemed worse than ever. He stood and waited for the explanation.

"That cockerel of a Roman officer had been here again, shouting his mouth off," he sneered. "It seems they are having trouble getting their supplies along the high way without losing it to some locals with a death wish. He reckons someone around here is informing to the rebels. What do you know about it?"

"Nothing," Arbin shrugged. "No one on this estate would dare. They know what's good for them."

"That's what I thought," nodded Tirtos. "But if there's a different profit to be made from these Romans then I want to know about it. Get Tala to ask some questions around here. I think it would be a good idea if you spread a bit further than usual. Have a wander up across the high way and visit the valley beyond. The piss-poor dirt grubbers there are hardly worth a second look, but they are closer to the road than we are. Someone might have got a bit ahead of themselves. See what you can find out."

"As you say," said Arbin, and sauntered off cheerfully to find his brother. He was very happy with his orders. It would make a change to get out of Beindubn for a while and get out of the shadow of the big man and his temper.

9

Without knowing it, Mog and Tilek helped Tirtos out of his tricky situation with the Roman garrison at Corinium.

They decided to stand down their fighters for a while. The constant ducking and diving, the hand-to-hand combat, it had all taken its toll. Many of their band were recovering from injuries, and tiredness soaked through their bones.

Also the daylight had lengthened again, restricting much of their movement. Uban shone with welcome warmth; it would be good to put down their weapons for a while and help with the new season's planting back on the farms. There was no use fighting for freedom without food to feed them through the next winter.

And Mog had more plans, plans that reached into the mountains of the Siluros and beyond. It was now time to make contact with other resistance groups and find out what was happening further afield. The Roman army had sharpened up, increasing their armed cavalry and actively hunting out suspected pockets of resistance in the villages. To renew any assault on them was a daunting prospect with the few reserves they had left. Mog had decided to go and find Caratacos for advice and maybe some reinforcements.

When she heard this plan from her cousin, Kele was not pleased. "Mog, I get you all home in one piece, just about, and you say you are going away again! You are tired and not thinking straight. Galete, you've got some influence here. Support me!"

But Galete knew Mog well enough. "No Sister, I can't. I agree with Mog. We need as much information as possible. There may be better ways to make trouble for the Romans. The Siluros will know where Caratacos has got to."

"Once I am across Savren I can move quickly," said Mog. "I'd like to see how far the Romans have got beyond their new base at the river. I'm guessing not that far. The land changes fast in a few days' travel, and the mountain passes are perfect for defence and attack. I'm sure the Siluros have not whimpered and rolled over at one sight of a Roman spear."

"How long do you think you will be?" Kele asked anxiously. It was time to distract her, and Galete thought fast.

"Long enough to miss some fun!" announced Galete with forced cheerfulness. "Mog, you do what you must. We stay-at-homes will enjoy life without you! Kele, let's plan a proper feast. We can ask Kirin and Ribby to stay for a while. It will do us all good. How are the stores these days?"

"As you would expect, after a long winter," considered Kele. "But the new lambs are arriving now. We can spare an old culler for a roast, and there's barley for more brew. I'll go and check." She bustled off, something new to think about.

Mog, Galete and Tilek looked at each other and smiled briefly. "Good thinking, Cousin," said Mog.

"Can I go with you?" Tilek asked Mog. Galete held her breath. She did not want him to go, but there were greater things at stake than her peace of mind.

"No," said Mog. "I'll travel best alone. One is less threatening than two. I'm not sure what my welcome will be, to be truthful. People have learned to be careful the hard way."

"We won't know where you are," said Galete. "I've heard it's a wild land still beyond the river."

Mog smiled. "The gods and my sword have been good to me so far. Let's hope that stays true."

THE MESSAGE TO stand down was passed back along the network. When it got to Kirin he accepted the decision as gladly as anyone else, though he had not been allowed near any hand-to-hand fighting. He had burned to join in, but Mog had insisted there was enough to worry about without looking out for an old man with creaking knees.

The news that his cousin was off to find Caratacos, without a companion, did bother him however.

But Ribby was not so worried. "Mog is right to do this, Kirin," she said. "There must be many other tribes, far from us, who still want the Romans gone. If we unite, that could make a difference. Maybe this Caratacos can send help. Remember, I have Siluros blood in my veins, I know the people of the mountains. I am sure Mog will be treated well."

Tilek's messenger had also brought their invitation to the family feast. It was very welcome; it was so long since they had had a chance to relax together, like old times.

Kirin and Ribby decided to leave pretty much immediately. Samos was happy to stay with the animals and supervise the spring work in their fields, so they agreed to take a chance and call on Lad on the way. It would be in daylight, but he needed to hear the message from the resistance as soon as possible. If they took the drovers' route to Elebyrig, then drop down to Tilek and Galete's farm, they could divert briefly into Lad's valley without losing much time and avoid any close Roman attention. They packed quickly and set off as soon as they could.

As it happened, they caught sight of Lad sooner than they expected, as he trotted up out of the dip and turned northwards. He was heading for them, it seemed. At the sight of strangers in the distance, riding towards him, he reined in and slowed to a walk. He rarely saw anyone up there on the top, let alone riders.

"Pona's greetings, old friend!" called Kirin as soon as he was within earshot.

Lad realised who they were and perked up.

"You two made my blood run a bit colder, just then!" he declared. "What are you doin' here in the day? I didn't 'ave you fer Roman scouts on they little ponies, tho I weren't sure with my ole eyes. Phew, my mouth is runnin' dry after that." He wiped his brow on his sleeve and reached for his water bag.

Ribby could see the strain on Lad's face. The stand down would be good for all of them. "We come with news," she said. "Tilek has called a halt to the attacks for now. You can stop watching the road until we get word."

"That do make my life a bit easier, Cuda knows," said Lad. "I been up an' down that slope more times than I likes to think, checkin' what the children 'ave spotted. I was comin' today cause it were a good'un. Two slow waggons with they funny lookin' jars packed in straw, an' so many soldiers guardin' em you'd think they was the gods' babies."

"Roman oil for the Savren camp," said Kirin. "Mog tells me it's good stuff. But not worth dying for, and not worth you running such risks. Come, old friend; we are on our way to visit Galete and Kele for a few days. We will see you to the standing stone and then say farewell. You need to get home to rest a little and we need to get on our way."

Lad turned his pony, and the three of them trotted back along the way together, glad to chat for once about happier things than fighting and fear. It was soon time to part, and after a final wave, Kirin and Ribby set off southwards on the track for Elebyrig and Lad headed down the hillside towards the farm.

As he got closer to the ford he realised a man was standing at his pig pens, looking about him. Melis and the children were nowhere to be seen.

Something about his confident stance made Lad's stomach

turn again.

"Cuda's breath," he sighed. "If I aint 'ad enough to worry me today." He splashed across the shallow water and dismounted stiffly.

At the sound of the horse, the man had turned. He pointed to the pigs. "These yours?"

"Mine they are," said Lad cautiously. "Who's askin'?"

"Arbin of Beindubn, if you must know," the man replied. "I'm just having a little look around. Is that a problem?"

"No," grunted Lad. "I s'pose. Not often we gets anyone from Beindubn over 'ere."

"You've heard of my master? Tirtos?"

"Sort of," said Lad carefully. "Don' need to know much. Always got on fine, we 'ave, stickin' to our little valley. Not botherin' anyone."

"Good. Keep it like that," said Arbin. "He's a hard man when he's crossed. You stick to your pigs and stay in your valley and I'll be happy. And then he'll be happy. Get the message?"

"Not sure what yer talkin' about, but I don' plan to upset anyone. We got a good life 'ere."

Arbin sniffed. He gave another look at the farm buildings and then turned to head back up to the high way. He stopped, a curt comment directed back over his shoulder. "You'll see me again," he said, then set off up the slope, leaving Lad to breathe a little better.

"A grubby pig man with a good pony?" Arbin muttered to himself, as he climbed. "Interesting. Yes, you can lay a bet on seeing me again, old man."

BEINDUBN HAD NOT been a good place for a long time, even for Arbin and his brother. They were the men who put Tirtos's orders into action. They were the men who ordered frail old people into the fields, or denied food supplies in winter. It had been worth it for the power and favour with their master, but these days things were getting worse.

It was uncomfortable to watch their best livestock being driven out through the gates in the embankment and off down the trackway to the Corinium camp. It was much harder to stomach the sight of a desperate mother as her children were forced from her and sold to the Romans. Tala and Arbin were used to doing pretty much as they pleased but now Tirtos was everywhere, stung into action at the thought of losing any bargaining power with the army. The vicious old man heaved his considerable weight around the place, poking into everyone's business, suspicious of all. No one was safe from his demands, or questions, or his terrible mood swings.

So Arbin got out of Beindubn and returned to the quiet valley sooner than anyone there knew. It was a good excuse.

There was more to find out as well, he was certain. A peaceful few hours, sitting and watching, would be a very good idea. The weather was dry and still, with that fresh cut to the air that only the spring can bring. He settled in amongst the bright green of a hedge that overlooked the farm and the slope to the ford. Only a stone's throw below him, the man and a woman went about their work around the tumbledown huts and pens, and a tall girl helped a toddler scatter scraps for some ducks in the mud, all unaware of their silent observer.

On the third morning of watching and waiting something much more interesting happened. The quiet was broken by the younger children shouting and laughing as they rushed down out of some trees to Arbin's left.

"Tarn says the Romans are coming! Tarn says the Romans are coming!" they called as they danced down to the farm.

The woman stood up from scraping out a wooden trough and

shook her head at their excitement.

"Shush, you two!" she shouted, stopping them in their tracks. "We've told you, your father doesn't need to know for now. Stop your noise and get back up with those hogs. Any reason for nonsense with you two, isn't it! The Romans can get on their way without telling your father today."

The man poked his head out of the stable. "An' without tellin' the trees around, Melis my lovely! Keep yer voice down!" he called.

Arbin's eyes narrowed.

None of them could know then how much damage had just been done.

10

Lad decided he had to deal with the problem of Arbin by himself. He guessed Kirin and Ribby would have returned from their trip to the Savren valley, but he dared not visit them at the moment. No, he would wait for the next full moon and his usual midnight meeting to tell Kirin.

The man had become a constant threat, intimidating and depressing. Lad would look up and see him standing over at the ford, or spot him sitting in the sunshine on the grassy bank opposite. And Lad assumed he was often watching from somewhere nearby, even if he could not see him. Now he could be sure that he had heard the children that day and wanted more. They had forbidden the children to roam out of their sight. Tempers were getting frayed and Melis blamed him for it all. She was probably right.

As Lad walked the hogs himself one morning, trying not to look over his shoulder all the time, he thought it all through. Kirin and the resistance expected nothing from him right now, but the man did not know that. All this hovering and watching must be to frighten, to stop him making contact with any allies. Or maybe the man wanted to push him into a mistake. Why couldn't he pretend that it had worked? He could lead him a bit of a dance and send him back to Beindubn wishing he had never bothered. He sat for a while on the soft leaf litter, smiling to himself as he formed a plan, while around him the hogs made the most of their extra snuffling time. When he returned home he told no one.

Lad got into action the very next day. First of all, he had to capture his audience. Very early, before the last of the stars had faded, he crept quietly from their hut and fed and watered the pony. He tethered her ready behind the stable and tied on his water bag and a cloth bag with a bit of food for himself. Then he marched off, up through the trees, keeping in sight the gully that led up to the high way and beyond to Beindubn land. He chose a useful hiding place just before the final rise to the top. It was his turn to sit and spy.

He had timed it right. After a short while Arbin appeared, striding down the path. He passed close by Lad, humming tunelessly to himself.

Ain't fed up yet, then, thought Lad.

As he disappeared on down, Lad creaked his joints into action and trailed him carefully. He watched as Arbin slowed a little and then veered to the right to drop behind the hedge on the ridge and settle himself in the bushes above the farmstead.

"Got you," smiled Lad. "Fraid yer prey is ahead of you this morning, Master Fox."

He retreated back a short way then crept back around and down through the undergrowth to the huts and pens. He found Serun outside, about to collect fresh water for the morning.

"You got going early, Father," she said. "I heard you move before dawn. Are you well?"

Lad decided it was necessary to tell her some of it. "I'm good, my lovely. I got a bit of a plan goin' on. I'm goin' to head off with me pony right now, and you an' yer mother ain't to worry. If you sees that Beindubn feller go after me, well that's wot I want. An' if 'ee don't, then you know nuthin' bout wot I'm doin'. Don't make sense now, but tis best that's all I tell you."

Serun did not argue, nor ask more. She knew enough of what had been going on lately.

"Be careful, Father," she said quietly. He looked weary this morning, with a brittle excitement about him. She hoped he knew what he was doing.

"Oh, that I will. You go inside for a bit now, and leave me to it," said Lad.

Serun watched around the doorpost of their hut as Lad walked his pony round to the front and clambered on. She kept her eye on him as he walked the pony across the ford and follow the river until out of sight. And very soon after that she saw the man from Beindubn move up the slope after him.

LAD AVOIDED HEADING on up their home valley any further. There were more small farms ahead, just like his, at intervals along the stream. It would be wrong to put his neighbours under suspicion. He decided to get up on to the open stretch, to the north of the mound with the standing stone, then lead the man down to the spider's web of deep streams and cuttings beyond. He had picked his way through there a couple of times before, setting traps for game during a hard winter. It wasn't a patch he knew perfectly, he had to be honest, but it would stretch the man's legs. More importantly, it would lead him away from the north and any idea of where his contacts really were. With a bit of Cuda's luck he could lose him down there and circle round for home.

He kept the pony at a plodding pace as if it was all it could manage. If the man was hooked it would not do to lose him. As he covered the open ground on the hilltop, Lad tried to appear calm but his mind worked at speed, assessing the ground cover and visibility. He needed an opportunity to check if this was a waste of effort. He planned to get to the edge of the treeline ahead and find a place to hide and look behind him.

Cuda was kind to him. Just before he reached the trees a fine young stag emerged, directly in front of him, and gave Lad a look that froze him in his tracks. After a casual turn of his head towards others following, he leaped off at speed and passed by Lad and his pony so closely he could feel the air churning in his wake. Then wave after wave of beautiful deer, all sizes, all ages, came out of the woods, skittering in surprise at the sight of the man and his pony in their path. Lad had to dismount quickly and hold the horse firmly. As the herd rushed by he took his chance and turned as if to watch them go. In his sudden sweep of the open horizon behind he spotted a lone figure dropping quickly.

"Got you, my lovely," he whispered.

Now he could relax a little and enjoy himself. Lad wove his pony downwards, as steeply as he dared, dodging overhanging branches dotted with fresh soft buds uncurling in the spring light. His pony's hooves made no noise on the new green poking up through the woodland cover of last season's leaves.

"There'd be worse days to do this, fer sure," said Lad to his pony, sitting up straighter as they reached the stream and a bit of a clearing right at the bottom. "Now, let's take 'im up t'other side!"

He reached behind and slapped the pony's rump lightly, with a loud "Hup!" of encouragement.

But that was too much in the quiet of the hidden valley – too much for a temporary resident resting in the grass. With a wild cry of alarm, a large grey goose rose suddenly and clumsily in front of them, beating its wings in the pony's face. The little mare squealed and reared up, as scared as the bird, and Lad was thrown backwards to the ground. He landed awkwardly and gasped as a sharp pain shot up his arm. He lay face down in the damp and for a short while could not think or see ...

When he opened his eyes he was looking at scuffed leather boots. A voice broke through the haze in his head.

"Ha! Nobody gets the better of me, do you understand now?" it jeered. "Trouble is now on your head, old man, not mine. I have a fine new mount in exchange. Think hard before you try to make a fool of me again!"

The boots disappeared from sight and the pony's hooves followed. Lad closed his eyes again, drifting back into pain.

11

Before the daylight had finally faded, and well after Serun and Tarn had persuaded the younger ones to lie down for the night, their parents stumbled up to the entrance of the hut. Lad was in a bad way, leaning on Melis and hardly managing one foot in front of the other.

"It's his arm, mostly," said Melis, breathlessly, as the children helped get him lying down on a pallet. "I went up to the old stone. There's always a good view from there, and sure enough I met the old fool stumbling back. The horse is gone. Cuda knows what might have happened if I hadn't gone looking. If I'd known he was going to take on that Arbin ... Well, what's done is done. There's no stopping him once he decides, is there?" She flopped down to the floor next to him.

Lad looked dreadful. He sipped at the water that Serun held for him, his eyes dulled with pain. After a moment he was able to speak. "I'm 'ome, Cuda be praised. Now I needs to rest me arm ... I needs to ... sleep." He closed his eyes and passed out. His limbs lay heavy on the bedding.

Melis had got her breath back and knew what they had to do. She struggled to her feet and gathered her hair back into its usual knot.

"Serun, we need strips of cloth. Cut the new stuff from my loom. Tarn, light another lamp and get some sticks from the kindling, as straight as you can find. I think his arm is broken. We will need to bind it." She turned to the three children watching in scared silence from their bedding. "Anba, Cam? Fetch more water. Kirin, be good and stay in your bed, please, while we help your father. Blessed gods, let's hope he feels nothing for a little longer."

Day and night then blended into one. The fever was the worst. Serun would take over and watch her father as he shivered and mumbled into his beard, while Melis tried to get some sleep over in the corner. It was a scary time for them all.

The brace on his arm stayed in place, though, and there came a dawn when Lad seemed to be sleeping more easily. Serun wiped his wrinkled brow and for the first time sensed that things were improving. It seemed that Lad had got past the worst.

Not so outside. The younger children had done their best with the feeding and watering of the animals, but the woodpile was low, the winter growth of weeds were still strangling Melis's vegetable patch, and the grain bin for their bread was nearly empty. Young Anba had proved herself a useful baker and had taken to grinding dried beans into what was left of the wheat, but without those beans the soup was a thin and miserable offering to hungry children. This was the time that Lad would have set off, upstream and down, to barter the spring piglets with their neighbours for summer fattening, and come back with the stores they could not grow or forage themselves.

Serun looked at her mother as she moved wearily around their stone hut, trying to put things back in their place and create a little order in their tumbledown home. Lad stirred and opened his eyes. He watched her too.

"I worn you out, my lovely," he said quietly. "Stupid ol' sod that I am."

Melis stopped and knelt at his side.

"Old, yes. Stupid? Most likely." She patted his good arm. "But we are glad to have you alive, ain't we, Serun?"

"I was thinkin' I could beat that Arbin, but all I did was bring you trouble."

"We are doing just fine. Shush, now," said Melis. "All you got to do is rest and mend that arm. And hope Serun and I got it straight enough for you."

Tears came to Lad's eyes. He closed them slowly and fell back to sleep.

Serun left them and went outside. In the distance the children could be seen trying to drag a dead branch out from the edge of the wood, with Kirin crying loudly and angrily over something or other.

She sighed. "We are not doing fine, not fine at all."

An idea came to her. She walked round to Lad's workshop, the rickety lean-to against the wall of their hut, its lid of thatch looking ready to slide at any moment. She knew his workbench so well. For a moment, a lump came to her throat when she saw the carving of Cuda waiting there. It dawned on her how distracted her father had been for some time. She stroked the stone folds of the goddess's gown and sent up a prayer that her father's arm would one day work well enough to finish it. Then she turned to what she had gone looking for.

Scratched lightly into many of the propped timbers was his daily tally, irregular little marks making their way down the stripped wood like the broken teeth of an old bone comb. She had asked her father a long time ago what they were for. She smiled; it was many moons ago, in fact, for they were Lad's recording of the faces of Hatane. She knew why he kept that record. She was used to seeing him slip off quietly under a full moon. Where he went to on those midnight walks? Well, she had heard the quiet conversations meant only for her mother. She always knew that the next morning he would have a bit of news or a funny story to tell.

Serun didn't know why it was such a secret, and right now she didn't care. She knew of the man, the grown up Kirin that her youngest brother was named after. She was sure that must be who Lad met, and when. Serun came to a decision. She and her mother needed help, and her father needed his friend.

She took a deep breath and concentrated. Lad's tally was out of date, and she and her mother had been far too busy to moon watch. Carefully she followed the pattern and then tried to work out how many nights it had been since her father had left on his pony that day. Eventually she came to a result, and checked it twice. She could hope for Hatane's full face in two night's time. And if the man wasn't there? Well, she would keep trying until he was.

"Serun? Serun!"

Melis's call broke into her thoughts. There was so much work to do and Serun knew she should be getting on with it. Her own plan was made now, and as secret as any of her father's. Her mother had enough to worry about as it was.

THIS TIME IT was Kirin's turn to be surprised, very surprised in fact.

He did not know who the girl was at first. He found her there, shivering a little in her thin cloak. In the fitful moonlight that came and went through the blow of the clouds he was taken back in time, back to another pair of dark and shadowed eyes that had once pleaded for help, or mercy. Not so far from this spot either. For a moment he was lost for words. But the girl was not. She spoke urgently.

"Are you Kirin, friend of my father?"

"Ah, I see!" Realisation dawned. Who else could have known about their meeting place? "Yes, I am. And you are perhaps... Serun?"

She nodded. "I'm here for him, well, for us. He doesn't know, nor does my mother. You see, he is not well. He was thrown from the pony ..."

Kirin went to interrupt, but she shook her head, tears starting. "His arm is broken and he has a lot of pain." She brushed her face with her sleeve. "We straightened it for him but the hurt keeps him to his bedding. We are doing our best but it is not enough. Mother is worn to nothing. The others are getting hungry and sad. I wondered if you … if you could help at all?" She finished on a whisper.

This was unexpected, and a problem to all of them. He had to weigh the risk involved, risk to others that that the girl could not be expected to know. And need not know, he swiftly decided. The resistance had their heads down for now. Lad was in trouble. There was no doubt in his mind.

"Of course, Serun. Of course we can help. Look, go back now and try to get some sleep, you have done the right thing. I'll ride home and talk to others. Tell your mother to expect me, at least, by tomorrow evening."

Serun's face lit up. "Thank you, thank you! Cuda's blessings on you!" she said, as she wrapped her cloak around her and ran off.

As Kirin rode home he wondered how Lad had come to be thrown off his horse.

12

Tirtos suspected everyone. Sometimes he suspected secrets in the wind. Right now he suspected that Arbin's loyalty to him was not as reliable as it should be. He had certainly been following his orders to investigate beyond Beindubn very thoroughly. He had hardly been on the estate, yet where were any results? His brother Tala could not properly account for what he had been up to. And now, apparently, he had turned up the other day with a sturdy little mare that was as good as any in their meadows. He had heard that from Kenet last evening, as casual as you like, as if it was alright for some minder to make a little profit of his own.

Kenet was nursing a reminder of where his loyalties should lie across his cheek. It was quite clear that son of his should wake up and start to take on some responsibility. Come out from behind his doting mother. Spoilt stupid. Tirtos grunted crossly at the effort he was having to make. Why was life such a struggle at the moment? Every bone ached.

So now it was time to deal with Arbin. Luckily he soon found him at the back of his hut, rubbing down his new mount with handfuls of dried grass.

Scowling, Tirtos lowered himself slowly onto a woodpile. "Explain!" He was not in the mood for wasting time.

Arbin sighed into his pony's neck. He had known this would happen. He didn't imagine the pony would be his for much longer unless he told his story right. He had something and nothing; a few ideas and no proof. Not a strong position to be in with a master who did not tolerate weakness.

He turned and faced Tirtos.

"I got it from a stupid pig farmer over the hill. Where you told me to poke around. I heard something that made me wonder about him, about that trouble with the soldiers. I followed him the other day to see what I could find out and … he came off his horse and I took it." Arbin didn't want to give much detail.

But Tirtos wanted exactly that. "He came off his horse. What was he doing? What did you find out?"

"Nothing, really," Arbin had to admit. "I heard the kids shouting about the Romans coming up the high way and the parents said they weren't interested. Well, weren't interested anymore. That's what made me think. That's why I followed the man. He didn't go anywhere helpful, just down through the woods. Waste of time, really."

"Except for the pony," said Tirtos.

"Yes, except for the pony."

"Hmm, maybe you found out more than you think. Or maybe he did." Tirtos's eyes were sharp in calculation. "So who are these people?"

"Typical valley rubbish, as you thought. Getting along by trading hogs. Man, woman and a handful of noisy kids. They seem to know what they're doing, though a hard winter would probably see them off. Don't think they are worth any more of my time."

"That's your problem, you don't think. See, Petronius called in yesterday. It seems the convoys have been reaching Glevum without any attacks recently. Wanted to thank me for my efforts, knew I would be glad to keep the favour of his great and glorious Empire, blah, blah blah. It was all I could do not to knock him off his horse. So, maybe these dirt dwellers know something we don't. You can keep your pony for now, though the gods know you don't deserve it. And you can use it to join me for a ride over the hill tomorrow. And tell Kenet he's to come along too. It's time to dig for some truth myself."

13

When Serun announced that help was on its way, and who was bringing it, her parents were not as pleased as she had hoped. The worried look that passed between Lad and Melis was obvious, though Lad quickly tried to cover it with a tired smile. He sat himself up.

"Well, if Kirin thinks 'tis alright to visit, then that's what we goes by. Though you should 'ave spoken to me or yer mother first."

"He said yes, straight off," Serun said evenly.

"Serun, my lovely, you'm a brave girl. What's done is done. Think no more on it now and we shall see what 'appens. Maybe he'll think better of it in the daylight. He an' Ribby don't offen come this way, fer lots o' reasons. Look, I'm movin' better today, so I'll soon be back with me hogs an' the work. Keep helpin' yer mother like you do, my lovely, an' we will all pull through."

Serun did as she was told, but the excitement of her midnight adventure had faded fast and she felt deflated and stupid. Her mother obviously did not want to talk anymore of it, so Serun kept herself and the children out of her way, trying to get a bit of order to their wood-collecting up in the trees. Even the spread of spring bluecaps and star ransoms could not cheer her. The children, a little subdued by her frown, for once did as they were asked straightaway.

So it was a huge relief for all of them to get back to their hut in the middle of the day and find her parents sitting outside with the man Kirin and a lady, and to see everyone smiling.

"You must be Serun, I'm Ribby," the lady said, getting up to greet her.

"And who are all these workers?" She grinned at Serun's raggedy bunch of young woodsmen. The children dumped their sticks and rushed forward to announce themselves, apart from little Kirin, who rushed instead to hide behind Melis.

"I expect you are hungry after all that," Ribby said. "Kirin and I have brought some extra supplies with us. Melis, may we fetch it all from the ponies?"

"Yes, and we'd be right glad of it. Wouldn't we, Serun." Melis stood and put her arm round her eldest, and Serun knew she was forgiven.

The unloaded basket was a joy. Potted hare, a pile of flatbreads, sheep's cheese, even some of last season's apples. The children could hardly believe it. At first they held back, but Kirin and Ribby encouraged them and soon everyone was eating heartily out in the fresh air.

"That's what you need, Lad," said Kirin, handing a laden flatbread to his friend. "Lots of good food to mend that arm. We will stay and wait on you for a while, but don't get too used to it!" For once, Lad was too tired to argue.

Even little Kirin found his nerve again. The sight of the food brought him forward to sit and eat on the grass with his brothers and sisters, and for some time he sat in silence looking the man Kirin up and down. Eventually he stood up and walked over to him. He reached forward and touched the beads that were threaded on the thongs of his belt. "I like it," he said.

Everyone stopped chattering in surprise at his words.

"I like them too," answered Kirin. "Each one reminds me of something. My father gave them to me when I was a boy like you."

"The belt's 'ad to grow a bit, tho' Kirin," chuckled Lad. "More leather than stones now!"

"Very true," agreed Kirin ruefully, patting his middle.

The little boy didn't move, looking into Kirin's face and ignoring the laughter around him.

Kirin looked steadily back at him. "I had a good father, like you," he continued. "And a respected grandfather ..." He stopped suddenly, and then said, a bit surprised at the thought, "I must show you the gift he gave me."

He lifted the flap of his leather purse and took out his small knife, holding it out by the blade for little Kirin to see. The boy said nothing. He stared at the bronze head, then cautiously stroked its smooth neck. The other children stopped eating and went over to see as well. They crowded round but none spoke, as if they half expected the strange animal to speak first.

And to Kirin, it did. He became conscious of a faint trembling in his fingers, and a quiver in the ground beneath them. He caught his breath and looked over the children's heads to Ribby. She noticed immediately.

"What is it?" she whispered.

"Get the children inside," he said. "You and Melis. And stay there. Do it now!"

Ribby moved quickly. "Come along everyone, your father and Kirin need to talk about something important right now. We must go into the hut." Nobody argued as she rounded up the younger ones and hurried them to the hut door. Melis and Serun followed her, confused at the tone of her voice. In a moment Lad and Kirin were left alone on the log benches.

Lad was mystified at the sudden change in Kirin's mood. "I don' get it, Kirin. What's happened?"

Kirin tucked the knife away and looked at his friend. "Lad, how did you come to fall off your horse?"

Lad's face paled as he began to understand.

"I was bein' followed. I led 'im downaways an' off the track but me pony got frighted and threw me. Then 'ee took the mount and left me hurtin' on the floor."

"He?" Kirin's mouth was dry.

"Arbin ... of Beindubn. I think 'ee had picked up on what we 'ad been up to."

Kirin nodded and took a deep breath. "Then the knife is right, Lad, as it always is. Today it tells me trouble is on its way, and soon."

It was very soon. Even as he spoke, three riders appeared into view from the right, trotting down towards them. Lad recognised the second man and sighed. "That's 'im Kirin. Cuda's breath, friend, but I'm sorry for this. I don't know t'others."

"Oh, I do," said Kirin, darkly. He stood up. "Leave the talking to me."

Tirtos slowed his horse to a walk as they got closer, and then pulled up. A youth sullenly reined his horse to a halt a few paces behind, too similar to his father for Kirin not to know who he must be. Kenet had not been pleased to be roused for this ride. For a while there was silence as the men stared at each other.

Then Tirtos spoke. "I might have guessed," he sneered. "A pig-stinking midden, catching any rubbish that blows down the valley. Where did you blow from, nephew? I thought you well gone."

He looked down at Lad, nursing his arm in its sling. "Now I'm beginning to understand. Friends in low places kept you alive? Useful, if you are a worm." He turned back to Arbin. "You've managed to dig up a couple of good ones here."

Kirin shook his head in disgust. "Nothing has changed you then, Tirtos," he sneered. "Still clinging on in your tiny world? Still thinking you can bully your way to what you want? Well, some of us have got on better without you ..."

"Better? Better?" Tirtos moved his bulk with unexpected

speed. He slid off his horse and took two strides. Before Kirin could react he had grabbed Lad by his injured arm and slipped a blade to his throat as he pressed him down into the dirt. Lad hissed through his teeth and closed his eyes at the pain, unable to move.

Tirtos glared across at Kirin, his breath rasping. Suddenly he registered a sharp and shocking new cramp of pain at his core, starting to grow from inside, eating at his arm. He shook his head to try and clear it, eyes burning in his red and sweaty face. "I'll tell you what's best for you now!' he managed, clinging on to Lad feverishly. "A little visit to the Roman camp. A few hours explaining yourself at the end of a Roman sword. That, or your miserable friend will drop back dead … into the mud he's crawled from! Arbin! Get over here, and bring the rope!"

Arbin hesitated, still on his pony, shocked at the sight of Kirin again after all these years. Tirtos couldn't believe it – his word always sent people scurrying. His control was slipping away, he realised, of his world and of his body. Someone has done this to me, he realised. Someone has done this …

His face purpled with anger and panic. "Kenet!" he yelled, "You! Now!"

A voice shouted clearly from the doorway of the hut. "Think hard young man! Think hard before you do what he says!" A voice with authority.

It was Ribby. She walked slowly down towards them. "Do you really want to obey this monster?" she called to Kenet. "This man, who bought me and was going to sell me without a twitch of worry! Who drove Kirin from his home!" Kenet stayed where he was, in shock. This was not what he had expected at all. He glanced nervously at Arbin, who was just as fixed as he was, trying to decide where his own best interests lay.

Ribby sauntered over to Tirtos, head held high. "Well, I survived you! I survived your cart, and your bruises, all those years ago."

Tirtos stared up at her, chest heaving, his hands starting to shake. She moved nearer, without a trace of fear, and bent close, her face in his.

"Remember me now?" she said. "Do you see? You didn't win then. And the gods know you're not going to win now!"

His jaw dropped, but no sound came out. His face turned from purple to a strange yellow as he looked from her to Kirin, and back again.

And suddenly ran out of breath. With a puzzled look he let go of Lad and toppled back clutching at his chest, gasping like a fish. Kirin took his chance and got between him and the others, snatching the blade. Ribby rushed to support Lad.

Tirtos could do nothing about it. He rolled on the ground clawing at his left arm and struggling as the rope of pain tightened around his chest. This could not be happening! There had to be someone to blame! Then sudden clarity brought an image of his pathetic wife, fussing and plying him with food while growing weariness dogged his steps. And he knew.

A movement from Kenet drew his eye. He had flung himself down from his pony and was finally coming to help. Through gritted teeth, Tirtos ground out, "I'll kill your mother for this. I'll kill her."

Kenet's pony shied as his hand tightened on the reins. Shock changed to horror. He moved no closer.

Kirin closed in on Tirtos with contempt.

"You once said I would never lose you your living again, Tirtos," he said. "So now I'm going to watch you lose it for yourself. I hope Volkos has a special torment waiting for you!"

Tirtos stared up at him, mouthing desperately. Then, with a final gasp for air, he fell forward in the grass and breathed no more.

It seemed an age before anybody moved. Then Kenet dropped to his knees by his father, his face an awful mixture of disbelief ... and relief.

Arbin dismounted and walked slowly past him to Kirin. He held his hands up, no weapon in sight. He shook his head, unable to speak.

"You have a choice now, Arbin," said Kirin, coldly, "after you have tied this heap back on his horse and got him home. There are two tales to choose from. One tale will bring more suffering to this family; it will also bring down such revenge upon your head that you will dare not sleep at night. The other tale will let the Beindubn families start again, take their chances out of the shadows, and leave us all here to get on with our lives."

Arbin was suddenly conscious that a weight had just been lifted from his shoulders. And was no longer confused. He cleared his throat. "Kirin, you should come home now to Beindubn. Where you belong. Tala and I will support you ..."

Kenet rose to his feet and joined them. He looked older, changed, standing taller. He nodded. "We must get back. I must tell my mother what has happened." He looked around him, from the body of his father on the ground up to the silent faces peering from the doorway of the hut above. He rubbed his own face roughly and squared his shoulders. "You and your family would be welcome, Uncle," he said, "but no one will disturb you here if that is your wish." He looked Arbin in the eye with new confidence and the man nodded quickly.

Kirin glanced across at Lad and Ribby, as they waited for his answer, pale and drained by shock. The offer was tempting, but the fight against the Romans was not going away. He couldn't put that at risk. Nor could he involve the Beindubn families. His voice softened. "No. Those days are over. Beindubn can manage without me now." He turned to the body of Tirtos. "This dead man was my last connection there."

It took some effort to put that heavy body back on the horse and fix it securely. Nothing more was said until Arbin and Kenet were about to leave. Then the young man said to Kirin, "You can rely on us. There's no reason to see either of us here again." He got on his pony and turned it to leave.

"I'm glad of that," said Kirin, then he added "You should know, Arbin, if you want to make some changes at Beindubn, I could send someone to help. Someone who used to know his way round your fields better than you."

Arbin looked puzzled.

"Your father, Samos," said Kirin. "I know where he is."

He pointed to Melis and the children, coming out of their hut. "If this family stays unharmed, then you could get yours back."

A slow smile spread across Arbin's face. He nodded once to Kirin, then turned the horses and followed Kenet as they headed off for the path back over the hill to Beindubn.

14

Beneath them the Romans' road took a straight line into the distance, heading across the wide river valley for the camp at Savren. Alongside it, Kirin could make out cleared patches within the areas of woodland where new construction was appearing, smoke rising, pointers to unwelcome change.

He shook his head, half to himself, half to Ribby at his side. "Like mould through old bread," he grumbled. "These Romans are getting their fingers into everything."

Ribby was getting used to this view but not resigned to it. Every day she held fast to the belief that Mog would return with a new plan and new confidence. Surely this Roman advance was not inevitable. She shivered a little and squeezed Kirin's arm. "Thank the gods we are up here above it all. Come now, I should think Lad will have finished checking those pigs and will be grateful for a brew."

They made their way back, hand in hand, along the network of animal trails that crisscrossed the old banks and ditches above the steep drop. Around them the summer birds wove their own wild paths in and out of each other, wheeling and squealing. Here the insects were carried to them on the upward breeze. It was easy feeding for their young ones.

Soon they reached their favourite spot. They turned once more and gazed across to the sleeping giants on the Savren plain, the smooth humps of hill now seeming to float above the evening mist.

"This is where I want to end my days, Ribby. Sleeping like that, with you. Stretched out and at peace, on this ridge. With the birds to watch over my old bones and the world beneath me."

"Perfect," smiled Ribby, putting her arm around him.

"That's how it must be then, one day." He gently patted the leather purse at his waist, then stroked Ribby's cheek. "And whoever goes first, the knife – and Nema's mirror – goes with them. We'll protect some things from these Romans. They will help us find each other in Uban's world above, or below."

A chuckle behind them made them jump. "Cuda's breath, but ain't that too sad a talk on a lovely evenin'?" laughed Lad, as he joined them at the viewpoint. "Only one who's in danger of dyin' round here is me – dyin' of thirst. I've checked that ol' mother and littl'uns out, an' Serun's new beeswax dressin' will take care of the cuts on those two scrappin' hogs. I've separated 'em till they learns better."

"Thank you, Lad," said Kirin. "Truth is, we have missed Samos since he went. It's good of you to come and help like this."

"Oh, Samos is in the right place, enjoyin' having a couple of sons to wait on 'im. 'Ee still manages a walk over the hill to tell us the news from time to time. An' there's plenty o' that. Sounds like they're all doin' better. The son Kenet an' his mother are lettin' those that know about the metal makin' an' the farm sort the work out, while they deal with the tradin'. She has a pretty smile for any o' they soldiers from Corinium, as they calls it, so there's not much bother from them. Seems she can make a good bargain. The families are keepin' their kids, thank Cuda, and got more in their food bins."

"But what about that son?" said Ribby. "He has his father's blood in him, after all. Should he be trusted?"

"Well, only the gods know I s'pose. But they families learned some 'ard lessons from that Tirtos. Can't see Tala and Arbin lettin' Kenet get that bad, ever. Anyways there's plenty o' entertainment to keep 'im busy down in Corinium. 'Ee loves the Romans, I'm told. Seems to do alright."

Kirin frowned. "Too many like him, I'm afraid. Too many now turning enemies into friends. How can we make a proper stand for our birthright? For our Dobunnic lands?"

Lad's attention was caught by some movement. "Ere comes someone who might 'ave an idea!" he declared, grinning.

They turned and looked in the same direction. A rider had appeared out of the trees onto the upper grassland.

"Mog!" cried Ribby, her voice cracking with relief.

"Uban be praised," breathed Kirin, as the three set off running.

Mog slid slowly down from the pony, arms outstretched in greeting. Kirin was so happy to see his cousin, apparently unharmed, obviously exhausted, but with the same warm smile lit by their reunion and Ribby's tight hug.

"I came as soon as I could," Mog said, catching Kirin's eye over Ribby's shoulder. "There's much to tell. I've seen the others already. There are messages from the mountains. They need us to keep going, and I've learned much from Caratacos … but …"

The look and the words made it clear to Kirin. Mog was not going to answer easily any of their prayers, today or tomorrow. The path from here was going to be up to them and them alone. It was a daunting thought.

But Mog's safe return proved to Kirin that there was always reason to hope. That evening, together up there on Cuda's breezy hilltop, he could be sure of only one thing, but it was the most important. With the support and love of friends and family, he could face the future. Whatever the gods had in store.

FOLLOWING IN KIRIN'S FOOTSTEPS

FASCINATING OBJECTS IN museums and ancient remains in our landscape represent real human conversations, lives and experiences that are closer to our own than we might think at first. Dip into the evidence yourself and the stories will shout out at you. Follow your own trails into Kirin's world, and the world of others that have come before, and start to feel part of a greater community; a community that has always been there behind you and just needs a voice.

It is always very useful to have a car, but with a bit of planning and some careful use of timetables you can explore Kirin's world by public transport. I have included some information to help. Then I have added some notes on the creation and pronunciation of the names in the story.

Finally, I have many people to thank.

SEE THE ARTEFACTS FOR YOURSELF

START WITH THE mirror and the knife handle. They are real, and waiting patiently for you. Visit *The Birdlip Treasure* display at the Museum of Gloucester, and you can see them alongside many other beautiful things from Iron Age and Roman Gloucester. Perhaps your time-travelling will begin there, just as it did for me.

The discovery of these exceptional grave goods, in the nineteenth century, remains an enigma. The site of the graves was not recorded accurately, nor do we know whether all the finds were handed over. Experts still disagree about whether they were buried with a man or a woman, and you don't have to decide. What I did decide, however, was that collection of threaded stones would have been very heavy to wear as a necklace.

The museum has a drawer containing a collection of Dobunnic coins or 'staters'. There are always clues to the names of powerful people on coins, but not enough here to be sure who exactly they were up on the Cotswold Hills, or where they lived. From archaeological digs we know that many were minted at Bagendon, north of Cirencester, and have been found spread across a wide area. Why did they make the effort to bring heavy ore from the Forest of Dean to make them and other goods and who organised it? You see now how my story quest began, and 'Beindubn' and its tribe emerged into print.

Kirin's descriptions of the Beindubn settlement were based on Bagendon, Ditches and Woodmancote, north of Cirencester. To find out more about the evidence behind this Iron Age settlement, the Corinium Museum in Cirencester is not to be missed.

In the Prehistory gallery, you can sit inside part of a reconstructed roundhouse, see real tools, pots and Dobunnic coins, even see an Iron Age dog skeleton and imagine lanky Kuno.

Look for the museum display labels that say 'Ditches', and you'll see objects that were once handled and used there by working families. There is an iron door latch on display that I like to imagine Tirtos slamming in a show of temper!

Carry on through the Roman displays to see the evidence for the timber military fort that soon replaced the first Roman army camp at the crossroads of Akeman Street and Ermin Street, then explore the riches of the town of Corinium that developed from there.

There is a great deal more on display upstairs that has been very influential on Kirin's story. The first is the *Religion and Mother Goddesses* display. It features limestone carvings to gods respected by the local people, including images of mother figures. Number 6 in *Local Cults* is a carved piece that was unearthed in the same valley as Lad's home. The word *Cudae* has been found inscribed and *Cuda's Wold* has been suggested as an origin of the name Cotswold. Lad had a great deal to thank Nema and Cuda for. You can think about who might have carved these stones, and why.

In the 1980s archaeologists excavated circular crop marks on the hillside at Ditches. They found the remains of an enclosure and much evidence of people living there in the late Iron Age. To everyone's surprise, they also found the remains of an unusually early Roman villa within the perimeter ditch. The objects they dug up around it included fine pottery, coins and jewellery. I like to think Kenet built his house for Eberia.

The tiny carved semi-precious stones in the *Dressed to Impress* ring display are very like the real intaglio of the young man that was found during a field walking survey on the Ditches site. The ring underlines the link between those fields and Roman society. Whatever the story is of how it came to be there, we can be sure that someone in the past was very upset to lose it.

Another highlight is the *Mercury: God of Travellers* display. I have always been drawn to the association of Mercury's purse and cockerels in representations of that popular god. On the edge of empire, Corinium must have seemed like a backwater for the Romans for much of the time. Perhaps it was enlivened by cruel blood sports and gambling and the worship of Mercury for good luck.

So, consider the evidence for yourself:

Museum of Gloucester, Brunswick Rd, Gloucester, GL1 1HP
www.museumofgloucester.co.uk

Corinium Museum, Park St, Cirencester GL7 2BX
www.coriniummuseum.org

Public transport: *currently* the 882 Tetbury to Gloucester bus, via Cirencester. Travels between The Forum, Cirencester and Gloucester Transport Hub, Station Road, Gloucester. www.bustimes.org www.stagecoachbus.com Liable to yearly and seasonal change of timetable so ALWAYS check.

FINDING THE ARCHAEOLOGICAL SITES

WHEN YOU ARE ready to explore Kirin's world in more depth, two Ordnance Survey maps are very useful for your quest. They are the Landranger Series Sheet 162 Gloucester and Forest of Dean, and Sheet 163 Cheltenham and Cirencester.

The following are a selection of tours you can make by bus and train to take in the key locations, and some further reading ideas including original reports and sources. Take a look, that's how I discovered a severed head was excavated at Bagendon.

CIRENCESTER TO GLOUCESTER: LAD'S VALLEY, KIRIN AND RIBBY'S SETTLEMENT, AND THE BIRDLIP TREASURE SITE

THE 882 STAGECOACH West bus that runs currently between Cirencester and Gloucester is a great route to start with. Departing from The Forum in Cirencester, it zigzags its way on and off the fast A417 dual carriageway, which follows much of the Roman road of Ermin Street, so there is no better way to see the impact of Roman road building on a quiet landscape.

Begin at Cirencester. Going north, as you approach the village of Winstone, the upper levels of the Cotswold Hills stretch westwards towards Uley Bury – *Elebyrig* – and Lad's valley rises up from Middle Duntisbourne to meet the old drovers' route. The standing stone is still out there somewhere on its barrow mound, though too small to see from the bus route.

As the bus continues northward, you soon reach the edge of the escarpment, with views of Crickley Hill hillfort, and Gloucester in the Severn Valley below, with the Malvern Hills in the far distance to the north-west.

A small Iron Age settlement has been excavated near Birdlip and the Barrow Wake area. The Birdlip Treasure was uncovered somewhere near this site. This is the evidence I chose to recreate Kirin and Ribby's final home. As I write, new road improvements are underway to relieve the congestion of the A417 near Birdlip, and fresh archaeological investigations are already revealing further secrets of this interesting Iron Age and Roman landscape.

Barrow Wake National Grid Reference SO930152

Hoar Stone Long Barrow NGR SO965066

Further reading:

Prehistoric Gloucestershire (2ndEd), Darvill T, 2011, Amberley

www.bgas.org.uk click on Resources to search the Transactions, Vol 5, 137—141, *On some Bronze and other Articles found near Birdlip,* J Bellows 1880-81, Transactions of the Bristol and Gloucestershire Archaeological Society

www.bgas.org.uk Vol 116, 25—92, *Excavations near Birdlip, Cowley, Gloucestershire,* C Parry 1998

Trow S, *Britannia* Volume 13: pp322—323, *An early intaglio found near Cirencester, Gloucestershire. 1982. (Britannia* is a series of journals published by Cambridge University Press on behalf of The Roman Society, unfortunately not free to access online. Your library might have a set available, if not then see *Prehistoric Gloucestershire* Darvill T, 2012, as above, p228)

The Tribe of Witches: The Religion of the Dobunni and Hwicce,
Yeates S, 2008, Oxbow Books

www.cotswoldarchaeology.co.uk for the latest reports and information

GLOUCESTER TO CIRENCESTER: A VIEW OF THE BEINDUBN PLATEAU

RETURNING FROM GLOUCESTER towards Cirencester, when you travel southwards on the A417 from Barrow Wake, the split level in the carriageway crosses one of the highest points in the Cotswolds. On a clear day you can see across the Upper Thames river valley to the route of the ancient Ridgeway on the hill line far beyond Swindon. Up here is where the quiet route from Lad's farm to Kirin and Ribby's settlement would have had to cross the new Roman road. Further along to the east, tree plantations mask some of the views but there is a useful gap at the turning to Duntisbourne Leer. There you get a brief glimpse of the fields that hold the remains of Kirin's family roundhouse and Kenet's later villa, at Ditches. They are across a very steep valley that would have been very difficult to manage with an exhausted pony and cart. Look for the line of pylons striding across the Bagendon site and you will get your bearings.

The current bus turns off the dual carriageway onto the quieter road to Stratton and Cirencester. You can enjoy then the gradual drop down to Stratton and Cirencester and imagine Lad striding southwards on his mission to investigate the new Roman encampment, later known as Corinium.

Bagendon NGR SP017064

Ditches, Woodmancote, North Cerney, NGR SO996093

Further reading:

A Biography of Power: Research and Excavations at the Iron Age 'oppidum' of Bagendon, Gloucestershire (1979—2017), Moore T, 2020, Archaeopress

Bagendon, A Belgic Oppidum, Excavations 1954—1956, Clifford EM, 1961 The Bingham Library, Cirencester. (A fish hook p152, a severed head p268)

www.bgas.org.uk Click on Resources to search the Transactions, Vol 106, 19—85, *Excavations at Ditches hillfort, North Cerney, Gloucestershire, 1982—83,* Trow S

UP THE CHURN VALLEY

THE STAGECOACH 51 from Cirencester to Cheltenham takes you along the A435 and the Churn river valley. The Perrott's Brook stop, where the little stream that waters the Bagendon – *Beindubn* – valley meets the larger Churn, is the place to get off. The quiet village of Bagendon sits on the valley side, to the west of the main road.

Try to imagine the much busier and sometimes industrial atmosphere of the Iron Age estate down where water was plentiful and the sunny valley beyond was alive with animals and working people. Retrace your steps a little then walk up a peaceful lane alongside visible earthworks, using your OS map to find the site of Ditches at Woodmancote. This is where the remains of the large Iron Age roundhouse and enclosure, and the early Roman villa, were found.

Of course, never walk on anything other than public footpaths or roads; the present-day farmers and residents need as much respect as the Iron Age people we are investigating. From

Woodmancote you can walk back down eastward to the river and main road at North Cerney to catch your bus, and think of Galete struggling with her fishing along the river bank nearby.

Bagendon NGR SP017064

Ditches, Woodmancote, North Cerney, NGR SO996093

Further reading:

As above

GLOUCESTER TO CAM:
EXPLORING KIRIN AND RIBBY'S
ADVENTURES BY THE RIVER SEVERN

JUST LIKE KIRIN you can explore beyond the Cotswolds. An interesting trip to make on the east side of the River Severn is a small train journey southwards from Gloucester Station to the Park-and-Ride station of Cam and Dursley, and back again. The service is a regular one on the GWR line to Bristol; but the stop is basically a car park. Take a sandwich with you if you don't wish to walk a while to find lunch.

From the train you can look up at the Cotswold escarpment and, with map in hand, spot many of the important landmarks in Kirin and Ribby's journeys: the gap in the hill line above Stroud and Stonehouse where the River Frome emerges into the Severn valley, the barrows on the skyline at Selsley Common, and from Cam the wooded promontory of Uley Bury – *Elebyrig*.

The train crosses the ridge of higher ground that they followed westward to Barrow Hill and the Severn crossing at Arlingham, and speeds past the settlement of Frocester on the valley floor that has been there since prehistory.

If the weather is kind you will be able to see the opposite hills and woods of the Forest of Dean that protected Ribby's family, and the viewpoint at Blaize Bailey above Newnham. As you return to Gloucester you are following a very similar route taken by that cheerful group of friends on their way to the summer solstice celebration at the Severn crossing.

DURSLEY TO STROUD: A VISIT TO ELEBYRIG – ULEY LONG BARROW

A VISIT TO Uley Bury is so worth the effort. I have found that a good way to get there at the moment is by the bus that runs between Stroud and Dursley along the B4066, getting off at Uley. I hesitate to give the route number as rural routes are so vulnerable to change. If you can then follow one of the published circular walks that use the Cotswold Way National Trail as a starting point. Don't try to walk up the road from the centre of the village; the path peters out and it is too dangerous. There is a narrow car park near the entrance to the hillfort at Coaley Wood so if you can persuade a friend to drive, or you can save for a taxi, there is somewhere to stop. If you don't wish to walk at all, the sight of the ramparts of the hillfort from the bus as it climbs up from Dursley to Uley will give you some idea of Kirin's wonderful vantage point at the start of the story.

As you continue your ride to Stroud you will spot some of the 'Mounds of the Old Ones' – Round and Long Barrows – that dot the Cotswolds. They must have fascinated the Iron Age people. Uley Long Barrow – also called Hetty Pegler's Tump – is the one nearest to Uley Bury and English Heritage have made it safe to enter.

Nearby is the site of the Uley Shrine, West Hill, which has

been excavated and recorded and can be investigated virtually by reading the report (all the sites in Kirin's story are based on real archaeological finds and reports).

As you follow the edge of the Cotswolds, you will pass Coaley Peak viewpoint and the Nympsfield Long Barrow. The view of the Severn and across to the Forest of Dean can take your breath away. Stop there for a while if at all possible.

Uley Bury Hillfort NGR ST784989

Uley Long Barrow 'Hetty Pegler's Tump' NGR SO78960003

www.nationaltrail.co.uk *Cotswold Way Circular Walk 9 Hills and Hillforts*

Further reading:

www.archaeologicaldataservice.ac.uk search *Uley Shrine* in the Archsearch section, and choose West Hill Romano-Celtic Complex

www.heritagegateway.org.uk search *Uley Bury*. From the Historic England Research Records click on the records for Gloucestershire County Council: Historic Environment Record and choose HER 261

www.english-heritage.org.uk search *Uley Long Barrow*

GLOUCESTER TO CINDERFORD AND SOUDLEY: EXPLORING THE FOREST OF DEAN AND THE DEAN HERITAGE CENTRE

THE WEST BANK of the River Severn and the Forest of Dean have their own remarkable characteristics and atmosphere, so different from the Cotswolds. One of my favourite bus routes is from Gloucester to Cinderford via Littledean, but again, check the latest bus number and information with bus websites. The earlier you start with public transport the better, many rural routes do not operate outside shop or business hours.

Crossing the Severn is easy in modern times, but the viaducts and bridges across separate channels of the great river as you leave Gloucester will give an idea of how tricky that must have been in the past. After Minsterworth the road follows the Severn's banks closely for a while. The Severn Bore Inn is a reminder of the regular tidal phenomenon up the river that has entertained and mystified across the millennia. Prehistoric people will have had their own explanation for it I am sure.

After Westbury-on-Severn you get a glimpse across the width of the Severn between Arlingham on the east bank and Newnham on the west, where Kirin and Ribby crossed. I'm not sure I would have been brave enough to cross that in a small boat, but it is a recognised crossing point in historical records so probably was in prehistoric times as well.

Turning to Littledean and then Cinderford, the bus takes you higher through red stone and red soil, up carved valley routes with views behind across to the Cotswolds. The weather can't be controlled of course, but with a bit of luck a stop in Cinderford will reward you with open sky, miles of treetops in the distance and the facilities and friendly cafes you need for a break in your trip.

There is an important site in the story that would be good to visit, if at all possible. I was able to pick up a bus at Cinderford that took me down the B4227 through Ruspidge to Upper Soudley, but at the time of writing it has been removed from timetables. It may return in summer months. Instead, there is currently a bookable public bus service called 'The Robin' operating in this area which you could try via their website or phone app. You need to get organised well in advance to use it, but your efforts will be rewarded. Steep woods close in around you, the sky space above gets smaller and smaller as you venture properly into the Forest of Dean.

Ask the driver to let you off at the White Horse Inn at Soudley and walk through the village towards the Dean Heritage Centre. On your right the stream cuts below you and between the houses before the trees rise steeply. On your left, after the school, is a raised shelf of ground that has interested archaeologists for years, with various attempts to confirm its archaeology. To us, it is Ribby's family settlement, attacked and abandoned. When she and Kirin emerged from the woods high above, the silence in the deep shadows would have been truly shocking to her. A few minutes further takes you to the Heritage Centre, well worth a visit. There you can learn all about the Forest of Dean: geology, history, archaeology, wildlife and, most of all, its people and their way of life. And get a cup of tea. Perfect. You will have so much to think about on the way home.

Ribby and Kirin had a little more walking to do beyond Soudley before they found safety. North of Blackpool Bridge in the Ruspidge area there is a boulder in the ground with two ancient cup-marks worn into it. It is called the Drummer Boy Stone. I was lucky enough to be driven there, and was immediately taken by its name and how that had come to be. If you have the determination to get to it on foot, or by bike, or have the gift of a car ride then see what you think. I'm glad it is hard to find. It stays almost a secret, which is how the forest people would like it.

Dean Heritage Centre, Camp Mill, Soudley, GL14 2UB
www.deanheritagecentre.com for opening times and public transport information

'The Robin' bookable bus service www.gloucestershire.gov.uk

Barrow Hill, Overton Lane, nr Arlingham NGR SO730102

Soudley Camp, Lower Soudley NGR SO 661105

The Drummer Boy Stone, Ruspidge, FoD NGR SO6547089

Further reading:

www.heritagegateway.org.uk search *Soudley Camp,* choose Gloucestershire County Council: Historic Environment Record Monument 444 Soudley Camp

Prehistoric Gloucestershire, Darvill T, 2012, as above, p92, The Drummer Boy Stone

Facing the Ocean: The Atlantic and its Peoples, 8000BC to AD1500, Cunliffe B, 2003, Oxford University Press

CIRENCESTER TO STROUD: SECRET VALLEYS AND OPEN SKIES

TO COMPLETE YOUR modern day tour of Kirin's world by public transport you have to take a bus between Cirencester and Stroud. Currently there is a direct bus that provides for college students (Cotswold Green 54X), and a slower one (Cotswold Green 54 and 54A) that dips into the valley villages, either one will provide the contrasting view of wide uplands and the deep 'Golden Valley' of the River Frome. The villages of Sapperton, Frampton Mansell and Chalford are the larger and most accessible modern settlements on Kirin, Ribby and Lad's westward route to the Severn Valley.

Further north, the first stage of the river cuts its valley just as insistently and privately as it ever did. The steep lane from Winstone to Miserden, crossing at Bull Banks, is as close as you can get to Kirin and Ribby's flight to safety from Tirtos's anger in the dark.

I have reasoned that the most level drovers' way would pass above Cherington, Glos NGR ST905977, and continue past Kingscote NGR ST814962 (where I have placed the home of Kirin's grandfather at Comelris), before crossing the modern A419 at Chapman's Cross NGR SO938019, on to Winstone. There it would pass the Hoar Stone Long Barrow NGR SO965066 and then make the final push to Woodmancote and Bagendon. A minor road follows this route today, with notable wide grass verges in places.

www.bustimes.org

Sapperton, Gloucestershire NGR SO9403 can be walked to directly along the Broad Ride from Cirencester, by permission of the Bathurst Estate, Cirencester Park. See their website for times and conditions www.bathurstestate.co.uk

NAMES AND PLACES

THE NAMES IN this story do take a little getting used to. I created them from Gaulish/Celtic roots or Iberian/Celtic roots to reflect the cultural crossover that must have existed in Kirin's part of Britain during the Late Iron Age. I have relied on the extensive, and sometimes controversial, work of others to do this, notably Patrick Sims-Williams, Barry Cunliffe, and the analysis of the Tartessian inscriptions by John T Koch. To add to the mix I have taken liberties with Welsh derivations, and enjoyed the interchange of 'b' and 'v'.

Whichever side of the many debates on the origins of Celtic culture you settle on, there is strong evidence that the Atlantic seaway brought people and culture from the Iberian Peninsular – modern Spain and Portugal – and even the Mediterranean to British shores. The Silures tribe of South Wales were described as having dark curly hair by Roman writers. Influence from eastern Britain and Gaul, across the Channel, must have been just as strong through trade and sea transport. Contact with the Roman Empire was regular and usual in the Late Iron Age in southern Britain, before the Romans had to invade to protect their invaluable sources and trade links. The Dobunnic tribes were well positioned to take advantage of all cultural influences in all directions – but a young boy growing up inland would still have discovered many unusual habits and customs out of his home area.

When I read a story I always want to know how to pronounce names like the author intended, so here are my suggestions where necessary:

Alisne – *Alisnay*

Arbin

Assuna – *Assoona*

Bane – *Bannay*

Beindubn – *Bayndubbon* – the hillsides above Bagendon and North Cerney, Gloucestershire

Belin – *Bellin*

Bulva – *Bullva*

Calleba – *Kalleeba* – Calleva Atrebatum to the Romans, now known as Silchester

Caratacos – *Karatahkos* – leader of the resistance, now known as Caratacus

Colios – *Kollyoss*

Corinium – the military camp at the road crossing over the River Churn, now Cirencester

Cuamena – *Kooameena*

Cuda – *Kooda* – a goddess of home and fertility

Comelris – *Komellriss* – somewhere near Kingscote, Gloucestershire

Dobunni – *Dobooni* – an important tribe controlling pre-Roman Gloucestershire and beyond

Eburia – *Ehburiah*

Elebyrig – *Ellaybirrig* – Uley Bury, Gloucestershire

Fomorik – *Fommorik* – a demon of the sea

Galete – *Galaytay*

Hatane – *Hatannay* – a moon goddess of the night

Kalte – *Kaltay*

Kele – *Kellay*

Kenet – *Kennett*

Kerdos – *Kerdoss*

Kirin – *Kirrin*

Kuno – *Koonoh*

Lad/ Sheep Boy

Marcus Claudius Petronius – an administrative legionary, or beneficiarius in the Roman army

Melis – *Melliss* – with Serun – *Sehrun* – Tarn, Anba, Cam and Kirin

Mog

Nema – *Neema*

Pona – *Pohna* – a horse goddess

Rianbe – *Reeanbay*

Samos – *Sammoss*

Savren – *Savrenn* – The River Severn

Siluros – *Sylerross* – a tribe controlling large parts of what is now South Wales, now called the Silures

Tala

Tass

Terb

Tilek – *Tilleck*

Tirtos – *Tertoss*

Tovisac – *Tovvissack*

Turaius – *Terayus*

Uban – *Oobann* – a sun god, giver of life and death

Venetes – *Veneetees* – a navy defeated by the Romans in battle

Volkos – *Vollkoss* – a god of trouble and conflict

ACKNOWLEDGEMENTS

SINCE THE EARLIEST days of starting to write this story, enthusiasm from others has been priceless. Tim, the generous gifts of your time, expert knowledge and extensive library, and those first car trips to deep corners of Gloucestershire helped shape my ideas and create new ones. I hope my public transport suggestions go some way towards helping others who don't know a Tim. Shan, when I finally dared show someone my first draft, your encouragement then meant so much, and has never wavered. Since then friends and neighbours – including Bron, Karen, Rob, Emily, Kate – who read and commented on various drafts have all contributed to this printed version. Lauren, I hope you enjoyed correcting your old primary teacher's work. Talk about turning tables.

Mike and Julie, Tabby, Jessica – getting advice on the final version from practising archaeologists and those 'in the know' was a privilege. And Lorna, from Crumps Barn Studio, I cannot thank you enough for your editorial and design skills.

If I have missed anyone out I am so sorry. I can only blame the long time it has taken me to learn to produce something readable. To you, and the past pupils I expected to just turn out stories at short notice in busy classrooms, I apologise. And I thank you all.

Anne Buffoni

ABOUT THE AUTHOR

ANNE BUFFONI IS a former primary teacher with a passion for education, archaeology, landscape and the natural sciences.

Growing up on a farm near Cirencester, Anne joined summer archaeological excavations as a student, before beginning a lifelong interest in writing for all ages and encouraging independent investigation of the past and its treasures all around us.

When she isn't writing, she volunteers as an environmental archaeologist. She is currently involved in a Neolithic long barrow site in the Cotswolds.

If you loved this book, you'll love our other historical fiction titles ...

Crumps Barn Studio
www.crumpsbarn.online

JUST CAUSES
GEORGIA PIGGOTT

Dorset, 1625

Alice knows she shouldn't be here.

She has been careful, watchful, deceitful even, to get to this point. But now the time has come, her heart is pounding with the enormity of her plan ...

Alice Edwards is on her own and fighting for all that she holds dear. In a time of deadly plague, hope lies in herbs and remedies. But sickness is not the only danger.

Who is the mysterious child who has fallen under her care? And how can Alice tell friend from foe when the shadow of a murder is haunting her steps – and heartache awaits at every turn?

The gripping and authentic first book in The Alice Chronicles, from a new voice in historical drama

A HAZARDOUS GAME
GEORGIA PIGGOTT

England, 1626

You are mistress of High Stoke now, Mistress Jerrard ...

After escaping her Dorset village, Alice is building a new life with husband Henry Jerrard at his beautiful but impoverished home, High Stoke. But behind the crumbling façade, someone is playing a deadly game.

When a maidservant is murdered and an innocent man is named, the crime reveals a web of lies. Alice can trust no one – not the witnesses, not sinister steward Isabel, and certainly not the coroner Sir Malcolm, who seems more interested in pursuing an old gambling feud than the facts behind the case.

How can Alice uncover the truth when every wrong turn means risking more innocent lives?

There are secrets in Alice's new home. This is a game of high stakes that she must not lose ...

The captivating second historical mystery in The Alice Chronicles, full of twists and turns